CHARLES BEAMER

LOVE'S MAJESTY

HARVEST HOUSE PUBLISHERS
Eugene, Oregon 97402

LOVE'S MAJESTY

Copyright © 1983 by Harvest House Publishers
Eugene, Oregon 97402

Library of Congress Catalog Card Number 82-084071
ISBN 0-89081-325-6

Printed in the United States of America.

7067055

This book is dedicated to the memory of those who were...and whose story I have told in this fiction form with all the love and grace given me.

CONTENTS

Alex's Courting

T he cemetery was silent and the sun fell warmly on my back as I knelt by my parents' graves. Not far away, pale green wild asparagus sprouted and "bouncin' Bets" bloomed small and lavender-white. My husband, son, and daughter walked near the white fence, looking at the dark green cedar trees and at the white frame Pleasant Ridge Church—the focal point of so much that had happened. I looked at the headstones:

Lucy Mary Smith Walker
April, 1883-April, 1977

Victor Flute Walker
March, 1877-June, 1963

"That shouldn't be," I thought. *"Dates tell nothing. Not how blessings are born of tragedy...how years of hardship bear golden fruit...how ordinary events accumulate and become rich joy...how the silver thread continues to run between seams of coal...or how love's majesty...."* I stood abruptly and rejoined my family; they looked at me in surprise, watching my smile where I suppose they had expected tears. "Let me tell you," I began, taking my son and daughter's arms and leading them toward the church, "who these people were, and how 'ordinary' can be very, very special...."

• • •

Alex Walker felt a tender, budding love that threatened to burst free despite his careful restraint. Fearful of displaying his emotions, he tightened his restraint and hoped that Mr. Smith soon would go to bed. Like a benign guardian, Mr. Smith sat across the farmhouse parlor from his daughter Lucy and her "feller." Alexander sat on the edge of the horsehair sofa and waited for Lucy to lower the stereoscope so he could again gaze into her blue-gray eyes and try to communicate his feelings through his look.

In the meantime, he studied the pure white skin of Lucy's wrists—fine wrists with almost-delicate bones. It occurred to Alex that she was not a worker. But then he realized that the daughters of well-to-do farmers were not supposed to be. He chided himself; to be successful in making this step up, he knew he would have to get used to such differences between what he was accustomed to in Lower Tennessee—his section of the county—and Ravanna, her section. He sighed; *her* work was displayed in the shadow embroidery around the edges of her sleeves and on her collar—embroidery such as he had seen only in pictures. No one he knew in the county, except his mother, did such work, and he felt proud to be with Lucy. A vision formed in his imagination, a vision of how lovely she would look going up the path to the Pleasant Ridge Church, how admiringly his brothers and sisters, his parents and aunts and uncles would smile at her, how he would feel standing with her before the minister, how he would feel united with her at the altar....

"Trafalgar Square," she said in a soft voice that was trying to become mature.

"What?" he asked, and immediately felt foolish. He knew he began to blush because she smiled briefly. He tilted his head to ease his neck against the hard celluloid collar and took the viewer.

"It's in London," she explained, as if she were speaking to her younger brother rather than to a man nearly ten years older than she was.

"Oh," he said, moving the card-holder until the picture came into three-dimensional focus. "Yes, it's nice," he said lamely. It occurred to him that there were advantages to having an education; he knew she had finished the eighth grade, and he knew that she knew he had stopped at the sixth. He wondered if she held that difference against him. "I never had time for much geography," he explained, knowing that it would do no good to explain but feeling an urgency to do so; he spoke even more loudly now, knowing that her father was listening rather than reading the *Post-Telegraph*, as he was pretending to do. "But I have been to St. Louis."

"That's nice," she said mildly. "The last time Mother and I were there she bought me the prettiest crushed-velvet rose. I put it on a beige-gray felt hat I have. I'll wear it for you sometime."

He looked at her soft brown hair, swept up in back and arranged atop her head in the fashion of that year, 1899. Alexander quickly and vividly imagined how lovely she would look wearing the hat and velvet rose. He glanced at her solemn yet somehow sensuous features. His voice, when he managed to speak, was so thick with emotion that she barely heard him say, "You're as pretty as a Dorothy Perkins rose."

She blushed and looked quickly toward her father to see if he had heard, then looked at the stereoscope picture cards in her lap.

Her father, whether or not he had heard, stood decisively. "Time for bed," he announced, folding his newspaper and dropping it onto the chair. His blue-gray gaze went from his daughter to Alexander with gentle admonition—an urging, Alex thought, for patience.

"Yes, Sir," Alex said, standing. He handed the stereoscope to Lucy but held onto it when she took the handle. "May I come by Sunday afternoon?" he asked her. "We didn't have much of a drive today, and I thought maybe you'd like to go up toward the Jewell farm, to see their new barn."

"I'd like that, she said softly, holding the stereoscope close against herself when he let go of it. She looked at her father.

He nodded, coming toward them to usher Alexander to the door. Alex caught one final glimpse of Lucy as he went out the door into the chill February night air.

Mr. Smith followed him outside and closed the door. He waited until he heard his daughter's footsteps running up the stairs inside, then cleared his throat and said, "I'd be careful going home."

"Yes, Sir," Alexander said, settling his hat onto his head.

"Might spend the night in Ravanna if I was you."

Alexander looked at the older man, noticing how the lamplight from the house made the white hair among his brown stand out; his beard, though, was darker and shadowed. They were the same height, just under six feet, and he looked directly into Mr. Smith's eyes. "I'm not afraid of them."

"Carrying a pistol?"

"No, Sir. Daddy doesn't allow any of us."

Mr. Smith smiled faintly, a satisfied smile that, Alex thought, seemed to be about the limit of the emotion he would allow himself to reveal. "No," Mr. Smith said slowly, "thought not. You...um, you serious about Lucy, are you?"

Alex grinned, then laughed to relieve the tightness of his stomach muscles. He was glad Mr. Smith had broached the subject. "Is it all right with you...and Mrs. Smith?"

" 'Bout time you got married, isn't it?" Mr. Smith answered with mild evasiveness. "How old are you—25?"

"Four."

Mr. Smith's gentle, almost rectangular face became more serious. "Lucy's not but 15, you know."

"I can wait," Alex said—more from a sense that Mr. Smith wanted him to say that than from any desire to wait. "*Tomorrow...tomorrow would be....*" He nodded, tightening his lips. "I can wait."

"Best you do. She's got a lot to learn yet."

Alexander smiled at Mr. Smith, really liking the understated way he protected his daughter. He held out his right hand to the older man, and they shook. "Good night, Sir," he said, going quickly down the porch steps, down the walk, and through the gate in the picket fence.

He heard the door softly close behind him as he picked up the iron "anchor" from beside his lead horse, coiled the rope, and unhooked it from the horse's bridle. He laid the anchor and rope in the floorboard, climbed onto the front seat of the spring wagon, and untied the lines from the stanchion. "Getup!" he said, slapping the lines on the bay geldings' rumps. Blowing frosty breaths, the horses started off at once, glad to be moving again. The wagon wheels snapped loose from the ice and began crunching over the frozen ground of the driveway. On the road, the wagon lurched from side to side until Alex settled it into a pair of ruts. Then he let the lines hang slack and let his thoughts drift back...toward her lighted window covered by lace curtains. Alex smiled, hardly feeling the numbing and still night air.

By ten o'clock or so he had gone through the tiny village of Ravanna—without seeing even one light burning—and had turned onto the road that ran east from Princeton through East Pine. In a mile or so he passed Robert McCargue's farm, and in two miles or so more he passed the Fairly holdings. Now he felt uneasy watchfulness replace the pleasantness of having been with Lucy, even as the chill of the night had replaced the warmth of being in her home. Alex looked toward the Fairly house, thinking about the "Fairly Gang," as the three younger Fairly boys, several of the McCargues, and the two Trask boys had come to be called. It was against that "gang" that Mr. Smith had warned him—as if he needed warning, Alex thought, annoyed at the very existence of the gang members.

But it was late, and it was the middle of the week, when little was going on to draw the gang together. He slapped the lines on the horses when the thought occurred to him that he had come courting and had stayed late with those facts in mind. Was he afraid, or was this courting a test he had set himself? His father's friends had been plaguing him unmercifully about "gettin' too old to catch anythin' but a spinster or a Clark" and about "wantin' only the best but bein' afraid to go down 'Fairly Road' without an army." The men at Rouse's Dry Goods and at the Gregory Grocery had made such teasing the automatic topic of conversation whenever Alexander showed his face in town. He almost had had to do something, but once he had done it, he had fallen in love.

His thoughts went back to Lucy...and having to wait. In a way he wished his mother would settle for someone closer to home, someone from a Lower Tennessee family, someone he felt more comfortable with or more equal to. But Alex knew his mother well. She didn't put on airs or think herself better than other folks, but she had her standards nevertheless. She never talked openly about her standards, because if she had, her husband would have made fun of her. But somehow she had communicated her expectations to Alex more strongly than with words.

Part of it, Alex sensed, happened when they went to town and she either ignored certain people, spoke politely but briefly to certain other people, or stopped and engaged in conversation with still other people. It was subtle, Alex realized. He decided to talk with Victor about it.

He was startled from his reverie by the sounds of hoofbeats, quite a number of them, clattering along the road toward him. He pulled his team to a halt on the crest of a hill.

The riders appeared in the darkness—two, then two more, then three more. They gathered in a line across the road in front of his team, which was backing nervously, sniffing the newcomers.

"Who's there?" Alex called, squinting into the pale darkness. The moon, two nights past new, and the stars made such scant light that he could not identify the shadowy riders, though he knew who they must be.

Sarcastic chuckling answered his challenge from first one, then another of the riders. Their voices sounded young and cocky, and Alexander shook his head as he took up the lines. He watched the riders and their skittery, blowing horses, then abruptly shouted, "Getup!" as he popped the lines on his horses' rumps. They flinched and pulled ahead at once.

For a moment the two riders directly in front of Alex's team held their mounts steady and close together, but they yanked their horses aside as the wagon clattered toward them. Alex braced his feet on the floorboard against the sideways tossing caused by the ruts in the frozen clay; he did not look back, though he heard sharp curses and thudding hoofbeats coming up behind him.

"Where're ya goin', mud-dauber?" shouted the rider who came up on his left. "Runnin' home, are ya?"

Alexander looked at the rider, whose face was half-hidden under a wide-brimmed hat, and recognized Tom Fairly. "Say, Tom," he called pleasantly, "Isn't it past your bedtime?"

A rider pulled up on the right of the wagon and cried, "Hey, cradle robber! What's an old man like you doin' courtin' in *our* terr'tory?"

Alexander smiled as he turned and watched the other young man struggling to control his horse as it trotted in the grader ditch. Alex recognized the leader of the gang, Jim McCargue. "Evenin', Jim," he said amiably. "Since when is Ravanna *your* territory?"

Jim laughed, jerking on the reins of his horse when the animal stumbled. "Since Lucy Smith came of age!" shot his reply.

"Shame to waste all your energy buttin' your head against a door that won't ever open to you," Alex commented.

"Gonna waste it bashin' in yor face if'n you don't stay away from the Fairly...*and* Ravanna," Jim retorted sullenly.

Alex heard a horse come close behind the wagon as someone jeered, "Go on...I dare you!"

He felt the wagon sag as boots thudded into the rear. He turned to see a very scared-looking Weldon Trask, the town barber's son, climbing over the back seat. The boy, losing his hat and clutching wildly for it, laughed uncontrollably. Thin and stooped, the boy glanced back at the person who had dared him to jump—his sister Jane, Alexander figured, who affected the dress and personality of Calamity Jane Canary. Alex saw her mannish figure on the horse beside Weldon's, holding his reins; when she saw that Alex recognized her, she spat tobacco juice and yelled at Weldon, "Go on...chicken!"

Alex stared at Weldon as the young man laughed and said, "Thought you'd need some ex-pert help with yor courtin'!"

With one hand Alexander reached back, grasped Weldon tightly by the front of his coat, and hurled him over the side of the wagon toward the rump of Tom Fairly's horse. Weldon screamed a curse word as he hit the horse and slid toward the ground. Tom's horse ducked its hindquarters and reared, and the horses of the two riders behind Tom pitched into each other trying to avoid Weldon, who was scrambling away. With confusion reigning behind him,

Alex slapped the lines on his horses; they broke into a fast trot as the riders behind helped Weldon remount, then galloped in pursuit. Alex took the buggy whip from its socket and held it ready, listening to the sounds of the horses closing on him.

When the first horse came up beside him, Alex lashed out for its nose, missed, lashed again, and popped the animal below the eyes. It shied, twisted, and went down, sending its rider sprawling across the frozen clay ruts. Once again the sounds of confusion spread into the otherwise silent night. Rising above the sounds came Tom Fairly's voice: "We'll get you, Alex Walker! You jist wait! We'll get...." His words were lost in the sounds of clattering wagon wheels, protesting springs, and thudding hooves.

• • •

Miles away, amid field and forest-blanketed hills, a kerosene lamp cast a sphere of pale yellow light in the living room of a small farmhouse. Daddy Walker was deeply settled into his chair by the large cannon stove. Mrs. Walker was sitting nearby, stitching together a quilt top from brightly colored squares of cloth.

"Courting Lucy Smith?" Mrs. Walker asked, beginning to rock. She glanced at her husband. "I guess it's about time he began seeing someone nice." She sighed, stilling her chair and focusing on her stitches.

"Give up on him, most folks have," James said unhappily. "But one of the Smiths? Ravanna Pennsylvania Dutch folks? Her daddy is Franklin's brother, and Franklin was a Union officer, dyed in the wool. 'Sides, none of those Ravanna folks have ever looked very kindly on us Lower Tennessee people." He sniffed, gripping the broad arms of his chair.

Susan continued sewing, making sure each stitch was as close to the previous one as possible. Some women would settle for stitches an eighth of an inch apart, but hers....Quietly she stated, "Those Smiths needn't think their daughter would be lowering herself any if she married our Alex." She nodded, tightening her lips.

James stood abruptly, went to the stove, and shook the grate handle to settle ashes from the dying fire. "But how'll Alex make a livin' for such a girl?"

Susan's eyebrows slowly went up as she peered down at the pattern lying beside her chair. Soon she selected another piece of cloth from her basket and began sewing it into place. "Alex will do for her just fine," she said placidly.

James sat heavily, with a sigh, and stared at his wife. "I s'pose you like the idea."

She glanced at him. "Only if it's the Lord's will."

"Well...yes," he said, leaning back in his chair, "but it's easy for you to look forward to a Smith daughter-in-law, you bein' a Ruth—'scuse me, a *Routh*—and all."

"Something wrong with that?" she asked mildly.

"No," he admitted. He listened to the sound of the fire popping. The other children—except the oldest son, Alex, and Ella, the oldest daughter—were in their rooms: Madison or Matt, who was 22; Victor Flute or "Fluty," who was 21; and the "baby," Nanny, who was 18. James sighed again. "Mark my words, though: It'll only bring trouble. For one thing, he's got to cross the Fairly ever' time, and you know—"

"If you start imagining trouble, you're liable to call it up." She laid her sewing in her lap and looked at him, at how impatiently he sat, how he seemed unable to contain the energy that had made him one of the best farmers in Lower Tennessee. She also thought how, despite her love for him, she still considered the whiteness of his forehead where his hat covered his head from the sun to be funny, almost as funny as his red, curling hair. She smiled to herself, loving him more because he did have humor—in his curling red hair, his twinkling blue eyes, and his smile, when he let himself show it. She glanced at his red-brown arms and hands, hands becoming gnarled, hands that had the strength in them to manage everything that might happen—except waiting for a son to come home. She smiled, picked up her work, and resumed making tiny evenly spaced stitches.

In sidelong glances James admired his wife's auburn hair, neatly done in a bun—hair the same color as Victor's hair. He let his thoughts drift to Victor, the "special" one. In the long silence that followed, James yawned several times, continually listening for the sound of wagon wheels crunching the remaining skiff of ice. When at last Susan folded her work, placed it and the design into her basket, and went to bed, James began to doze.

●　●　●

When Alexander crossed the narrow wooden bridge over Fairly Creek, he let his team slow. They pulled the hill into Princeton, the county seat, and he let them take their time going through the town. He hoped they would make as little noise as possible lest someone notice him and spread the word that he had been courting. The team crossed the Rock Island railroad tracks, sped up going down the hill to the fertile bottomlands near the Grand River, and began passing the farms of the people Alex had known all his life—people who were like pillars in his memory, supporting him and his family with friendship, with their presence in times of joy and of trouble, and simply with the fact of their existence as parts of Lower Tennessee.

Alex let the team take their time crossing the stone bridge over the Grand River, for the horses could sense the drop to the ice below, and they shied away from the edges. A half-mile more and he turned the horses northward, toward the heart of Lower Tennessee, toward the farms that, like his father's, lay near the Pleasant Ridge Church and schoolhouse. The road began climbing and winding among hills covered by winter-plowed fields on which thick snow remained—fields separated from one another by hedgerows of trees whose bare branches etched the nighttime sky. Alex began to feel that he was home as the wagon wound among the hills, and the air itself smelled richer and less prairielike than it had over in the Fairly. A great horned owl ghosted across the road, making the horses prick up their ears even though the bird's flight was absolutely silent. Off in the densely forested creek bottom to his right a lone wolf howled. The wild, sharp cry sent chills over Alex's neck and shoulders and made him think how the ten-dollar bounty for a wolf's ears would help toward building a house for Lucy Smith.

In another half-mile or so he turned the team into the drive that led to Daddy Walker's farm—his farm someday, his father had promised. He stared at the starkly black, bare branches of the apricot, peach, and pie-cherry trees near the drive, imagining how the orchard would look when it bloomed out in three months or so. Beyond the orchard to his left was the largest cornfield, which he and his father and brothers would plow in about six weeks. The rich brown clay soil would be shiny where the plowshares sliced it, and it would have its special pungent odor.

He frowned as a bad feeling crossed his mind. He considered the feeling, then tried again to think of plowing and planting, of the orchard blooming out and....

But his mind went blank as if it had a black curtain drawn around it. He clucked to the horses as they passed the house and whickered at the mules in the barn. The horses blew and shook their heads, jingling the harness, glad to be home at last.

Alex, although sleepy and cold-numbed, lit a lantern and carefully rubbed down the horses after unharnessing them. He was proud of them, of their sleek bay hides and firm flesh, and he wanted no chill or illness to strike them. They shook thoroughly when he had finished, and they nuzzled his back as he broke the ice in their water tubs. He blew out the lantern, left the barn, latched the doors, and went toward the house.

As Alex crossed the kitchen, his father's voice came from the living room: "That you, boy?"

Alex knew from the abrupt sound of his father's voice that he had been sleeping but didn't want to sound like he had been. Alex went into the living room. "How'd it go?" James asked, putting his hands to the small of his back and stretching with a grimace.

"Went fine," Alex allowed. "Lucy's real nice."

James took up the lamp that was burning with a down-turned wick on the table near his chair and carried it toward his bedroom. "Any trouble?"

"Nothin' I couldn't handle," Alex said, heading toward the bedroom he and Victor shared with Matt. He heard the ceiling boards creak, and he wondered if Nanny had been awakened by his coming home.

"The McCargues?"

"And Fairlys...with those Trask kids."

His father grunted and went to his bedroom, blowing out the lamp. In the instant before the light was extinguished, Alex glimpsed his mother in bed, covered to her chin with layers of quilts, her long auburn hair spread luxuriantly over a lace-bordered pillow. He felt mildly ashamed for having seen her with her hair unbound, but he straightened, treasuring the image, and went into his own room.

"That you, Alex?" asked the sleepy but strong voice of Victor. Alex smiled, thinking how reassuring Victor's voice always was.

"Yes, it's me," Alex said. He removed the chimney of a lamp, lit it, and carefully replaced the chimney as he adjusted the wick to its lowest yellow-flame level. He took off his tie and un-snapped his collar; he laid them on the bureau beside Victor's Bible and a china bowl of their "treasures." He put his stickpin and cuff links in the bowl and began undressing. In his long, woolen underwear, he slid into the bed, shivering from a chill.

"Did everything go all right?" Victor asked, sitting upright and pulling the cotton inner blanket and the quilts up across his chest.

Alex squirmed around to make the feather mattress fit his shape, then looked at his brother in the pale light. Victor was shorter than he or their father, but he was as strongly built; he had a kind face with a rather wide mouth, large ears, a longish nose, and their father's twinkling blue eyes. Something about Victor's face was as comforting to Alex as his voice. Alex sighed, feeling that finally he could open up.

"Fluty, she's the finest girl I've *ever* seen. She's...she's like a dream, an angel. She holds herself straight but not stiff, confident but not overproud. She seems solemn, but I think she's just bashful...though she can look right at you without giggling or blushing. And she's *been* places—St. Louis and even Chicago."

Victor sighed. "But was there any trouble?"

"Some, like I told Daddy." Alex squirmed slightly, making a nest for his head in the fluffy feather pillow and wishing his mother wouldn't starch pillowcases. "What're you and he so worried about? Don't you think big brother can take care of himself?"

"It's not that," Victor said slowly. "It's...I've been having a dream...the same one over and over. It's given me a bad feeling."

Alex quickly sat upright, and Victor and he watched each other. "When I was driving into our place, I got a bad feeling, too," Alex said. "What d'you think your dream means?"

Victor thoughtfully lay back with his hands under his head. "I can't say for sure."

"Well, I wish you'd figure it out." Alex muttered uneasily, thinking about how both sides of their family always had considered Victor "set apart." "Remember when you were eight and had that dream? When you had *it* figured out, you got all us kids and cousin Maude and Ellie together out back, stood up on the stump, and preached us the *best* sermon I've ever—"

"How do you feel about courting Lucy?" Victor interrupted.

Alex's smile faded. "Like Mr. Smith is watchin' me, trying to figure out if I'm good enough for his precious second daughter. And I was thinking on the way home about how Ed and Henry and the other men have been plaguin' me...and about how," he added in a whisper, "Mama wouldn't like it if I didn't marry someone...." His words trailed into silence.

"Better than we are?"

"Yes."

Victor spoke with care. "Mama wouldn't mind who you married as long as you were satisfied that you were marrying a good girl. Look how she was when Ella married Fred. He's 'just' a farmer, doesn't own more than 50 acres."

"But he'll stand up in church and give testimony, and he'll be something some day," Alex returned, "Besides, Ella is Ella—with her dun hair and timid ways. Folks said it was a blessing she was married at all, 'specially to a strong-willed man who can take care of her.''

Victor said nothing, and Alex began feeling guilty for having spoken disparagingly of their sister. He knew that Victor always had defended Ella because of her meek, timid ways; he considered her precious and had fought the only fight of his life because a boy in school had called Ella a ''dun cow.'' Alex whispered, ''I'm sorry.''

Victor resumed speaking as though he had heard neither Alex's running down Ella nor his apology. ''I just hope you feel certain that courting Lucy Smith is right in every way. Seems that things most often go wrong when somebody forces something.''

''I know,'' Alex said, suddenly feeling very tired. He lay back, pulled the soft quilts up to his chin, and closed his eyes. ''Fluty,'' he said as he drifted into sleep, ''she's the prettiest...gentlest....''

Victor heard his brother's breathing become regular, and he looked over at him, then leaned up to see if Matt was awake. In the soft light, Matt's fiery red hair was dimly visible above his bed.

Matt, who was older than Victor but younger—though ''wiser''—than Alexander, whispered, ''He'd better watch out. You know what Clay George said: If you step on a sleeping sow, like that Fairly bunch, you're liable to get a whole lot more'n growl an' bark.''

Victor said nothing, and he lay back with a silent prayer that his recurrent dream would end. *''Please, not that...not that...!''* He whispered, ''Matt, are you still going down to Spickard tomorrow?''

''Sure,'' came Matt's sleepy but eager voice. ''Mr. Holbein says he'll pay me 50 cents a day if I'll work for him till his foot heals.''

''While you're gone,'' Victor said tensely, ''will you pray for Alex?''

''Yeah,'' Matt casually replied, then added, ''You know me, though.''

Victor laughed to cast off the lingering bad feeling and hopped out of bed to go blow out the lamp—thinking how often Alex hurried by something, leaving someone else to finish it. As he hastened back across the cold floorboards, Victor told Matt, ''You just be careful about those Spickard girls. I hear they're mighty pretty.''

''Yeah...I'll do that,'' Matt said.

The comforts rustled faintly, and the brothers fell asleep.

Saturday Night Dance

During that night and the three that followed, Victor slept without dreaming any dream he could remember. When he felt sure that his recurrent dream had ended, he also felt as if he had committed a form of betrayal or denial by asking that it stop. And in lieu of an interpretation of the dream, he felt a personal obligation to protect his big brother. He decided to go with Alex when his big brother again went courting—beginning the next Sunday.

He and Alex left home soon after church; the sky was clear, and the northward returning sun was speeding the early March thaw. The roads were so muddy that Alex and Victor took along an extra set of clothes, knowing that they would arrive mud-spattered and wet.

Their appearance did not, however, seem to dampen the spirit of Lucy Smith. She hurried from the house the moment Alex stopped the wagon in front of the gate. "Afternoon, Flute," she said to Victor as she waited just inside the fence for Alex. Behind her, Mr. Smith came onto the porch, coatless but still wearing his suit pants, leather suspenders, and white shirt from going to church. Mrs. Smith was waiting in the doorway. Past her, throwing open the screen door as he burst outside, came Samuel Franklin Smith. He was about 12 and, Alex thought, was spoiled rotten because he was the only surviving boy in the family of five sisters. Close on his heels to see Lucy's feller came Catherine, nine, May, five, and little Clara, who was called Blinky because she once had drunk milk so sour that it made her blink. Alex picked Blinky up in his arms, and the three-year-old proudly squinted down at Sammy and May and stuck out her tongue.

"I want to go, I want to go!" Sammy cried, tugging on Alex's left sleeve. Lucy frowned at him hard enough to wilt flowers.

"You're not going anywhere," she snapped, leading Alex and Victor up the steps onto the porch.

"Oh, take the boy, if you're still going riding," Mrs. Smith urged, her lively brown eyes twinkling and her face creased by smile lines. She was short, with graying brown hair, and she was famous roundabouts for the entertainment she provided for the young people who visited. "He's been cooped up in the house all winter; it'll do him good to get out." She laughed pleasantly, holding open the screen door so the others could go inside. Victor and Alex immediately smelled fresh bread and....

"Rhubarb pie?" Victor inquired, turning with a grin spreading his rather wide mouth and lighting up his eyes.

Mrs. Smith waved one hand toward him and frowned as if disgusted that he so quickly had guessed the surprise she had been saving; she went past him and into the kitchen at the back of the house. When he stopped in the kitchen doorway, she glanced at him. "Would you believe it," she said, "the rhubarb's already shootin' up—just as bright red as current jam! Chloe'll need it, since she's been complaining of stomach trouble. By the way, she and Park are in the parlor." She looked at the clothes Victor was holding and at his muddied trouser legs. "You can change upstairs," she said, dumping a cooled loaf of bread out of a pan. She turned to watch the hired girl carefully take a roast from the oven. "Papa!" Mrs. Smith called. "You can come and start carving!"

When Victor and Alex had come back downstairs from changing their clothes, Victor saw that Chloe, who was 17, and her fiancé had come from the parlor into the dining room. Victor. studied her as Mrs. Smith and the hired girl brought dishes and platters of food from the kitchen and lined them up along the center of the long dining room table. Chloe was taller than Lucy, Victor noted, and had darker brown hair; it framed her rather small, pale white face, large eyes, and small nose and mouth, giving her a vulnerable but beautiful look. Park Robinson seated her at the dining table as they all sat, and Victor recalled that the serious-looking young man was a "city feller" from Trenton who had come to Princeton to open a pharmacy; Park seemed anxious and stiff as he glanced from Chloe to her father, then stared at his plate.

Dinner was all too soon over, and two pies had been consumed. The young women carried the dishes into the kitchen and remained to help the girl and Mrs. Smith clean up. The younger children, meanwhile, were shooed outside. Stretching, Alex and Park went with Mr. Smith into the parlor. Mr. Smith sat in his chair to the left of the organ; Alex sat across the room from him in front of the lace-curtained windows, and Park took a chair near the chintz-covered, round table with its hand-painted globe. By it was the double doorway into the entry hall where the rope portiere hung. Silence prevailed until Victor came in. He laughed, holding his stomach, and sat on the sofa. "*That* was a good meal!" he declared loudly enough for Mrs. Smith to hear him in the kitchen.

Mr. Smith beamed, placed his forearms on his thighs, and leaned forward. "Thank you, Fluty. It was almost as good as that meal Mrs. Walker cooked us all that Easter we ate over at your place. I'll never forget that goose."

"Neither will Nanny and Ella," Victor said, chuckling as he crossed his legs. "They swore that goose had more feathers than the Lord allows on one bird."

"That reminds me," Mr. Smith said, crinkling the crow's-feet lines at the corners of his blue-gray eyes as he smiled, "Preacher over at Otterbein Church this morning spoke on pluckin' the bird—and he wasn't talking about a rich man's purse, either. What he said was to the effect that we ought to pluck out the fancy ways of living that're becoming so popular." He looked at Park to see his reaction. "Preacher said we ought to go back to a simpler way of living."

"Can't argue with that," Victor said, his eyes twinkling almost merrily. Some people said that his auburn hair turned bright red over religious discussions, but now calmness seemed to dominate him.

"You mean a Baptist agrees with a Brethren?" Mr. Smith asked teasingly, hoping for a good discussion as "exercise" after the meal. "I thought you were the one who wanted to join Teddy and his Rough Riders in the last war."

Victor's expression settled further into calmness. "I did," he said. "I thought—and I still do—that it was our duty to help the country, especially after Congress declared war."

"That war was nothing but a whoop-de-do stirred up by the Eastern newspapers," Mr. Smith asserted, leaning back and folding his arms with a satisfied expression as though he were glad a topic had been found that would spark some talk.

Lucy, closely followed by Chloe, came hurriedly into the parlor, then slowed to a halt, clasping her hands in front of herself when she saw her father's look. She turned to Alexander and began to smile again. "Ready to go riding?" she asked, going toward him. "Chloe's going, if Park wants to, so we can leave Sammy." She turned uncertainly toward her father, then toward Victor. "Oh," she said, "I forgot...."

"I'll be glad to stay," Victor said easily, smiling at her and noticing for the first time that everything Alexander had said about her was more than true. "I'd enjoy talking with your father, and maybe playing a few tricks for the kids." When her expression became inquiring, Victor took a coin from his trousers and held it toward her. She reached for it, but he flicked his hand and made the coin vanish.

She laughed a girlish, delighted laugh, lookly briefly at him, then turned toward her father. "Is it all right if we go on?" she asked.

"Surely," Mr. Smith said, nodding. "Up toward the Jewells' to see their new barn, is it?"

"Yes," Lucy said breathlessly, turning back toward Alex. "Oh, and before I forget," she added as they and Chloe and Park went toward the front door, "there's to be a pie supper and dance over at Fairly School Saturday night, and Mommie says Chloe and Park are going and I may if they'll take me and see that I get home." The front door closed behind them, and Victor and Mr. Smith heard the couples laughing as they went quickly toward the Walkers' spring wagon.

"Now, then," Mr. Smith said, sitting back down and resting one hand on the highly polished, carved organ, "about the war. You know, of course, that when I was 15 or so my father refused to let me join the Union army. Despite my brother Franklin's views, my father steadfastly declared that that and all other such conflicts—"

Victor listened, nodding occasionally as his thoughts went with the two couples...and strayed unwillingly to Lucy Smith...to her smile and the delighted way she had laughed at his simple trick.

• • •

On their way home, as the sun was setting, Victor bided his time, watching his brother smile faintly to himself. They went through Ravanna, nodding to several families they knew who were walking to the evening service at the Otterbein Church. The brothers went on in silence, past the Mercer farms, and turned west at the junction. Idly they gazed southward toward the rent farms of Olphin Thogmorton, the owner of the Princeton State

Bank. Then, to their right, they looked toward Robert McCargue's rambling old farmhouse, and dimly heard loud laughter and whooping. Only after they had gone a few miles more and had passed the Fairly main house did Alexander speak.

"Judge Jewell's built himself a fine barn," Alex said, leaning forward with his elbows on his thighs, the lines slack in his hands.

"Has he?" Victor said, smiling to himself. He knew that when Alex had so much to say that he was about to bust, he became more silent than usual until his excitement settled down. After all, there were few things worse—for anybody at any time—than an emotional outburst.

Alexander nodded solemnly, as if the new barn were the most significant thing in the county. "Copper cupola. Trotting horse and sulky weather vane, too."

"Um...interesting."

"Double doors, both sides."

"Don't say?"

Alex looked sideways at Victor, and slowly his brown eyes lit with laughter. "Yep...do say."

"Well," Victor said seriously, gripping the iron railing at the end of the seat as the wagon lurched down to the bridge over the creek bordering Fairly land, "that's what he gets for being elected state representative—that and William Junior getting accepted to Harvard Law School."

"So we heard," Alex said, his mirthful expression simmering and appearing about ready to blossom. "He's home now, though. We talked to him some. Not every day you meet someone who's going to a back-East university."

"First one from Mercer County, Daddy said."

"Course Quincy Thogmorton went to University of Missouri."

Victor nodded. "It's a good school, too."

"Bigger'n Maryville State Teachers' College—where Quincy's wife, Lorna Routh, graduated last year."

Victor tilted his head and stared at gray clouds that were slowly gathering overhead from the west, obscuring what had been a nice sunset. "Heard Lorna was going to teach up at the Burrows School—upper grades."

"Olphin Thogmorton's daughter-in-law teach school? Not likely," Alexander snorted.

"Nothing wrong with teaching school. I heard Grace Bohring was planning on going to Maryville."

Reflectively, Alexander said, "Now there's a beauty for you. Too bad her mother's half-Indian."

"Didn't hurt her looks any."

"Which one?"

"Grace."

"No," Alexander said, still reflectively.

"Have you seen her brother lately?"

"Ira? Nope, can't say I have...and can't say I'm sorry I haven't. Wonder who his daddy was, dark as he is."

"Sure wasn't Dad Bohring, not with his white hair, beard, and skin. Looks like he was made of writing paper. Ever talk much to him?"

"Can't say I have," Alex said, watching the sky darken.

"Knows more about gardening than any man I've met," Victor said, watching the horses raise their heads and sniff the air. A coachwhip snake writhed across the road, and the horses shied sideways.

"Hup!" Alex called, slapping the lines, "Nothin' but a snake," he added with disgust. He looked skyward again. "Hope it doesn't rain next Saturday. It'd spoil the dance."

"So we're going."

Alexander looked at him. "Got some shoe polish?"

"You going to polish your shoes tonight, or wait'll tomorrow?"

Alexander laughed and shoved Victor playfully, then spread his arms wide and began to sing to the horses and the coming night:

> Oh, the moon shines tonight
> on pretty Redwing,
> on pretty Redwing.
> The wind is sighing,
> The night birds crying,
> for pretty Redwing,
> for pretty Redwing.
> But Redwing's weeping
> her heart away....

In the morning the Walker family sat down for a meal of biscuits and gravy, fried eggs and cornmeal mush with butter, and buttermilk. Afterward, while Nanny was clearing the table, James looked at Alex and Victor with a twinkle in his blue eyes. "If you boys aren't too tired from all your hard work yesterday, I need you to go into town." He pulled a five-dollar bill from one pocket. "Mama, what'd you need?"

Mrs. Walker had been pumping water into the sink; she paused and turned. Patiently, as if she already had told him several times, she said, "Sack of Blue 'D' flour, sack of beans—the red ones, and have Elijah open the sack and check it for stones—a pail of cane syrup—"

"Can't we get syrup from Jess Lewis?" James asked, tisking his tongue behind his teeth, peeved at having to buy things that the neighbors made.

"He's out. And buy a pound of brown sugar. Oh, and some dried apples if they're not brown."

Alex suddenly laughed, folded his arms, and leaned back. "Fluty, remember the time you was left—"

"Were left," Mrs. Walker said, pumping hard and making jets of water splash into the sink. She began washing dishes.

"*Were* left with Nanny and Ella and decided to cook them some dried apples to eat with cinnamon? Filled a big pot with them, didn't you?"

Victor laughed ruefully, glancing at his father. "I kept adding water and the apples kept swelling until I had every pot in the kitchen filled with apples."

"We had 'em for a week," James said, snorting.

"Mama, couldn't they get some Castile soap, too?" Nanny pleaded, taking dishes from her mother to dry them. "Your lye soap burns my skin, and Ellie said, 'Oh, you still use *homemade*! I can smell it.' "

"Bet she said, 'I *kin* smell it,' " Alex muttered, looking at his mother.

"If you have an extra nickel," Mrs. Walker said, sighing, "buy her two bars of soap."

"Lavender- or rose-scented?" Alexander asked prettily, sneaking up behind Nanny to untie her apron strings. She squealed and tried to pop him with the towel.

Mr. Walker followed his sons to the back door. "You should have about two dollars left out of the five I gave you. Go 'round to Rouse's and buy two singletrees and two breeching straps. If he doesn't have them, see if Kelly Combs'll make you some. Mind you get hickory singletrees, and check 'em for knots."

"Yes, Daddy," Alex said, winking at Victor as they hurried toward the barn. "And we'll make sure we get a left-hand and a right-hand breeching strap, too!" He laughed with Victor, and they looked back to see their father impatiently wave them on.

"He's in no mood for teasing today," Alexander noted, opening the barn door. "Must be thinking about plowing."

"It's his back," Victor said, taking the harness from the pegs. "He's getting old."

Alexander took one bridle and followed Victor into the horse pen. "He's not but 52."

"He's been changing," Victor said, cornering Mack, the lead horse. He slipped the bridle over Mack's head and forced the bit into his mouth, clicking it against his teeth and making sure his tongue didn't ride over it while he worked the head strap over the stiff, furry ears. "Haven't you heard Daddy mutter, 'Wore out...just plum wore out'?"

"I thought Mama was the one getting old," Alex said, bridling Lazy, the other gelding. "She's nearly 54."

Victor paused in scratching behind Mack's ears. "Have you noticed how Mama's been holding her head—like she had a pain in her neck or top of her back? And I don't hear them talking in bed like they used to."

Alexander grinned at his brother. "Then for sure they're gettin' old. You know what they say...."

Victor led Mack through the pen gate before Alex could tell one of the stories the younger men in town liked to plague the older ones with. In silence, the brothers hitched the horses to the wagon.

Almost three hours later they were in town, driving slowly around the square. Off to one side of the lawn of the square near the bandstand, a carnival troupe was setting up a large merry-go-round. Victor looked at the brightly striped tent covering the gaily painted horses, camels, and elephants, and he noted the upright steam engine. A boy was between the engine and the back of a wagon, shoveling coal onto the ground. "Want to stick around for a ride?" Victor asked Alex as they stopped in front of Gregory's Grocery. Alex snorted as he tied the horses to a post and climbed the steep steps.

"I take enough ribbing around here without acting *that* foolish," he muttered, opening the green screen door and the gold-flowered and design-painted inner one.

Smells greeted them first: cheddar cheese in a block that had been partially whittled away, molasses, vanilla beans, pepper, tea leaves, aging vegetables, and coffee spilled around the upright red mill. Victor separated each scent as he and Alex went toward the back, where the stove and tall stovepipe were—and four chairs around a checkerboard set on a cracker barrel.

"Well, mornin', Alex...Victor," came the cheerful voice of the tall, patriarchal-looking store owner. Elijah Gregory's paunch was covered by a clean white apron, and his gray beard came squarely down onto his chest; his keen black eyes flicked from Alex to Victor. Behind him, two men were playing checkers, and two men were watching them; all four men looked up and nodded to the brothers. One of the watchers was Clay George, the sheriff, and Alex in particular was glad to see him; the other men wouldn't plague him so heavily with Clay around, knowing that Clay was a good friend of James Walker.

"Hello, Alex," Clay said, standing and coming around the cane-bottom, ladder-back chairs to shake hands with the brothers. "Victor," he nodded. "You boys livin' west o'town or out east these days?" The expression of his weathered face with its thick brown eyebrows and forceful brown eyes seemed innocent, but he was pulling at one end of his broad mustache as if he were hiding a grin.

"East somewhat," Alex swallowed, slumping slightly to one side.

"Last feller who got to likin' that Fairly road was took sick," Clay said a bit more seriously. "Somethin' called Fairly-McCargue plague."

"You don't say," Alex remarked, glancing at the checker players—Mel Hickman and Spenser Lowry, both haulers and odd-job men.

"Do say," Clay replied, lowering his hand from his moustache. His hand came to rest on the handle of the .38 holstered at his belt. With his other hand he reached behind and pulled a pouch of tobacco from his hip pocket. He unfolded the top and opened it, then held it out toward Alex and Victor. When they each shook their heads, he took a wad of molasses-smelling chew and folded it into one side of his mouth. "Fact is," he said, working the chew around, "Tom Fairly's been shootin' off his mouth to the crowd over at the blacksmith's shop."

"Guess he needs to get rid of his hot air somewhere."

Clay chewed thoughtfully, then said, "Forewarned is forearmed."

Alex nodded. "Guess you've told Park Robinson, too."

"He don't count," Clay said, chuckling and glancing at Elijah

Gregory. "Park's store's comin' along, though, and so's his house over on Mayhew Street. Seen it?"

"Passed by," Alex said, turning to the grocer as Clay went back to his chair by the checker game.

The brothers made their purchases, carried the sacks to the wagon, and walked across the corner of the square to Rouse's Dry Goods and Hardware. The floorboards creaked as they went toward the back of the store, glancing at bins of seeds and larger bins of screws and bolts and still larger bins of nails. Woodworking tools were arrayed on cabinet doors, and garden tools hung along the upper walls. Counters displayed knives of all shapes and sizes and a multitude of kitchen utensils. Crockery was stacked on tables down the middle of the narrow, long store, and china and tinware were stacked on the farther back counters. Half a dozen men were sitting on nail kegs around the stove, occasionally spitting into the ash box; two were whittling, their laps covered with shavings, and two others methodically were sharpening their knives. All the men looked up and nodded, tipped a forefinger, or spoke when the brothers stopped near Mr. Rouse, who, as always, seemed frail and anxious. Alex told Mr. Rouse what they needed, and he went into the harness room in back to look for the singletrees and breechings. One of the whittlers, Rory McDougal, looked at Alex with one gray-black eyebrow raised.

"Seen you comin' back from courtin' the other night," he said, taking a curl of pine from the inside of one leg of the hunting hound he was carving.

"Spring's comin'," Alex said with a quick grin. "Sap's risin'."

The men chuckled, glancing at him.

"Heard you was courtin' trouble, too," the other whittler, Tilden Kauffman, said. "Ed said Clay told him he was lookin' for you."

"He found me," Alex said nonchalantly. "Lotta hot air goin' 'round town lately."

"Blowin' mostly from the east," Tilden said, glancing at Rory with a slow grin. "Liable to blow a man's hat clean offen his head."

" 'Less the man's got it settled in place," Alex retorted.

Mr. Rouse returned with his arms laden with the singletrees. "Out of breechin's," he said as Victor took the singletrees and began examining them. Watching Victor anxiously, Mr. Rouse added, "You boys need rings or pivot pins...anythin' else?"

"No, Sir," Alex said, digging in one pocket for the silver dollars Mr. Gregory had given him in change. He paid Mr. Rouse and was given a 50-cent piece in change. "You boys don't work too hard, now," Alex said, grinning at the whittlers and their companions.

Outside, going along the sidewalk under the bright new awning of the refurbished Burey House Hotel, Alexander whistled, "Whew! This's hard work!"

"Two down, one to go," Victor said consolingly.

They drove the team off the square and one block downhill to Combs's Livery Stable. Through the double doors they could see a straw-covered aisle lined on each side with stalls; a tortoise-shell cat sat in a spot of sunlight, washing one paw. Kelly Jr. was coming past the cat, carrying a hayfork. "Mornin'!" he called cheerily, waving his free hand.

"Mornin', Freckles. Your daddy around?" Alex asked, climbing down from the wagon.

"He's out back. Some gypsy's tryin' to sell him a horse. Lame in a back leg, though. Won't fetch more'n three dollars." Kelly Jr. put the hayfork into a tool room by the front doors and turned to lead the brothers toward the open back doors, halfheartedly kicking at the cat as he went by it. Victor inhaled the sweet smell of red clover and timothy hay, and he heard the shuffling and stamping of four or so horses in stalls. The smell and sounds reminded him of when he had been a boy and had dreamed of buying a real Arabian mare from Mr. Combs's father, Kelly John. Victor, feeling almost childish, looked over each stall door to see if an Arabian mare might be inside. There wasn't.

When Mr. Combs joined them, he asked, "Now, what can I do fer you?" Alex told him.

As Mr. Combs cut two breeching straps from a hide and punched holes in their ends, he talked about the man from whom he had just bought a horse. "Feel sorry for them gypsies, I do. Folks 'round here can't stand 'em any better'n Mormons or Indians, but all the talk about child-stealin' and puttin' spells on people is nonsense." He handed the straps to Alex and took the 50 cents Alex offered him. "Just nonsense. Folks who say such things don't know what it's like comin' to a new country, bein' among strangers and foreigners, livin' from hand to mouth." He shot Alex, then Victor, a sparkling but hard look. "But I do." He followed the brothers to their wagon and put his hands on the horses to steady them as Alex and Victor climbed up. "My father, rest his soul, brought me and Mama and us kids over in steerage in 1851. I was only two, but I remember the people yellin' out when they died—starved, sick, desp'rate."

"You're a good man, Mr. Combs," Victor said, reaching down to shake his hand. He smiled as Kelly Jr. came to stand beside his father. "And so'll be your son there."

Mr. Combs smiled broadly, looking at his boy and tousling his flame-red hair. "Got more freckles'n anybody in Mercer County."

"Maybe in all of Missouri," Victor called back as Alex clucked to the horses, who had begun slowly moving down the street.

As the brothers rode the next two blocks, they both could hear the ringing of a five-pound hammer against the "live" anvil in Big Jim McCargue's blacksmith shop. When Olin Gray had been the town's blacksmith and the brothers had been boys, the ringing sound had been cheerful, making them think of the strange and wonderful things not even their father could produce at their farm's forge. But when Mr. Gray had become feeble and Big Jim had bought him out, the sound of the ringing hammer had become ominous, almost a death-knell. Now, Victor saw, there was little traffic along Hill Street, and the two houses across from the blacksmith's shop were decrepit and rented, their yards weed-grown.

When the wagon passed the shop, several young men wandered out, their hands stuffed into their pockets or their thumbs hooked behind their overall straps. Jim and Todd McCargue were foremost among the lounging youths, and Jim cupped his hands to his mouth and reared back to shout, "You 'member what Tom tol' you, ya hear!" Laughter followed his shout, rising and falling, then rising briefly again. The ringing of the hammer resumed.

For the Walker family, the remainder of the week passed in the routines of work: up at five, breakfast before dawn, to work by five-thirty, dinner at noon, supper at sunset, to bed by full dark. Alex, Victor, and their father put the plow and corn-planter in order, repaired harness, greased wheels, made horseshoes, and reshod the mules and horses. They took the racks of seed corn down in the bin—where ears hung two by two over poles, with their dried husks braided together—and shelled the grains into sacks so the hoppers on the planter could be filled quickly and easily. And while they shelled the corn, Alex looked frequently at his hands, thinking how rough they were becoming and how smooth Lucy Smith's skin was. Once he gazed plaintively at Victor. "She sure won't want to hold *these* hands while we dance," he mourned.

Victor smiled, but he had disturbing thoughts of his own. His regret about asking that his recurrent dream be taken from him had deepened. He continued to feel that he himself was somehow responsible for Alex, and he had been spending quite a bit of time trying to remember the awful sound he had heard in his dream. It was a sound he knew he should know, but it wouldn't come to him. He stopped shelling corn and reached to pet one of the cats that had wandered in, sniffing around for rats. She arched her back and stared at him, blinking her green, yellow-centered eyes. Victor almost asked her what the dream-sound was, so greatly did he want to remember it. His father walked in then and gave him a strange look when he saw his son petting the cat. "If you make her tame," James said bluntly, "she won't hunt." With a sigh that was almost a groan, he sat back on a sack of seed corn near his sons, took up an ear, and began twisting the ear back and forth in his hands to send the white-yellow kernels rattling faintly into an open sack at his feet.

By Saturday afternoon everything was ready for plowing and planting season. The weather was clear; the snow had melted except in long, ragged patches on the shady sides of hills and under the trees and hedgerows. There was the smell of spring in the air—moist, fertile, rich with earth scent, and heavy with the promise of budding trees and burgeoning plants. After work, as the brothers walked to the house to take baths, they glanced at the two roosters—the smaller, yellow-and-white-tailed brown one chasing the heavier, red-and-black-tailed one, then strutting off to crow brazenly before chasing after a hen. The Jersey cow lowed from the west pasture, and Ed Kauffman's bull bellowed back in the southern distance, a hill and a pasture away.

Their mother had been heating water in four big kettles on the stove. Seeing the brothers, she and Nanny each took a handle to carry one of the steaming kettles into the bathroom. Alex and Victor took the two other kettles and followed, and Victor nodded toward their mother, frowning at the way she was struggling. Her head was held back, and her legs jerked with each step. As Nanny and she poured the hot water into the old zinc tub, Victor asked her, "Mama, are you all right?"

She turned, wiping her pale, sweating forehead. "Just tired," she said. "You boys scrub the ring before you leave," she said as she went past them.

They flipped a coin to see who would go first, and Alex lost. "You always win," he complained, taking the empty kettles out. "But you'd better not leave a silt layer in the bottom!"

When they were decked out in their Sunday best, with white shirts their mother had ironed to a fare-you-well, they appeared in the kitchen for her inspection. She turned from her cooking at the stove and sized them up. "What's that I smell?" she asked, going closer to them.

"Potatoes boiling?" Alex asked innocently.

She sniffed at him. "Lavender. You used Nanny's soap, didn't you?"

"Would you rather us smell like the bay rum Mr. Trask sells?" Alex asked teasingly.

"Lands, no!" their mother said seriously, rerolling a sleeve that had come undone. She turned back to the stove. "You be careful," she said. "I don't like you going to a dance—least of all one over in the Fairly."

"It's in a schoolhouse," Alex protested mildly.

"Some school that would have a dance," she muttered.

Instead of driving down south and over to Princeton, Alex guided the team north past Pleasant Ridge Church, then turned the horses east. They crossed the hills as the sun was slanting westward, and Victor sat up straighter on the bouncing, creaking seat. "Nice piece of land over yonder," he said.

Alex looked. "By the creek?"

"And eastward," Victor said. "Who owns that?"

"Old Mrs. Scholwalter, I think."

"Works in Casteel's Clothing Store?"

"No, her mother...a widow, I think. Land doesn't look worked."

Victor said nothing further, but he continued gazing at the fields and pastures. On far hills was forested land that looked virgin, so tall were the shadowed trees. "Lewises live over yonder, don't they?" he asked, pointing toward the northeast.

"Luther and Mott—Martha. Heard he was buying cows for a dairy herd. Mama says Mott's settin' up a loom. Going to do rug weavin'."

"Rugs would be nice in winter, wouldn't they?"

"Um. No more dancin' quickstep 'cross the floor to the stove to get dressed," Alex said, laughing slightly.

They said nothing more, crossing the Grand River and then the railroad tracks in silence. They turned south at the road that ran between Princeton and Centerville and passed a number of "middlin' " farms in the two miles before they sighted Fairly Baptist Church. Next to the church was a cemetery, and beside it was the Fairly School, a square, one-room, board-and-batten building with a shake roof.

"Lots of buggies," Alex noted as he turned the team into the schoolyard. Light streamed from the open double doors of the school, and they could hear the sharp notes of a fiddle being tuned. Standing outside were several couples—Celia McCargue, a wild, red-haired teenager known for her fighting, and Fred Fairly among them. Neither Fred nor Celia said anything as the Walker brothers went inside the school, taking off their hats and looking to the left of the door for the rack.

They stood gazing around for several minutes, absorbing the sights of a flurry of young women in reception dresses, nervous and stiff young men in suits that all looked too small, and older men sitting on benches around the dance floor while their women fussed with a large number of pies and the punch bowl, makings, and cups.

Victor leaned toward Alex and whispered, "There's Ed Ash and Grace Bohring."

"Ed looks as waxy as a candle," Alex whispered back. "Wonder what Grace sees in him."

"And there's Lizzy Casteel with Raymond Bearden."

"Bet Lizzy wishes Papa had kept little brother Hub at home."

Victor grinned. "Pruett and Olin Blakesley."

"Lookin' like horse thieves. Remember when Olin called Ella a dun cow?"

Victor ignored Alex's disgruntled comments as he looked among the crowd. "Fred Ash's got the fiddle," he noted.

"Wonder why Tom George wasn't hired?"

"John Henry Bein's still seein' Maude Fisher," Victor commented, nodding toward a solemn young man and his worried-looking companion.

"That's not a couple; that's a disaster waitin' to happen."

They moved toward the refreshment tables. Alex nodded to Mrs. Fairly, who seemed to be in charge of things, buzzing around like a bumblebee. Mr. Fairly, "Anvil," stood against the far wall, looking as though he were brooding about the money he'd spent on the dance. Mrs. McCargue, Robert's wife, was helping set pies in order and was overseeing the other women who were cutting them into slices. A number of the other wives were nearby, talking, sampling what one another had brought, and glancing toward the dance floor, then toward their husbands. The menfolk had gathered near Mr. Fairly but weren't talking to him, so glum did he appear. Then a buzz passed through the crowd, and most heads turned toward the door.

"Chloe," Alex said, his excitement showing, "Park...and...." He moved in a direct line toward the door, excusing himself as he brushed people and they turned to stare at him. "Miss Lucy," he said quietly, but not as quietly as he thought. People smiled, and heads went together as whispers began. Park hung his hat on the rack and moved toward Fred Ash, a friend of his; Chloe followed, and Lucy and Alex trailed behind. Soon they were out of the center of attention, and more arrivals changed the course of the whispered conversations.

But the talk stopped when those inside the school heard the sound of a number of horses and loud whooping. With a storm of slapping hats, in came the Fairly Gang—Tom and Lloyd Fairly, Weldon Trask, Tom and young Robert McCargue, followed in a moment by Jim and Todd McCargue. Outside by the horses, some people glimpsed Jane Trask—in pants and a man's shirt—lounging with Fred Fairly and Celia McCargue, her back turned as she slipped the couple a pint bottle. The young men who had come inside went toward Mr. Fairly, who looked as though wild hogs had just erupted inside his parlor. "You boys settle down!" he commanded in a low, thudding voice.

For a time, the young men obeyed—until two groups of young women arrived, first the Hunters, then the Clarks from down around the marshland. Those girls' coming set the young men into a spate of foot-stomping, whooping, and cries for the fiddler to get started. That commotion almost covered the arrival of a pair who caused the ladies who noticed them to stiffen and the young men to leer, winking at one another: old Corn Hart, the half-Indian from over Goshen way, and his "daughter," Half-Millie. The young woman's hair was coal-black and almost hid her attractive but puffy-looking face; her face, however, was not what the young men were looking at. She went along the left side of the room to the corner without glancing at anyone present, followed by her "father."

In answer to renewed cries for music, Fred Ash was joined by the youngest boy in Big Jim McCargue's family, Robbie. Robbie hopped onto the low platform with his silver flute in hand, turned, and bowed elegantly to the crowd, which began clapping. Tapping one foot and looking at Fred, Robbie set his flute to his lips and began a merry tune that quickly had couples whirling and dipping sideways around the dance floor.

Tune after tune the pair played, reels and waltzes. At the fifth song, Alex ushered Lucy onto the floor and shyly took her hand, stretching it out in proper fashion. He was so self-conscious that he felt his blush surely was a red beacon, and no sooner had they begun to dance than his embarrassment was heightened by bumping into another couple. He turned and mumbled, "Sorry," then noticed that the couple was Tom Fairly and a Lewis girl. Tom glared at him, whitening, and muttered something. Quickly Alexander stepped away before Lucy could hear the oath, but he glanced threateningly back. Tom still was glaring at him, twisting his head no matter which way his dancing led him.

As the night went on, Victor stood by the punch bowl, watching the dancing couples. It seemed to him that Grace Bohring and Ed Ash made a good couple, for both were quiet and graceful. He saw that one by one the "gang" members stole outside and returned flush-faced and more boisterous than they had been. He noticed two or three young men slip over to Half-Millie after each dance to ask for the next one. He also observed that the "wiser" young men, like Ira Bohring—who had appeared seemingly from nowhere—hung close to Corn Hart, whispering to the impassive, shrunken old man. It was Ira who left with Half-Millie near 11 o'clock, followed shortly by Corn Hart. Others thereafter began leaving, first the older adults, then the younger people. When almost half the crowd was gone, Victor looked around for Alex and Lucy.

He saw Chloe and Park near the platform, and he made his way to them. "Where're Lucy and my brother?" he asked above the fluttering music of the fiddle and flute.

Park and Chloe both looked around, standing on tiptoe to see above the dancing couples. "There's Lucy, over by the door," Chloe said, taking Park's hand and leading him around the dancers.

Lucy was seated on a bench beneath the hat rack, her hands clasped in her lap, her gaze downcast. "Lucy?" Chloe asked, kneeling by her.

When she looked up, Victor saw that tears were brimming her lower lids. He leaned close. "Where's Alex?" he asked, barely able to keep his question from being a demand.

"He...went out," Lucy said weakly, looking quickly from Chloe to Park to Victor. She looked at Victor's eyes for a moment, then stared down, reclasping her fine white hands in her lap. "He told me to wait here."

"Who'd he leave with?" Victor asked more loudly, his heartbeat quickening as a dry knot rose in his throat. A throbbing began in his temples as he felt his dream beginning to return *The sound! What was the sound?* "Did he leave with Tom Fairly and that bunch?"

Lucy's frightened look shot to his eyes. "Tom said something...something bad to me, and Alex just left...without saying anything except, 'Wait here.' "

"He wouldn't," Victor muttered, staring out the doorway. The first thing he noticed was that the gang's horses were gone. Quickly, standing as tall as he could, he looked around the schoolhouse. The McCargue boys, the Fairlys, and the Trasks all had gone. He glanced at Park, dismissed him, looked around again, and spotted Russell George talking with Al Kauffman. Practically shoving people aside, he went to the two men—Russell, who had been sheriff and before then a Union Army officer, and Al, who once had been a prizefighter in Cincinnati. Both men saw the expression on Victor's face and followed him without hesitation.

Outside, Victor told them what he thought had happened. Al went to his wagon to get a lantern while Russell went to his horse to get an old Colt pistol from his saddlebag. Al reappeared with a lit lantern, almost running, as Anvil Fairly, Tilden Kauffman, and Spenser Lowry came from the schoolhouse and were told what was going on. The men gathered around Victor and watched Russell George. "Which way would they have gone?" Anvil asked the taller, still strikingly handsome man.

Russell squinted toward the cemetery that was between the school and the church. "They likely wouldn't fight right out here where anybody could see them and break it up," he said quietly, measuring his syllables as if measuring an enemy before a battle. "Let's look at the cleared ground over in the graveyard."

With Al Kauffman leading the way with the lantern's swinging, pale circle of yellowish light, the men went quickly into the cemetery. They cast around until Al softly called, "Here."

The men clustered, looking down at scuff marks deep in the damp earth. "And here," Al said, taking hold of Victor's right arm. Victor bent and picked up a stickpin.

"It's his," he said with a sinking feeling.

"But where would they have gone?" Spenser asked, his voice trembling.

From the distance, from the north, came a long, rising and falling wail—a train whistle. "The Golden State Limited," Al muttered, pulling out his watch and unsnapping the cover as he held it into the lantern light. "Midnight—right on time."

Again the long, rising and falling, terribly lonely sound came from the distance, slightly closer than it had been. "The dream!" Victor said, feeling nausea swelling within him. He grabbed Russell's arm. "Don't ask questions; just follow me."

They sprinted to their horses, and Victor vaulted into his wagon; he lashed the team, wheeling them around so fast that the wagon nearly overturned. Up the main road a piece was a short road that headed down to the tracks and the marshes beyond. It was a fishermen's road, little used, and when Victor turned his team onto it, he pulled them up short. Whipping the lines around a stanchion, he leaped down; even in the light from the half-moon he could see the hoofprints. "They've been here!" he shouted to the men who were dismounting behind him. "Come on...quick!"

The whistle of the express train sounded again, loudly now as Victor thrashed along the muddy, print-tracked road. He could feel the ground vibrating from the oncoming train, and he could see the embankment for the track rising ahead of him in the darkness. A light flashed along the rails, growing brighter...and illuminating a shape flung across the track. "Nooo!" Victor screamed, reaching forward as he ran.

The whistle of the steam locomotive became constant, warning, drowning his scream and the shouts of the other men. Over the limp shape thundered the train, its steam off, its drive wheels backing, its shrill whistle blasting through the night, through the woods and marshland to the distant farmhouses, warning...crying.

When the men caught up with Victor, they found him kneeling near the track, bent forward with his forehead on the earth. Above him were legs, severed.

By the time the train came to a stop, it was past the body. Men with lanterns came running back up the track from the engine and the observation car. They joined the silent group staring down. It was several minutes before Russell George managed to gain control of himself enough to say, "Al...you and Spenser ride to town. Get Clay out of bed if you have to. And bring Otterman and Blumequist."

Al and Spenser broke and ran as if released from some awful spell. The train's engineer slowly approached Russell. In a shaking, hesitant whisper, looking down at Victor huddled on the embankment, he said, "When I seen it...him...I tried to stop...but he didn't move. I blew the whistle," he continued as Russell took a deep breath and crossed the tracks. "You must've heard me...I blew it loud and long...but he just didn't move!"

Russell stuck his pistol behind his belt and knelt by Alexander's head. He straightened briefly, took another breath, and reached down. "Bring your light," he said in a low, hard voice. When one of the trainmen was shoved forward by the engineer and held his lantern over the grisly sight, Russell put two fingertips to the bloody, crosshatched swelling on Alexander's right temple. "Blackjack," the older man muttered angrily. He stood when he heard a number of questioning, calling voices coming down the short road. He recrossed the tracks and hurried down the embankment toward the oncoming crowd. "Stay back!" he shouted. "Just stay back!"

"But why...what's happened?" a dozen voices asked.

Russell George straightened, turning to look for Anvil Fairly. When he caught the man's eye, he said, loudly enough for the crowd to hear, "Alexander Walker has been murdered."

Spring of Mourning

A wailing cry came from the rear of the crowd, and a girl almost luminescent in her white dress came running around the staring people. Lucy was followed by Chloe, who was clutching for her arms, trying to stop her, and by Park Robinson. Despite her sister's efforts, Lucy ran to the embankment, looked down and saw Victor huddled there, then saw the body. She screamed, shuddering violently, and turned in a half-circle with her hands raised as if searching for something. As if suddenly drained of vitality, she went limp and fell beside Victor, her arms across his back. He slowly raised his head, wiped the hair and mud from his forehead, and twisted around into a kneeling position so he could take Lucy in his arms. She sobbed against him, clutching his lapels.

More and more people came to stand silently, watching from the end of the short road. An hour or so passed nightmarishly, and finally Al and Spenser brought the undertaker and the coroner from Princeton. The undertaker, Otto Otterman, and his assistant took off their hats as they stood over the body. Then Otto beckoned to his assistant. They returned to the road and soon came back to the tracks carrying a wooden coffin between them; a hammer bounced on the lid as they crossed the uneven ground. They put the body into the coffin and nailed down the lid right there. As they were lugging the coffin back through the crowd and the crowd began to follow, Lucy pried herself from Victor, stood, and looked helplessly around. A spot of white between the tracks caught her eye, and she lurched up the embankment to it. She bent and picked up the white object, folded it over and over in her hands, staring at it, then methodically stuffed it up one sleeve. Victor went to her with Chloe, and they supported Lucy between them as they slowly made their way to Victor's wagon. Russell George had tied his horse behind it and was waiting to drive Victor back to town.

Although it was the custom of farm families themselves to prepare their dead for burial, in this case Mr. Otterman took Alex's body to his establishment for embalming. Meanwhile, Chloe and Park took Lucy home...while an even larger crowd gathered in the Princeton square than had been at the dance. Angry mutterings rippled here and there: Everyone knew who had committed the murder, and it was simply a question of who would go out and get them. Clay George, his sheriff's badge pinned to his hat, went among the crowd, picking out a man now and then. He also gathered what information he could from his Uncle Russell and from Al Kauffman and Victor. Clay and Russell then led a large group of mounted men eastward out of town, leaving Ed Kauffman and Victor to precede the hearse to the Walker farm.

On their way, Victor and Ed stopped to pick up Ed's wife, Libbie, and her mother, Grace George. When the four of them drove slowly up the Walker farm drive, they saw two people standing on the front porch; pale light streamed from the windows behind them, silhouetting their still, dark forms. Ed stopped the wagon and helped his womenfolk down while Victor went to stand in front of his mother and father. As succinctly as possible, he told his parents what had happened. Even before he had finished, his mother was crying into the night, "Ohh...noo! Not my baby...not my baby!"

Mrs. Kauffman, a large woman, put her arms around Mrs. Walker and led her into the house, followed by Mrs. George. They placed Mrs. Walker in her chair by the stove and found a quilt to put over her legs, then pulled chairs close beside her. Reaching across, Mrs. Kauffman held Susan's hands as the latter continued to repeat her cry, softer now than the wailing, accusatory cry she had sent into the night.

Mr. Walker stood silently on the porch, staring off up the drive toward the orchard. His hands were stuffed into his overall pockets, his legs were bowed, and his shoulders were slumped.

Victor, still standing before the porch with Ed Kauffman beside him, looked up at his father. "Daddy?" James neither changed expression nor moved. "Daddy, it was partly my fault," Victor said quietly but distinctly. "I was given a dream, but I asked that it be taken away. It was. When I tried to remember it, I couldn't...until it was too late."

His father looked at him, his chin trembling, and slowly he sat on the edge of the porch, his elbows on his thighs, his face on his upturned hands. Victor sat beside him and put one arm around his back, and there they sat.

"I'll tend to the team," Ed said quietly, shuffling off into the darkness.

The next day, a hush spread gradually over Mercer County. Otterman had delivered the simple coffin to the Walker house, where it stood in the living room on sawhorses. Matt came on the ten o'clock train from Spickard and was driven to the farm by his Uncle Matt, who also brought Aunt Minerva. Soon, Ella and Fred Wilcox came, followed by Russell George and his wife, Jane Walker George. They joined the rest of the family around the coffin.

People from Princeton, the villages, and the countryside began arriving in a steady stream that increased after dinner. The people came in family groups, in pairs and trios, and even singly to the Walker home, spoke quietly to the family members, then passed by the coffin; they laid their hands on the dark brown wood as they stared down at it, then shook their heads and went away to stand in small groups and talk quietly. By suppertime, Mr. and Mrs. Smith arrived with Chloe, Park, and Lucy, who—like a pale birch wand—was sheltered between her parents. Soon thereafter, the crowd began to thin out.

When it seemed time for her to go home, Aunt Minerva stood—small and wiry and white-haired—wiping her eyes with her lace handkerchief, and went to Mrs. Walker. "It's hard, I know...but the Lord knows best. Likely He was sparing Alexander something we can't even imagine."

Susan Walker looked at her sister-in-law with reddened eyes, and they embraced. When they turned so Minerva could go to the door, Victor was standing in front of them.

"God didn't do this," he said quietly, his hands in his trousers' pockets. He looked from his mother to his aunt. "This," he said, glancing toward the coffin, "isn't the will of the Lord." When neither woman said anything, he resumed, "The Adversary intended this...and used human hands to bring it about. So let's don't think that God has hurt us and that we must bow to His will until someday we can understand. Let's just know the enemy and rely on our Redeemer to comfort us." He looked at the women, then at his father, uncle, brother, Ella and Fred Wilcox, and the Georges.

From behind Victor came a frail, quavering, but surprisingly determined voice singing, "Rock of A-ges..." They turned to see

Lucy Smith, hands clasped before herself, held by her father. "...cleft for me...Let me hide...myself in Thee." One by one, looking either shyly or gladly at Lucy, the others joined in: "Let the wa-ter and the blood...From Thy wound-ed side which flowed...Be of sin the double cure...." Swelling, filling the room, the voices united in parts poured forth, "Save from wrath...and make me pure." The voices grew still.

Mrs. Walker went to Lucy. Taking the young woman's hands, Susan said, "Thank you, dear...for what you did just now...and for what you were to Alexander."

Mr. Smith's strong arms braced his daughter as she pulled a white, bloodstained handkerchief from inside her left sleeve. She pressed it into Mrs. Walker's outstretched hands. Mrs. Walker stared at it, turning it over and over, then slowly she embraced Lucy. Mr. Smith straightened and put both arms around the women. Victor, Matt, Nanny, and Ella slowly joined the cluster. In a rich but rough breaking voice, Mr. Smith then began singing, "A-maz-ing grace...how sweet the sound...."

• • •

In the small steeple over the entry of the Pleasant Ridge Church, the bell began to toll as the hearse brought the coffin across the hills from the Walker farm. From Henry George's viewpoint—as he carefully pulled the stout rope to make the bell toll but not ring with its usual cheerful sound—the funeral procession appeared crossing a hilltop to the south, crept slowly along the one-lane, winding dirt road, then slowly disappeared behind the next hill, the hearse in front, its horses wearing black plumes on their headstraps. Behind came wagons and buggies, so many that eventually the entire churchyard and schoolyard across the road were filled. The bell fell silent, and the people followed the coffin into the small church, filling it so full that many people stood along the walls, their arms folded, their eyes downcast. Many others were forced to wait outside in the bright chill air, hearing the wind in their ears mingled with the words of the hymns and sermon.

No organ or piano accompanied the hymns Mrs. Walker had requested—"How Firm a Foundation" and "Jesus, Lover of My Soul"—and the voices in parts soared richly, building upon one another as they went out from the church and across the countryside. Old Reverend Turnbull from the First Baptist Church of Princeton—standing straight in his black suit, black tie, and white shirt beside the pulpit—preached the funeral sermon. Afterward the coffin was carried by men of the George and Kauffman

families to the nearby cemetery, where an open grave lay shadowed by tall, pointed cedar trees, trees bowing in the wind that
coursed over the swelling hills, undulating hedgerows, and field-
patterned farms in a broad vista as peaceful as the funeral itself.
During the walk to the grave, the people were silent. But as the
coffin was lowered on a cradle of two creaking ropes into the red-
beige clay, the hymns began again—although this time they were
spoken, with restraint. Solemnly, the people clasped their hands
before themselves, not looking at one another, and said the hymn
words in unison. Silently, individually, they asked for the Comforter...though many of those present knew He had been among
them all along; within, deep within, those people already were
being comforted...and felt a certain joy.

Tuesday, neighbor women still were in the Walker home,
quietly preparing food, tending to the house, consoling Mrs.
Walker. Victor nodded to his older brother, Matt, and they left
together, settling their hats onto their heads as they went out to
harness the team. They said nothing about the funeral or the
murder during the drive into town; it was as if the entire matter
were crated with the lid nailed down, waiting to be reopened at
a time when something could be done; but until then....

In downtown Princeton, the streets were lined with buggies and
wagons. Men were walking purposefully but unhurriedly toward
the courthouse, which was on Main Street, two blocks off the
square and next to the high school. The courthouse steps were
jammed with people who moved aside when they saw Matt and
Victor coming. The brothers went slowly through the aisle that
opened, down the hall, and into the district courtroom. There,
every bench was filled and people were standing all around the
walls. The young district attorney, James Wendell Holmes, was
questioning Russell George. A number of other witnesses were
seated on two rows behind the prosecutor's table for the coroner's
inquest, but nowhere in sight were any of the members of the
Fairly Gang.

When Sheriff Clay George took the stand, Judge Franklin Hall
had to bang his gavel on a marble block to get the crowd to quiet
down.

Mr. Holmes took a piece of paper from his table and went to
stand near the witness box. He asked several precursory questions, then asked, "And what did you find when you and the posse
reached the Fairly house?"

"Nothing."

"Sir?"

Clay shrugged, turning his hat around and around in front of his knees. He shifted his chaw of tobacco and said more loudly, "The only people there were the three older boys—Andrew, Oscar, and Howard. When Russell and I went back Sunday, we found the rest of the family—Mrs. Fairly and Thomas, and the younger boys, Tom, Lloyd, and Fred. We asked them what happened Saturday night. Mr. Fairly made his boy Tom speak out. Tom said there'd been a fight in the cemetery at Fairly Church. He said that Alexander Walker slipped on the mud and hit his head on a tombstone. He said that when he and the other Fairly boys and McCargues examined Alex, he was dead. How he got onto the railroad tracks, Tom said he didn't know. He said that when he and his brothers left Alex, he was in the cemetery."

"But young Tom admitted having a fight with Alexander Walker?"

"Didn't make no bones about it. Said Alex called him out. Said Alex thought he'd said something dirty to his girl and called him outside. Said, 'Course I had to go, even if he was older and bigger.' "

"And what of the threats Tom Fairly, Jr., is known to have been making concerning Alex Walker?" Mr. Holmes asked, growing frustrated.

Clay George turned his hat around and around in his hands, looking down at it and ignoring the buzzing crowd before him. "Tom said it was just a lot of hot air." The crowd whispered more loudly, and Judge Hall rapped for order. Clay glanced over at him and received a scowl in return. "Judge," Clay said in a pleading tone, "there just isn't any *evidence*." He glanced out at the crowd, then let his gaze settle on Mr. Holmes. "Russell and I couldn't find anything out at the church except signs of a fight. And the horseprints down on the load that leads to the track were so...so scurried around by the folks that came down that we couldn't make nothin' out."

"But Russell George, your own uncle, has just testified that when he examined the head of the deceased, he saw a bloody swelling on one temple that was marked as though a blackjack had struck it, and you've heard testimony by Mr. Combs and others that Tom Fairly frequently has been seen around town carrying a blackjack. And we've heard—"

"I *know* what we've heard!" Clay said, exasperated. He set his hat on the railing in front of himself and leveled one forefinger at the district attorney. "But we didn't *find* a blackjack. We can't *prove* Tom had one the night of the dance, and we sure can't *prove* he hit Alex Walker on the side of the head with one!" He sat back in his chair, looking at the judge with frustration.

The ruling of Coroner Blumequist was "Capital murder by person or persons unknown." The crowd left the courthouse thoroughly dissatisfied, some arguing that it had been an accident, that an older man—no matter how respected he was in the community—had no business calling out a younger man, even if that younger man was 20. Others heatedly argued that a gang of toughs shouldn't be allowed to run loose, making threats and carrying on as if they were the James Gang. Still others countered that if some people wanted to get hard with the Fairly Gang, they also could take on the Hunter bunch down at the Hunter...or the Hauk-Clark bunch over at the "Shorts." The more respectable people whispered to one another things like, "That's what comes of these dances! Nothing but trouble!" "Been drinking, I heard." "Who had?" "Why, the whole bunch of them." "Drunk and fighting, that's what!" "If I was old Tom Fairly...." "Well, if *I* was James Walker...!"

Matt and Victor generally were ignored or avoided as they quietly left town; it was as though people felt sorry or ashamed that no particular person had been charged with the death and safely locked up to be tried. Most people in town well remembered the last public hanging in Princeton, two years earlier—the awful finality of it, the hooded body swinging, the sense of completion of justice. But this...this was unfinished business, and it seemed to hover about the people like a stench that no one could locate but that bothered everyone into silence. The hush spread.

When Victor and Matt reported to their father and uncle and the others what had happened at the inquest, James Walker said nothing. Uncle Matt stiffened, his jaw muscles working, and stared out a window. Watching him, Victor remembered the story of how he, broke and landless after the Civil War, had ridden with the James Gang for a time; the story was that the James boys and Matt and some other men were hiding out in a cave near where Grant Creek ran into the Grand River. Russell George had been sheriff then, and he had led a posse in search of the Jameses. The story went that Russell, out in front of the posse, had seen Matt near the cave and, not wanting to embarrass his wife's people, had led the posse off in another direction. Victor studied Uncle Matt's weathered profile, wondering what he was thinking.

That night, Victor and Matt silently undressed and went to bed. Victor took his place against the far wall in the double bed and lay on his back, staring up at the ceiling for a long time. Gradually a wave of grief washed through him. The next wave was stronger, longer, colder. The waves then came in increasing speed, rising from the depths of memories, cutting his chest, his throat with anger, frustration, loss, until finally tears flooded his pillow as he tried to bury his face and the grief in it. Again and again the full realization of his loss seized his mind, his spirit, and shook him with desolation.

When finally the seizures of grief wore themselves out like a tide ebbing from the full, his tears ceased and he felt sleep approaching like a comforter, a healer. But as he was slipping into the forgetfulness of sleep, he thought of Lucy Smith—Lucy alone, with no one to comfort her except her parents, who had been necessarily secondary to her love. Victor was reassured by the fact that before the funeral Mr. Smith had been powerfully sustaining Lucy, and yet.... Victor felt a strong desire to see her, to be with her, for he feared that her grief was greater than his own. Then he tentatively reached across into the empty space beside him. As he felt a deep loneliness, the thought came to him, *"It'll be filled...the emptiness* will *be filled!"* For one of the few times in his life, he slept alone. And he did not reach into the empty space again.

● ● ●

As soon as the ground was firm in early April, plowing began. Victor and Matt took turns with the team of horses, the lines slung over their shoulders, their hands gripping the worn handles of the two-share plow. Their laced boots stumbled over the chunks of upturned, rich-smelling earth and clotted up with mud that had to be scraped off at almost each turn. Their father soon followed with the team of mules and the disc harrow on the newer ground, where rotted corn stubble and sod were thick, and Victor followed him with the harrow. When that was finished, Victor and Matt took turns riding the corn-planter and carrying seed corn to fill the hoppers. The only breaks in the labor were when Nanny brought their dinner at noon, when their shadows pointed north and they could "step on their heads." With their innards rumbling, they quickly unpacked the basket she brought and ate under the shade of whatever hedgerow they were nearest.

They worked steadily, almost with a vengeance, relishing the release of anger and grief through the straining of muscles, the fight against the resilient earth and the recalcitrant mules, and the silence of it all. Not even the popping of harness and chains, the turning of wheels, the hiss of plowshares cutting through and curling over the earth, or the clicking of the corn-planter as kernels were fed into the ground broke that silence. And whenever they heard the distant wail of a passing train's whistle, they would slap the lines on the rumps of the horses and the black-gray mules and shout, "Hup...heyyygetmovin'!" until the whistle had ceased and the silence of the countryside returned.

Mrs. Walker and Nanny rose each morning in the darkness long before dawn and built up the fire in the kitchen stove after opening the flue and scooping out the ashes from the day before. They sliced the dwindling supply of ham from hog-killing time the autumn before, fried it, and made redeye gravy; they mixed biscuit dough and punched out the circles, then baked them while they made grits or cornmeal mush with butter. They washed the breakfast dishes after the men left, and they went out to work in the garden before the day grew too hot.

Covered in starched, stiff-brimmed, long-tailed bonnets to keep their faces and necks from becoming tanned, and covered in gloves and long-sleeved dresses, they worked the earth which the men had plowed before starting the fields. Potatoes already were up a foot, and long furrows were made beside them, Nanny pulling the garden plow while Mrs. Walker watched carefully to make each row straight; if she didn't—she smiled to herself—she knew how James would sit on the back steps looking at her work and tisking. Then, from her basket of seeds carefully gathered and culled the previous summer, she planted radishes, lettuce, carrots, green corn, pole beans and yellow beans, and all the other vegetables she and Nanny would begin canning later in the year. The shelves in the "cave" near the house—their storm cellar and storage "cool room" for milk, as well as for the canned goods she and Nanny put up—were almost bare, and that worried her, as it did each year. She liked to have an overlap between the finishing of the canned goods and the growing of the garden so there was no gap between. She dreaded ever having to ask James to go into town and buy things they should have had from their own land. In their second year of married life, she had had to do so, and the look he had given her had sent her into their bedroom to weep, feeling a failure. She had failed to provide her part, and she never made that mistake again.

The orchard also required work—pruning and burning the dead branches, piling ashes around the trunks of the trees to keep borers away, and liming and raking the ground. Then there were the chickens, which Nanny fed by scattering scratch in the yard each day so they would lay better and the family would have a source of cash from the dozens and dozens of eggs carefully crated and taken to Gregory's Grocery. Nanny gathered the eggs and kept tabs on which hens had stopped laying. Those hens had one leg tied with a bit of string and would go into the stewpot when a meal required one. And each morning the Jersey cow—Bessie, Nanny called her—had to be milked and her calf fed. The milk containers were always scoured spotless, the cow's udder was washed before milking, and the milk was kept covered until it could be poured into the separator.

Nanny worked the separator, winding it up until the flywheel began to spin the lower compartment at its "singing" speed. When the cream rose, it flowed out into one container; later it would be churned into butter that Mrs. Walker patted into molds that left flowered impressions on the pale-yellow blocks. The skimmed milk went into a separate container and was mixed with "shorts" or bran and slopped to the three hogs. The "concert" provided by the squealing, grunting, jostling, snapping hogs at slopping time was one of the few things about which Nanny laughed. She was totally silent during the afternoon hours when she and her mother washed, starched, ironed, and hung up the clothes, did the mending and darning, and sewed new clothes.

Between them they made everything that each member of the family wore, from underwear to shirts, from knitted socks to dresses and trousers and coats. The only clothes they bought were two pairs of overalls for each of the men each year and, rarely, a suit for one of them. There also were sheets, pillowcases, towels, and quilts to make and embroider or sew lace onto or hemstitch.

Since it was spring, the curtains had to be taken down and washed, the windows cleaned, and the house thoroughly swept, including the corners of the ceilings where cobwebs seemed—as Victor jokingly once had told Nanny—to "grow in the night from cob seeds." Then there was dinner—fried chicken and fresh bread, potato salad and canned corn—followed by supper, often leftovers. After supper came more work on quilts, lace, crocheting, knitting, drawn work, or hemstitching. They seldom went anywhere except to church once or twice a month. They seldom saw anyone outside the family except when a neighbor was sick or had a new baby. And they seldom spoke; there was plenty to do and little to say. But when the work was done, when a space of quiet thought crept in, each member of the family found an emptiness in a footstep that did not fall, in a hearty laugh that was stilled, in a chair that was not filled.

When the men had almost finished planting the wheat and Susan and her daughter had almost finished planting the garden, Nanny began watching her mother. Mrs. Walker was setting squash seeds into small hills while Nanny came behind with a hoe and mounded earth over the seeds. Nanny saw that after setting each group of five seeds in a hole, her mother would place the heel of one hand on the top of her back between her shoulders, straighten, and wince. Several times her mother took off her gloves, straightened completely, and turned her head from side to side, one hand on the back of her neck.

"Mama, what's wrong with you?" Nanny asked, coming to her mother and watching her try to erase the lines of pain from her face. Her brown eyes kept the pain, though, and Nanny clearly could see it.

"Nothing, I suppose. Maybe I took a cold in my neck," Mrs. Walker said, picking up her hoe to make the next hole.

Nanny said nothing...until she caught Victor by himself. On the back porch that night, while they were sorting eggs—the larger ones for sale, the smaller ones for eating—Nanny looked at her brother. "Something's wrong with Mama," she said quietly, glancing toward the kitchen, where her mother was scrubbing out the milk containers with steaming water, lye soap, and a stiff brush.

"I know," Victor said, "but you try to get her to see a doctor. I told Park Robinson what she was acting like, and he mixed her up something he thought might help. But she smelled the alcohol in it and wouldn't drink a drop."

"Well, if you couldn't do anything..." Nanny said, letting her voice trail off as she carefully placed eggs in one basket or the other. "Say, how's Park doing?"

"His store's been open a week," Victor replied. "And his house is finished except for the porches and some painting. Whip Lewis went on a drunk and wouldn't finish the painting, so Park's had to hire someone else."

"When're he and Chloe getting married?"

Victor straightened with a slow smile. "The Wednesday after Easter Sunday."

"That's next week," Nanny said, brightening. "You going?"

"Wouldn't miss it," Victor said, holding up a small egg whose brown shell was sprinkled with flecks of dark brown. "Which hen laid this one?"

"That little Rhode Island Red-Cornish cross you bought."

"Thought so," Victor murmured, holding the egg higher into the lamplight from the kitchen. A shadow blocked the light.

"Boy, you sortin' or dreamin'?" his father asked when Victor looked up at him.

"Little of both," Victor said, smiling as his father stretched in the doorway, both hands on the small of his back. "Want me to rub your back?"

"Naw, it'll be all right," James said, turning and going back into the kitchen.

Victor followed him. "You go lie down on the floor...."

"The floor!" James asked, turning with an astounded expression.

"And I'll work on your back," Victor said, pushing his father toward the living room.

Mrs. Walker wore a full, black veil to church Easter Sunday, and she led her family into their pew at the Pleasant Ridge Baptist Church with quiet dignity as the other 30 or so members of the congregation stood aside, the men with their hats in their hands, the women making small gestures of sympathy. The kids just stared; after all, seeing the family of a murdered man was almost as unusual and fascinating as hearing the many stories about the murder itself. Because the church had no regular minister, Reverend Oral Painter from "up Centerville way" led the service. When the time for testimonies came, Mrs. Walker stood right up. Turning to look at the congregation, she said in a clear, firm voice, "I praise the Lord our Redeemer for being with us in our time of need and for taking our oldest boy to be with Him over there, where we'll all be together someday." She nodded and sat down as many of the men murmured, "Amen!"

After a moment, Mott Lewis, who had come alone, stood and almost shyly looked at Mrs. Walker and several of the other women. With her arms straight beside her ample figure, she quietly said, "I'd ask you to pray for my husband. He ain't saved yet, you know, and the Lord's not blessed us with children—I reckon 'cause He don't want 'em brought up by no man who won't bend a knee to Him. So please pray for us." She quickly sat down, embarrassed.

It went on for 20 or so minutes—first one, then another member of the congregation, standing shyly or boldly, speaking softly or overloud, giving testimony about children who had been healed, someone who needed praying for, and praising the Lord for their own salvation. When a long moment of silence came over the group, they turned toward Reverend Painter, who was waiting patiently on the low platform. "Shall we sing 'The Rock That Is Higher Than I'?" Murmured agreement answered him, and Jane George moved to the organ. She began pumping the twin pedals with her feet and started playing. "O some-times the shad-ows are deep, And rough...seems the path...to the goal..." they sang, the sopranos casting the melody above the answering bass voices, with the altos weaving their part in between.

Following two more hymns suggested by members of the congregation, Reverend Painter preached for an hour-and-a-half on the new life, now and to come, then closed the service with a prayer. Definite "Amens!" answered his closing, and the church members began making their way outside. For a time they stood idly about, and then the men began to gather separately from the women.

"Ed Kauffman's got new potatoes," one said, setting a foot up on one hub of someone's buggy. "Sure was proud. Claimed he was the first hereabouts."

"Naw," someone else said. "I'll bet Dad Bohring over yonder was the first. Usually is. Anybody talked to him?"

James Walker settled his hat on his head, looking northward toward the Bohring farm. "Don't know. But my corn's sprouted."

"Mine's up two inches," Otto Sparks said with a faint hint of pride.

"You've got more sun on your fields," James said, glancing aside at Matt and winking, "or else you've got a diff'rent almanac from me."

"Same almanac, same moon," Otto protested. "Your fields is just lower down than mine. Stay colder, 'specially early in the day when the sprouts need warmin'."

They soon drifted apart, some to call together their families and bid good-bye to their friends, and others to follow their wives into the shade of the hickory trees in back of the church ground for basket dinners spread on quilts.

•   •   •

The Robinson-Smith wedding was held at the home of the Otterbein Church minister, Philip Schonover, in Ravanna. Actually, the ceremony was performed in his front yard because his home was too small to accommodate the number of people who came. Judge William Jewell and his son and their families were in the forefront, near the various Smiths, Halls, Rouths, and Ruths. Mr. and Mrs. Thomas Fairly and their older three sons were present, as were most of the other families from Ravanna, the English, and the Fairly. James Walker and his family arrived just as the ceremony was beginning, and they stood in the back of the crowd. They barely could see Chloe Smith in her high-necked, frill-and-lace-covered, long-trained dress. When Mr. Schonover ended the ceremony and stepped back, Park slowly and awkwardly lifted Chloe's long white veil to kiss his bride. Mrs. Walker and many of the other women smiled and caught their breaths, their hands to their faces, clasped, or reaching to take their husbands' arms; the children giggled while the young men whooped. With her veil back over her wide hat, Chloe hurried to kiss her mother, then Mrs. Robinson—who had come all the way from Trenton for the wedding—and Lucy, in that order.

While the members of the wedding party went into the house, Victor followed them in search of Lucy, speaking to people he knew. A crowd of young men was in the parlor, gathered around Park, congratulating him. Victor heard the laughter and giggling of the young women upstairs where the bride had gone to change clothes for the honeymoon. In came Mr. Smith, urging everyone to eat cake and fill up on lemonade. Older men trailed after him, waiting for a chance to shake his hand and clap him on the back. He spotted Victor and went directly to him.

"Glad you could come," he said, shaking Victor's hand. "We'd have invited you to Lucy's birthday party, but Mrs. Smith said it was too soon."

Victor blinked. "She's 16?"

"Fifth of April."

More quietly, Victor said, "Do you suppose I could talk to her?"

"Sure," Mr. Smith said, smiling broadly. "Just a minute." He looked around and saw his wife coming down the stairs, merrily humming a tune. Leaning over the handrail along the staircase, he whispered to her. She nodded, nodded again to Victor, and hurried back up the stairs. In a while she reappeared and beckoned to him. He followed her up the stairs and into a sitting room at the front of the house behind the stairwell. She smiled courteously as she left the room and softly closed the door behind her.

Victor went to the window and pulled aside the curtains so he could look down at the crowd still standing around the minister's home. Near the white wire fence he saw his parents face to face with Mr. and Mrs. Fairly. He leaned forward anxiously, then saw the look on Anvil Fairly's face. It was a pleading look, and his dark eyes glinted faintly with moisture. James Walker nodded, nodded again, and shook Mr. Fairly's right hand when the older man extended it. Mrs. Fairly, tiny and bright-seeming in a dark purple dress with long sleeves and minute garnets on the lace trim, opened her arms and met Mrs. Walker in an embrace that lasted several seconds. Behind Victor the door opened, and he turned to watch Lucy come into the room.

"I'm so happy to see you!" she said gaily, hurrying to lightly hug him. He felt her cheek soft against his and smelled the sachet scent of her dress. When he released her, he was surprised at the reluctance he felt at doing so. For a few seconds they simply looked into each other's eyes, searching...and seeing that the pain almost had gone but the loneliness had not.

"I'm glad your father and mother let me talk to you," Victor said, going to sit on a love seat against one wall behind a small mahogany table. She sat on the edge of the seat, half-turned and facing him. He said, "I wanted to thank you...for what you did at our home. Your singing was lovely."

She reached across and touched the tears that had trickled onto his cheeks, then put her fingertips to her lips. She leaned toward him, and he raised one hand to her face, touched her cheek, then took her hands in his. They were sitting that way when the door opened and Chloe bubbled into the room, oblivious to everything except her own happiness. "Come," she urged, frowning playfully as she reached one hand toward Lucy, "we're going, and you *must* be there!" Lucy stood as Chloe seized her hand and practically dragged her from the room. Victor followed, smoothing the brim of his hat with one coat sleeve.

The crowd reassembled in front of the minister's home, the young ladies near the porch steps. With her mother and mother-in-law behind her and her new husband stiff and proud beside her, Chloe held her bouquet of forget-me-nots aloft, teasing the younger women with it for a moment. Then she threw it arching toward the reaching hands. She laughed, clapping with delight, when Lucy caught it and held it against the bodice of her dress to smell the bright blue blooms. Lucy turned and looked among the crowd until she saw Victor. Their eyes met for a moment, then Lucy was gone—swirled into the laughing, wheat-throwing crowd that pursued the newlyweds to the road to surround their buggy. Park had bought a new single-seat buggy with a top edged in purple fringe; his mare waited nervously under her fly netting, and she almost sprang forward when he slapped the lines against her.

"Good-bye!" shouted those following the buggy as it turned and began heading toward Princeton—toward the train station, someone told Victor, for the long ride down to Excelsior Springs. "Good luck!" "God bless you!" shouted the followers, the young boys in the lead, racing the mare, Sammy Smith in front of them all.

"Didn't she look lovely!" a woman said to a friend as the crowd began moving toward carriages and buggies for the drive to Mr. Smith's house for an afternoon and evening of eating, singing, and celebration.

"Oh, yes; that satin collar on the primrose faille," another woman said admiringly, "why, that must have cost 20 dollars!"

"I heard from Mrs. Scholwalter that the design was one Maude Adams wore in 'The Little Minister.' "

"Sure glad that boy got married," one of the Hall men said to his companion. "Maybe now he'll lose that studied look of his."

His companion, Arnold Jewell, laughed. "Glad he stopped calling that store of his a 'pharmacy' and put up a proper sign. Folks didn't know what a 'pharmacy' was, but they'll go to a regular 'drug store.' "

"Sure'll give Mr. Casteel and that old store of his a run for his money," another man put in, coming to the first two. He was a renter of Mr. Thogmorton's, a McClary, and the other two men stopped to look at him and hear what he had to say. Slightly flustered, Mr. McClary added, " 'Course Mr. Casteel's still got a soda fountain, and young Robinson only sells drugs and notions...but my wife, Ethel, she bought a bottle of Cardui in Robinson's for 89 cents, 'stead o' the dollar a bottle Mr. Casteel's askin'." The other two men thoughtfully nodded and walked on, talking between themselves. Mr. McClary grinned at the success of his little expedition and hurried back to his family.

On the drive home that evening, James Walker turned to look at Matt and Victor. "Spoke to Mr. Fairly," he said. He looked at his wife, who patted his right leg, then regrasped the seat railing beside himself. Mr. Walker again turned to glance at his sons. "Good man," he asserted. "Said he whipped his youngest three one by one till they told him the whole truth. He looked me square in the eye an' said, 'My son Tom did say something low to Miss Lucy, and Alexander rightly called him out. Tom and Alex took off their coats, squared off with their fists up, and were circling each other when Weldon Trask's sister put him up to sneaking around behind Alexander. He hit Alex on the side of the head with a blackjack.' " He paused to look at his wife sitting stiffly beside him, staring straight ahead, then resumed. "Said his boys took off right then, 'fore they even made sure Alex was dead. That Weldon and his sister talked the McCargue boys into helping them put Alex's coat back on him, then dump his body onto the tracks. Guess they thought they'd make it look like an accident." He sighed, glancing again at his wife, and turned back to face the horses, his shoulders slumped.

"Where's Weldon Trask?" Matt asked through clenched teeth.

"Took off," James answered without turning. "Jim McCargue gave him a letter of introduction to his brother out in Virginia City. Kid was gone by Sunday morning, him an' his sister both."

Victor let out the breath he'd been holding. "Well, I'm glad that's cleared up."

"Is it?" Matt demanded, giving him a fiery look. "Just who'll we go to to get our hair cut? I'm sure not settin' foot in Trask's shop!"

"I'll cut your hair," their mother said mildly, holding her head erect. "And your father's." She looked at him, and briefly they touched hands across the narrow space between them. Then she stiffened, arched her back, and put one hand to her neck.

"Mama?" Matt asked, leaning toward her.

"I'm all right," she said firmly. But her fingers remained pressed into her neck.

She went to bed as soon as they got home, and when Nanny came home later—escorted by Tom McClary and his parents from over Cainsville way—Mrs. Walker called her into the bedroom. Nanny said goodnight to the McClarys and went to her mother expecting to be fussed at about the McClarys being Mormons. But her mother simply said, "Dear, would you please heat some water for me? I think a hot compress might feel good on my back."

Nanny quickly took off her gloves and set to work. By the time she returned to her mother's bedroom, Daddy Walker and his sons had gathered uncertainly around the bed. "I'll be all right," she assured them, trying to smile. "I just strained my back."

But she wasn't all right, as they all knew. The hot compress only made her pain worse. They tried what few patent medicines they had in the house, but nothing had any effect on Mrs. Walker's pain, which steadily increased throughout the night. In the morning, Victor saddled Mack and urged him as fast as he would go into town to bring Dr. Powell.

When the doctor's buggy clattered up the drive, James and Matt came outside as Victor went on to the barn. The doctor, a kind and extremely gentle gray-haired man they had known all their lives, knew the condition of his patient by looking at the faces of her husband and son. "She's not good," James said, following the doctor into the house.

When Dr. Powell came out of the bedroom after examining Susan, he looked at the men who were standing up from the chairs around the stove and shook his head. "I could treat her better in town, at my hospital, but she won't go. She says she'll stay here."

"Doctor, if she's worried about the money—" James began.

Dr. Powell again shook his head. "No, I don't think it's that." He wiped his hands on his handkerchief, although they weren't dirty, and meticulously replaced the cloth in his coat pocket. He looked at James through his glasses, his head tilted slightly back, his mouth slightly open as if he were assessing James's strength of mind. "I think she knows she's dying."

"Dying?" James repeated dully, sagging against Victor as his son came to take his right arm.

"Yes," Dr. Powell said softly, taking off his glasses and pulling out his handkerchief to clean them. "She's not like some, who complain about the least pain and ache. She's kept going...until she couldn't go any further."

James searched the doctor's face, his expression, his eyes, ignoring the tears in his own eyes. "Doctor Powell, she can't...I mean, we just buried Alex. Did that—"

"No...no, I don't think so," Dr. Powell said. "I think this is something called spinal meningitis."

"What's that?" Matt asked, going to his father's left side. His piercing blue eyes were full of fight; his hands were clenched. "What can we do?"

Dr. Powell inspected his glasses, polished another spot, and resettled them on his nose. "There's nothing anybody knows of to be done. It's some sort of infection of the spinal cord. I wanted to give her an injection of morphine to deaden the pain, but she wouldn't let me. Said it was something she was meant to bear. But, if you want, I'll help Nanny make a tea with the morphine in it so she won't know."

"No," James said slowly, looking toward the bedroom door. "I've always been honest with her, and I won't change now."

"The pain...will become unbearable."

James looked at him, stiffening his posture and his expression.

"I know," Dr. Powell said, bending down to pick up his bag. He started to go, then paused. "If you want, I'll wait here till the end."

Panic flitted into James's eyes. "How long...do you think?"

"Well, like I said, she held out as long as she could. Now she's let go...given it to Him. I don't doubt He'll be merciful."

"Yes...well," James said numbly.

"I'll stop off and tell the Kauffmans and some of the rest," Dr. Powell said gently, laying one hand on Victor's back as he went toward the door.

When the men reentered the bedroom, Mrs. Walker was lying with her back arched, her elbows pressed into the mattress, her head thrown back. Nanny was sitting on the bedside, leaning partially across her mother, holding her hands and wincing as her mother squeezed them hard when the pain passed through her. Mrs. Walker's mouth was open, and she was breathing with difficulty. But she was making no sound. Periodically her back would arch still more...then gradually she would relax a bit...then stiffen again. Once she moaned, but when her menfolk moved closer to her, she focused on her husband and managed to smile. Weakly, distantly, she murmured, "You bear up, James. You bear up."

Before night came Ed Kauffman and his wife arrived. A few hours later the Henry Georges came, followed by the nearest Hickman family and Wilma Sparks. Mrs. Sparks was told the situation, and she left immediately. Near midnight she returned with a covered tin of tea which, she said, she had made according to a recipe of her grandmother's. Into the bedroom she went, carrying the tin and a cup. She poured the cup full, let Mrs. Walker smell of it several times, then supported her head while she drank. "Barks and roots," Mrs. Sparks said in a throaty, soothing voice. "Nothin' but barks and roots."

After that the pain seemed further away from Susan, and her breathing became easier. But near dawn, in the weak and gray hour, she bowed her back and cried out, "Now...give me grace...to set my spirit...free!" With James holding one hand and Victor the other, she smiled, looking toward the ceiling, and died.

She too was buried in the Pleasant Ridge Church cemetery.

New Life Comes To Pleasant Ridge

James Walker sold his farm—land, house, horses and mules, machinery, and all—to Ed Kauffman and his oldest son, Bill. With the money he took his remaining family down to Spickard. There he bought out Teeter Holbein, whose injured foot had developed the dreaded disease gangrene; Mr. Holbein was glad to sell. "Got to pay my bills," he said dryly. "And what good's a one-legged grocer anyhow?"

Daddy Walker and his family settled into the living quarters in the floor above the store. Some people back in Princeton said it was a shame that Mr. Walker was broken; others said they thought he was wrong going "away down in Spickard," though it was only about 12 miles from Princeton; but still others claimed they understood. "After all," they said, "a man can stand only so much."

The one piece of advice Teeter Holbein gave Mr. Walker when the new owner took over was, "Don't give nothin' to *nobody* on credit!" But he himself—Victor soon learned by going through the card file behind the counter—had allowed his neighbors to run up credit bills totaling more than 4000 dollars. As Victor patiently went around the town, making friends and renewing acquaintances, he learned that almost all the debtors of Holbein's store were good people, people who could, if they wanted to, have paid their bills. Discreetly he asked why they had not. He was told either, "It ain't none of yor business," or, "First things first," meaning that bank notes and mortgages and crop loans came before grocery and doctor bills. So Victor and his father put up a big sign that said "NO Credit!" Before long their trade dwindled to almost nothing.

While James Walker remained depressed and silent, Victor pitched into the work. The summer went by, and autumn came on. Victor learned who the best suppliers were, and he even went down to St. Joseph to see if he couldn't establish a better way of getting produce to Spickard. A new outfit using gasoline-powered trucks signed an agreement with him, but their newfangled contraptions broke down so often that Victor was obliged to continue to buy only what was available around the countryside—produce that if the people wanted, they could go out and buy themselves.

He talked his father into buying a meat-slicing machine to cut slab bacon and ham. From that beginning he developed something of a delicatessen—with different kinds of cold cuts, cheeses, and breads that were baked by a woman down the street. He installed six stools and a counter, and Nanny began serving sandwiches, fried sliced potatoes, and a glass of tea for a total of 40 cents for a dinner—or lunch, as it was called locally. The "lunch counter" kept them in business, but as the winter came and the country people came less to town, the Walkers began having to dip into their cash reserve to stay in business.

During the summer, fall, and winter, Matt worked for a local printer—a one-eyed scoundrel more likely drunk than sober who paid his employees irregularly but well. Mr. Whisnat seemed to be his name, although no one was sure how you were supposed to pronounce it since no one ever could understand the man well enough to tell. Mr. Whisnat appreciated Matt's energy and his ability to deal with the public, so he taught him everything he knew about the printing business, made him shop foreman, and disappeared on long drinking bouts. The job made Matt independent, and with his grand income of 12 dollars a month he rented a room in a boarding house—"away from the stink of rotting bananas," he said, but really, as Victor believed, so he could be closer to a Spickard girl he had started taking out. His going cast James even further into depression...and Nanny's "situation" did nothing to relieve it.

Nanny was red-haired and brown-eyed, with white skin, a few freckles, and ways rather like her mother. She had always been a quiet girl, but in her own usually unprotesting way she was stubborn—even more stubborn in her way than Victor was in his. She continued seeing Tom McClary, who drove down from near Cainsville each weekend to take her to some church social, chautauqua, or dance. The first two events James didn't mind, though he didn't like Tom McClary—neither his name nor his religion; but he vocally objected to her going to dances.

"I'm going and that's that," she said one Saturday afternoon, not raising her voice but not lowering her glare, either.

"Dances brew trouble," he father stated, rocking in his wife's broad-armed rocking chair in the living room-kitchen near the top of the stairs up from the store.

"Tom's asked me to marry him," she said, raising her chin so her jawline was straight and firm. "I said I might...or I might not. But if you force me out...."

When she had gone and Victor had closed the store for the day, his father began talking to him. And during the conversation Victor realized that what should have healed in his father had not; like Teeter Holbein's foot, James Walker's wound had festered and was spreading infection.

"I don't understand what's happening, Fluty," James said, pressing his fingertips against his temples. "Everything's changing. Automobiles're comin' in, and faster trains're goin' through. There's more noise...more busy-ness. And *she*...she talked back to me. I should've slapped her! She's too old to spank." He stopped rocking and gave his son a wavering look. "What's happened, Fluty? Things used to be so...so certain. I didn't used to wonder about anythin', and now I wonder about everythin'. I wonder if maybe we shouldn't give credit, if maybe we shouldn't go back home, buy another place while we still have some money left, go back to farmin'. I...I just don't *know* any more...I can't seem to *think*...not since Suzie died."

Victor flinched; it was the first time he remembered his father calling his mother by her pet name. "Daddy, you can't plant yourself in the past," he gently urged.

"But there is nothin' else!" James protested, spreading his hands apart. "There's no *future*...nothin' to look forward to! I...I can't even feel God anymore." He searched Victor's eyes for an answer. "Where's He gone?" he demanded. "Where *is* the God of mercy and comfort we used to know?"

Victor looked his father steadily in the eyes for a time, then spoke slowly and distinctly. "Daddy, God is right where He's always been. *We* wander away from *Him* a step at a time. With each step away we take, the Adversary puts shadows and fears and doubts around us. Pretty soon we look around and realize that something's different, something's gone. But because of the shadows and doubts and fears, we can't tell what's wrong...and we blame God."

"Is that what's happened to me, Fluty?"

Victor nodded slowly, wishing his father would let him comfort him.

James buried his face in his hands, rubbing it back and forth against his thick, callous fingers. He raised his face slightly and murmured, "Fluty, I don't like bein' a grocer. I can't smell the land. All I can smell is that...that *asphalt* they spray on the streets and the fumes those...those *automobiles* put out." He looked at his son. "And where's the future, Fluty? Why can't I see nothin' out in front of me the way I used to?" Tears brimmed his eyes, and Victor quickly moved closer to him. Awkwardly trying to hold him, he let his father cry against his shirt, his arms wrapped loosely around Victor's waist.

"Daddy, I'll give you a future," Victor said quietly, "but you'll have to run the store and make the best of things you can with Nanny."

"Where'll you go?" James asked, releasing his son. "You won't do like Matt's done, will you?" He slumped against the slats in the back of the rocking chair.

"No, Sir. I'll go up Ravanna way."

James wiped his eyes thoughtfully; when he focused again on Victor's twinkling blue eyes, he brightened. "Lucy Smith!" he said, snapping his fingers. "That's it, isn't it! You're goin' to start courtin' her." He laughed, rocking and looking up at the design of the embossed tin ceiling. "Mama said you were sweet on her even while Alex was courtin' her. But you wouldn't say nothin'... not with your sense of honor." He nodded emphatically. "And that day when Chloe and Park were married, I figured you slipped off to be with Lucy, but I didn't say nothin'."

"Daddy, listen to me," Victor said, kneeling in front of the rocker and stopping it with his hands on the arms. "I'll have to move up to Ravanna. I'll write Mr. Cox to see if he can give me a job and let me live in his store so I can save money. When spring comes, I'll go if there's work. In the meantime, we'll start giving credit—but we'll tell the people, 'Please pay us when your crops sell...or offer us something in trade.' I'd just as soon work on barter anyhow, if we could. Then we'll see how things go." He nodded and winked, patting his father's hands reassuringly.

His father made an effort to smile, but tears brimmed his eyes again. "That's fine, son...but...but I miss my Suzie." He leaned toward Victor, and his son held him tightly as he wept.

●　　●　　●

Early in the new year, Lucy Smith was standing in the kitchen
of her home, watching the hired girl take the last of the Jonathan
apples from a barrel. She watched the girl peel, core, and slice
the apples and spread the slices on drying racks. Her mother came
into the room and noticed her, then looked quizzically from her
daughter to the girl and back. "Lucy, what are you doing?" she
asked.

Lucy smiled brightly. "Getting ready, Mommie."

"To put up dried apples?" Mrs. Smith asked, tilting her head.

"No..." Lucy said bashfully, turning away.

Her mother went to her and gently turned her face toward her
with one hand. "You really figure he's coming back?"

"Yes," she murmured...and suddenly looked at her mother with
a burst of calm maturity. "It's right."

Her mother nodded, letting her eyelids drift shut as mentally
she let go of her daughter another "notch." Her mother set about
cutting up a chicken to fry, and Lucy came to the pan and held
out her hands for the plucked bird and the knife. Her mother gave
them to her, wiped her hands with her apron, and went to sit away
from the stove.

"Is that why you were out watching the sow being farrowed?"
Lucy nodded.

"And were asking Bill why he was holding eggs up to a candle?"
Again Lucy nodded.

"But, honey, surely you don't want to do all that—not the canning and washing, the sitting up with sick cows and watching
crops die in a drought. Couldn't you let Lon Casteel take you out
some more? Look how well Chloe did, marrying an educated man,
a professional man."

"I think she did well," Lucy said, bending a wing back from
the carcass and severing it with a jerk of the knife, "especially
now that she's going to have a baby. But all Lon Casteel can talk
about is how *they're* going to put an awning all across the front
of *their* drugstore and *their* clothing store and how his father is
actually letting the bookkeeper teach him how to keep books."
She stopped jerking and cutting the chicken and stared at her
mother. "Mommie, he'd make me a clerk. Do you want me to
wear a starched blouse and skirt and stand up all day waiting for
my husband to inherit...?" She laid down the knife and chicken.

"Better than scrubbing floors on your hands and knees and

watching your husband plant crops that may or may not make *anything!*"

Lucy gave her mother a raised-eyebrow, amused look. "You mean you would want me to become a city girl—after all you and Mrs. Hall and Mrs. Jewell have said about how town folks can't be trusted, how they spend their spare time sneaking around and having affairs, how they don't care about anything except money—"

"That'll be enough," her mother said firmly. "I will not be up-braided because I want the best for my daughter."

Lucy sighed, working on the chicken again. "Did you and Papa start out with this house and hired help?" She paused in her work and looked at the Cardui calendar on the wall over the sink. "Besides, with Victor it'll be different."

Her mother closely watched her. "How do you mean, 'different'? If Victor doesn't go back to farming, do you think he can make a go of it as a grocer? From what we've heard, their grocery in Spickard is barely making ends meet, and how's marrying a grocer so much different from marrying Lon?"

"That's not what I mean," she interrupted with a hint of secretiveness. She pressed down on the breastbone of the chicken to split it in half; she put one hand on the back of the knife and rocked down, a determined tightness on her face. She sighed with relief when the breastbone split and the knife didn't slip. "Victor *is* a farmer; he's part of the land. But he won't always be *just* a farmer."

Her mother's perplexed look returned, and she blinked, wide-eyed at her daughter.

Lucy felt her look and smiled at her. "I don't know what'll happen. But I do know that it's right." She nodded and wiped her hands on a towel so she could go and hug her mother; Lucy felt the wrinkled softness of her mother's cheek press against the smoothness of her own cheek.

The winter passed, the thaw came in March, and Lucy's seventeenth birthday approached. Her father fretted when he came from plowing or from tending the stock. At the supper table he frequently gave her solemn looks. Finally he spoke. "What am I supposed to tell Hubert Casteel and Ray Bearden and Bill Hall?"

"Tell them to keep their boys away from me," Lucy said pleasantly, offering her father a bowl of mashed potatoes.

He stared at her and slowly took the bowl as her hand was

trembling. "I...don't think I can tell them that. And I'm surprised at you. What *are* you doing?" He looked from Lucy to her
mother—who maintained an innocent expression—then stared at
Lucy again.

"Well, since I'm hardly an old maid yet," Lucy said, "I'm
waiting."

"Waiting," her father grumbled, looking at his wife with a sour
expression. "Ohh," he said brightening. "You still think Victor
will come back."

"Mr. Cox down at the general store said he'd had a letter from
Victor. Mr. Cox said he'd written Victor to say that yes, he could
use some help, what with planting season here and spring on the
way."

"But...Victor is so...so uncertain."

"He won't be when he comes."

Mr. Smith's brown, gray-shot eyebrows went up, and his attitude seemed to subtly change; an almost fearful realization crept
into his eyes. Thoughtfully he said, "No, I s'pose not."

When Bill, the hired man, came into the house the following
afternoon, he announced, among other news, that when he had
gone by the general store in Ravanna, he had seen a new man
working there. Lucy ran right out and found her father. Sweaty,
hot, and tired, he was driving the team of horses to the barn; he
needed only one look at her before he said, "Not now."

"When?" she asked, fairly jumping up and down as she followed
him into the cool, shady, sweet-pungent-smelling barn.

"Tomorrow...maybe," Mr. Smith said. Lucy heard what she
thought was a teasing sound in his voice, and she picked up a
handful of straw and threw it at him. "Or maybe the next day,"
his voice followed her, ending with a laugh as she hurried from
the barn.

But he didn't take her into Ravanna the next day...or the next,
and she was not about to go without him. At first she thought
it was an April Fool's joke, though he almost never went in for
pranks. And then she became hurt. When he came in, he didn't
talk. Lucy watched him, trying to figure out what the matter was,
but she couldn't. Finally she asked her mother.

"He's worried about Chloe, I suppose," her mother said.

"Chloe? What's wrong with her?"

Her mother continued sifting flour for Lucy's birthday cake.
"She's having trouble carrying the baby."

Lucy sat at the kitchen table, glancing at the eggs, butter, and vanilla extract bottle. "Is it just because she's gotten so big?"

Her mother seemed reluctant to talk about the matter, and she took a long time before answering. "She's just having trouble," she said at last, keeping her eyes on the large crockery bowl.

"She won't be at my birthday party then, will she?"

"No, I'm afraid not. The ride would be too rough on her."

"When's her baby due?"

"Any time now."

"Really?" Lucy asked, feeling more excitement over the prospect of her sister having a baby than she felt over her own birthday party. "You didn't tell me!" she added, noticing how uncomfortable her mother seemed to have become.

Her mother glanced at her.

"Mommie, how do women have babies?"

Her mother slumped and stared at the red gumwood ceiling, holding the sifter above the bowl. "They just...have them."

"No, I mean...how does the man...what do they do?"

"Oh, you've seen the cows and bulls," her mother said, very flustered.

"It's not like *that*, is it?" Lucy asked, horrified.

"Well, no...."

"Then...what?"

Her mother began adding the liquid ingredients to the dry ones, stirring the contents of the bowl with a wooden spoon so vigorously that Lucy laughed.

"Are you mixing a cake or making meringue?" she asked playfully.

Her mother snorted, slowed a bit, and held the bowl against her body to stir the batter deeply. "I...I just can't talk to you about it." She went on stirring, then abruptly set the bowl down. "All I can say," she resumed, staring Lucy in the eyes with a harried but determined expression, "is that it's not like what some women say it is: It's not...dirty or...or an obligation. When the Holy Word says that a man and woman become 'one flesh,' that's what it's talking about. It's special...and very, very beautiful...and I don't want to talk about it!"

After a moment's reflection, Lucy asked, "What's having a baby like?"

"A lot of work," her mother stated flatly.

"Does it hurt?"

"Yes, quite a bit...especially the first time. But you forget the pain. I guess you'd have to or you'd never have another." She laughed, going to get cake pans; when she returned to the table, she carefully floured the pans. "Besides, once you hold your baby, you realize what a wonderful blessing it is—a real miracle. And you hold it and feed it and play and play with it." She smiled at Lucy and leaned across to kiss her on the forehead.

"But how do you actually have it?" Lucy persisted.

"Land sakes! what questions you ask," her mother said, flustered again as she began pouring batter into the pans. "You'd think you'd been raised in a city 'stead of on a farm!"

Lucy stood, feeling very much a child still in awe of the mysterious realm of adults, adults she knew very well...yet at times did not seem to know at all. She frowned thoughtfully, suddenly unsure about her eagerness to join that realm. If it couldn't even be talked about with one's own about-to-be-married daughter, then maybe childhood wasn't such a bad thing...or at least wasn't something to be escaped hastily. "When can we go see Chloe?" she asked, watching her mother bend to place the cake pans in the oven.

"I'll ask your father. Probably tomorrow afternoon after your party." She straightened, closing the oven door, and wiped her hands on her apron. "It'd be nice to take her and Park some of your cake."

"Yes," Lucy said, "it would."

The next day Lucy helped her mother string the parlor with paper streamers they had dyed blue, yellow, and pink. Where the streamers met, her mother hung large paper flowers. She set a table in the center of the floor, then went off to begin making lemonade. Bill had been chopping up ice in the icehouse, and the lemonade would have floating chunks of ice in it, each with a mast and sail, making the huge bowl have a flotilla of "yachts" like they had seen in a magazine.

When the young people from the area began arriving, Lucy greeted them at the door before the hired girl could get there...and each time she lingered to gaze hopefully down the road toward Ravanna. Midge Hall, Lucy's best friend, came with her mother and little sister, Josephine, or Josie, each with a neatly wrapped gift. Gertrude, or Trudy, Jewell—Lucy's next-best friend—came with her mother, her sister Mary, and her brother Elwin. Their mothers went into the kitchen with Mrs. Smith; the girls, with

Lucy's sisters—Catherine, May, and Clara—and, of course, brother Sammy, all went into the parlor. Mrs. Smith soon came in carrying the birthday cake with 17 candles on it, and Trudy played the organ while they sang "Happy Birthday" to Lucy.

Then Lucy noticed Victor standing just inside the door. She approached him, silent and with her eyes downcast. Smiling—beaming, almost—he opened the door and let her go out onto the porch.

She went to the swing at the south end and sat, her hands in her lap, and still would not look at him. He stood in front of her and placed in her lap a long, slender package he had been holding behind his back. The package was wrapped in an illustration from a magazine and was tied in pink ribbon. Lucy quickly undid the wrapping, opened the box inside, and carefully took out a pair of tan kid gloves with black buttons up the wrists.

"Ohh...they're *beautiful!*" she whispered, feeling the leather with her fingertips. "Where did you get them?" she asked in amazement, glancing up at him.

"Sent off for them. Struther's in Kansas City."

"Struther's," Lucy repeated, slipping on the right-hand glove and smelling of the talcum powder inside it. "We passed it once, but Mother wouldn't let me go in. She said it was too expensive for us."

"Nothing's too good for you."

She looked shyly at him and put her gloved hand to her face, knowing how red it must be. "They're...lady's gloves," she murmured, leaning her cheek against the leather's incredible softness.

"For a lady," he said as he sat sideways beside her on the swing.

"I've got to show Mommie," she said abruptly; her reception dress swished as she hurried into the house. Grinning, Victor pulled his cuffs out from his coat sleeves and sat back to wait.

When she returned, she was wearing both gloves. "Mommie had to help me button them," she said, turning her hands over to show him the rows of small buttons.

"When we're married, I'll help you," he said, standing as she sat.

She quickly looked at his twinkling blue eyes, his auburn hair so neatly combed to one side, his fresh collar and neatly tied blue tie, and his blue serge suit, which looked freshly cleaned. He even smelled fresh, and she seemed to be seeing him the first time ever.

She lowered her gaze. "I've been waiting for you to say that," she whispered.

"I know."

She looked at him, then held her head back and her arms out. He began unbuttoning her gloves, and his touch...."How did you know?"

He simply looked at her.

Later in the day he rode beside Mr. Smith—with Lucy, Catherine, and Mrs. Smith in the back seat of the cabriolet carriage—as they went toward Princeton to take the remainder of the birthday cake to Chloe. They passed through Ravanna and were almost beyond the Fairly holdings before Mr. Smith spoke—to Victor but without looking at him.

"So, do you think you'll stay with being a grocer?"

"No, Sir. I've spoken with old Mrs. Scholwalter about buying her place over northeast of Pleasant Ridge Church."

" 'Cross from the Bohring farm?"

"Yes, Sir. There're 52 acres and an old house that isn't fit for much more than a barn. The back ten acres are woods that've never been cut. Grant Creek runs through it, and it's good land."

"You'd build a new house?"

"Got the plan from a book I've been studying."

"A book?"

"Yes, Sir," Victor said, smiling at him. "Figure on two bedrooms, living room, kitchen, and sleeping porch out back."

Mr. Smith stared at him. "But you got the plan from a book? Something odd about the house?"

"Well, it's sort of ready-made, like the ones you can order from the Sears-Roebuck catalogue. I can put together the walls and roof trusses on the ground, then raise them into place."

Mr. Smith continued to stare at him. "Never heard of such a thing."

"You'll have to come with me and see it. I'll be working weekends on it."

Mr. Smith looked behind Victor at his wife, twisted further around to stare at Lucy, then glanced back at Victor. "You planning on getting married when the house is finished, are you?"

"Yes, Sir...if you'll have me for a son-in-law."

Mr. Smith's face seemed to cloud. "Be glad of having you as a son, Victor. It's just that...well, I just can't seem to get used to the idea of Lucy marrying so soon."

Lucy caught her breath, suddenly understanding why he hadn't taken her into Ravanna when Victor came, why he had acted so strangely. He didn't want to lose her! *"Oh, Papa,"* she thought, feeling a surge of warmth for him, *"you do love me!"*

"The house'll be finished before winter," Victor said. "How would an October wedding be?" He looked at Mr. Smith, who did not answer, then turned to Mrs. Smith and Lucy.

No one had to say anything. It was accepted as fact.

Chloe was in bed when they arrived at Park's new house. She made an effort to get out of bed, but she could not. Mrs. Robinson was there, and she silently went about getting plates and forks. Mrs. Robinson was as slender and reserved as Park, and she did not seem at all happy with the way things were going. While Mrs. Smith and Lucy were helping her in the kitchen, she confided, "Your Chloe's not strong at all."

Mrs. Smith studied the taciturn old woman's face; her wrinkles accented what appeared to be a perpetual frown, almost a scowl. "No...no, I suppose she's not," Mrs. Smith allowed. "But this is her first child, so...."

"I had eight. And my husband was working for the Rock Island when they were building it, so I had to do everything by myself." She looked pointedly at Mrs. Smith. "Folks that can't take care of themselves sure make a heap of trouble for others."

"Well, I'm sorry you had to come all the way up here from Trenton again, Mrs. Robinson," Mrs. Smith said mildly, taking two plates with cake and a fork on them from her. "I'm sure you miss your home."

"Oh, it's just an old railroad house," the woman said. "But we done the best we could—by ourselves. Sent three of our children through college 'fore the mister retired."

"I'll stay with Chloe from now on," Mrs. Smith said, giving Mrs. Robinson a gracious smile. "My husband can do without me for a time."

So it was that after the "birthday party" at Park and Chloe's home, Mrs. Smith stayed with her eldest daughter. Mrs. Robinson went home on the morning train. The following day Bill brought some of Mrs. Smith's things to her. He returned to the farm with the news that Chloe had gone into labor, and he glumly told his employer that she had been moved to the Powell Hospital.

Mr. Smith at once took Lucy and Catherine with him and set

off; they stopped in Ravanna to pick up Victor. From there on he frequently clucked to the horses and slapped the lines on their rumps, forcing them into a fast trot on each flat section of the road. The girls and Victor were silent, watching the set of Mr. Smith's shoulders: they were bunched up toward his neck as if he were trying to avoid a blow. Lucy and Catherine looked at each other, and Lucy mouthed the words, "I'll bet he's remembering when Glen died."

Catherine winced and huddled against her big sister as Lucy put one arm around her back, biting her lower lip to keep from crying. *"Chloe,"* Lucy sent her thoughts speeding ahead, *"please don't let anything happen to you...or the baby. Please don't leave us!"*

Victor sensed her turmoil and reached back to secretly hold her hand; he felt its clammy coldness and saw in her eyes the same panicky helplessness he had seen the night Alex had been killed. For the remainder of the trip to town, he tried in his look and grip to fill her with his strength.

When they arrived at the hospital that night, they hurried inside, but they saw no one in the antiseptic-smelling, dimly lighted place. Mr. Smith went down the hall until he came to a closed door labeled "Delivery Room." He knocked softly.

Dr. Powell came out almost immediately and nodded to the Smiths and Victor. His face bore a grave expression as he stared toward Mr. Smith's feet. "She's already been in labor nine hours," he said, glancing at her father's face. "But she doesn't seem ready to deliver. She's not strong, and she's used most of her energy." He tried to smile. "However, we can always hope...."

Lucy was standing behind her father next to Victor, and she took one of Victor's hands. As he held her hands, he felt how much they were perspiring. He led her back to the waiting room and sat with her near the front windows. Catherine followed them and sat on a sofa like a doll placed primly; she stared fixedly ahead, and even her eyes became chinalike. In a while Mr. Smith joined them, rubbing the brown-white hair back along the sides of his head. He glanced at Lucy, then swung his gaze to Catherine and let it rest on her for a long time. Lucy sighed, realizing that Catherine would have a far harder time leaving home or getting married because her father likely would become more protective than ever. *"Please, God...don't let anything bad happen to Chloe; my Papa and Mommie can't stand any more."*

The night hours passed slowly. Periodically the waiting four were roused when faint cries came from the direction of the delivery room. The cries were weak, and they filtered from down the hall as if searching for strength and hope...then faded away as if they had found nothing but despair. Each cry seemed to torment Mr. Smith, who sat forward, staring at the brown braided rug and wringing his hands. Whenever he did so, Lucy turned to Victor with a pleading look; when he had comforted her, she sat back under his arm that was across the back of the deacon's bench on which they were sitting.

The cries of pain continued to come faintly from down the hall, with 15 or so dead minutes of silence between them—just enough time for the listeners to begin to relax and drift toward sleep. Finally Mr. Smith could stand it no longer. He strode to the delivery room and opened the door. Victor and Lucy heard him talking with Park and Mrs. Smith. Their hushed whispers were tense and spaced by lengthy silences.

Slowly the sky outside lightened. Grayness seeped into the waiting room. A nurse came to work, bustling. She blew out the lamps, smiled with automatic encouragement at the family, and hurried down the hall with a rustle of starched clothing. In minutes, Mr. Smith and Park appeared, apparently having been forced out of the delivery room by the officious nurse. Victor stood and shook Park's hand, trying in his grip to bring some life back into the man's haggard face and almost-limp body. Park looked at Mr. Smith—guiltily, Victor realized—and went to sit near the sleeping form of Catherine, who was curled on the sofa near her father's chair. Park clasped his hands between his thighs, his elbows pressing downward, the muscles in his forearms and jaw clenching and unclenching...clenching and unclenching.

"Park," Victor gently suggested, "why don't you try to sleep?"

"How can I when she's...!" Park burst out with such wild unrestrainedness that Victor had a sudden insight into why the young man usually was so "studied"; he maintained, Victor reasoned, a pose of calm so folks would trust a druggist who really was very immature. Victor smiled in a kind way, also realizing how much the young man loved and depended upon his wife, and how deeply afraid he was of losing her—and being the cause of her death. "Park, you mustn't blame yourself, no matter—"

"No?" Park snapped. He struggled for self-control, staring at his hands as he clasped and unclasped them. "Well, it's not fair," he muttered. He gave Victor and Lucy a burning look, seeing but not seeing them. "It's *just not fair!*" he whispered angrily. "We were so happy, especially with the baby. We'd fixed up the nursery, gotten all the furniture and everything. And now!" He spread his hands as if searching for an escape or an answer. "How can this happen?" he muttered to himself. "We're good people, never hurt anyone, never did anyone wrong." His face hardened, and he glared at Victor. "I'll tell you, it's enough to make me wish I'd gone ahead and done what I was tempted to do when—" He broke off when Mr. Smith gave him a penetrating look; he hung his head, a frown contorting his handsome features and narrow face.

They all flinched and stood when a scream, followed by the prolonged sob of a second voice, came from the delivery room. Lucy turned to Victor as she broke into tears. Then, toward the delivery room, she cried in a plaintive voice as if trying to call back her sister, "Chloe! *Chloe!*" Victor held her when she tried to run, and he forced her to follow Park and her father at a restrained pace. The nurse met them in the hall; she was holding Mrs. Smith, who was sobbing into a handkerchief she pressed to her face with both hands. Dr. Powell stood in the doorway. Behind him was a still form. It was covered entirely with a sheet. He shook his head, staring at his glasses as he polished the lenses with his handkerchief. He glanced at Mr. Smith and Park. "She just didn't have the strength."

"The baby?" Park asked desperately, trying to get past the doctor.

Dr. Powell held him out for a moment, then released him, letting his own arms drop slack by his sides. "The baby died, too," he said despondently. He put on his glasses and turned to watch Park go to the bedside, pull back the sheet as if in one final hope that death was a lie or fantasy, then fall weeping against his dead wife; his face was beside hers, and his right hand stroked her face.

Dr. Powell turned toward Mr. Smith, then faced Mrs. Smith, who was limp, supported by the nurse. "I thought for a while that we could save the baby," Dr. Powell said, mustering his strength and squaring his shoulders. "But its little lungs just seemed to close up." He shook his head, stuffed his handkerchief into a pocket, and made his way past the family.

Lucy turned to Victor, who was watching her without crying but with tears crystalline in his eyes. She opened his coat, put her arms around his waist, and got as close as she could, crying with her cheek against his breast. Mr. Smith stood silently rooted for a long while, then raised his head, turned and went up the hall, got his hat, and left the hospital, walking faster and faster. Mrs. Smith silently, vacantly watched him go...until she noticed Catherine watching from the corner of the waiting room, her face a china mask of questions. With a convulsive sob, Mrs. Smith went to enfold her in her arms. Lucy and Victor quickly joined them in their closeness...a closeness of emptiness in which only Victor's body and spirit seemed to have warmth to give.

Chloe Moriah Smith Robinson and her baby were buried in silver-embossed caskets in Otterbein Brethren Church cemetery beside the grave of Glen Walter Smith, on April 9, 1901.

• • •

Mr. Smith went into such grieving that frequently, at Mrs. Smith's request, Reverend Schonover came to the house to talk to him. But nothing Mrs. Smith or Reverend Schonover did seemed to have any effect on Mr. Smith. He would say nothing, hardly would move from his hickory rocking chair on the back porch, and scarcely ate. Finally, in response to her mother's urging, Lucy walked to Cox's General Store, taking Catherine and May with her.

Victor was standing behind the long, single counter wearing a white apron over his blue shirt and dark trousers when the girls came in. He came from behind the counter to meet them, and he took Lucy's hands when she made a slight movement toward him. "Victor, you've got to come do something," she pleaded, unaware that the girls had gone to the candy case and put their faces as close to the lemon drops, peppermint twists, and licorice ribbons as they could. "I'm afraid Papa's just going to sit and die unless...."

Victor nodded and went toward the house behind the store, taking off his apron. When old Mr. Cox came back with him, Victor put one hand on Lucy's back and began following her outside. Then, abruptly, he stopped, grinned at Mr. Cox, laid a penny on the counter, got a handful of lemon drops, and gave them to the girls—much to their delight.

The Smith home was silent when they arrived. Lucy explained to Victor that their mother had taken Sammy and Clara up to Jane Hall's for the day. Then Lucy took Catherine and May upstairs. Victor went down the hallway and through the kitchen, glancing at the hired girl, who was dozing with her arms and head on the table. Taking a chair with him, he went out onto the back porch.

Mr. Smith was rocking slowly, staring out over the almost-flat, plowed, bare fields toward a line of grayish oak trees on the horizon. Victor placed his chair near the farmer, who appeared to have aged five years in the previous few weeks, and began praying.

They sat silently for an hour...then another hour. Victor heard the girl begin walking around the kitchen, preparing dinner. Otherwise the farm was silent except for the desultory cawing of crows flapping sullenly over the fields and occasional communal sounds from chickens scratching around the yard.

Another hour passed. Victor heard Lucy and the girls come into the kitchen, eat quietly, then go toward the front of the house. The hired girl cleaned up, rattling dishes, then apparently went back to sleep. Still, Victor neither spoke to nor looked at Mr. Smith.

The afternoon went slowly by, and Victor became vaguely aware of the ticking of the Regulator clock in the front hall. Patiently he waited, continuing to pray. A warm breeze flowed across the porch with the smells of livestock and the hay in the barn. A horse in a pen by the barn whickered at someone passing along the road out front. The clatter of buggy wheels and trotting hooves faded into the distance northward.

Finally Mr. Smith stopped rocking. His shoulders trembled. He put his hands to his face, leaning forward. His hunched shoulders trembled more violently, and he began to weep. He soon stopped trying to control his sobs, and they became deep and despairing.

When at last he became still, he sighed and lowered his hands. Staring across the bare fields, he whispered, "She's dead." Turning his tear-stained face to Victor, he blinked. "Fluty, she's dead," he repeated as the muscles around his unfocused eyes twitched. His frown trembled as he appeared to accept the realization. When he at last focused on Victor's face, he blinked and tilted his head slightly as a strangely sympathetic expression came over his features; the young man beside him was silently crying...and Mr. Smith slowly understood that pain was not his alone to bear. "Oh, Fluty," he whispered, "I'm so sorry."

Victor continued to gaze at him, his look without defense.

"Fluty, please don't cry," Mr. Smith begged him, laying one hand on the younger man's arm. The farmer stiffened, sniffing.

"I'll be all right now. I promise." He half-smiled.

Victor still sat gazing at the older man.

Mr. Smith's eyes filmed with tears again, and he gripped Victor's forearm. "Glen...Chloe. Alex...Susan." He looked toward the fields and murmured, "How much you must've loved your brother and mother." He clenched his lips, sharply shook his head, and stood, holding one hand toward Victor. "Come on, son; let's rouse that lazy girl and have some coffee!" He smiled and pulled Victor to his feet as the younger man reached upward.

Thereafter, whenever Mr. Cox didn't need him at the store, Victor walked up to the Smith farm to help with the planting and later with the cultivating.

Victor also borrowed Mr. Smith's mare—an Arabian beauty—and went to visit Mrs. Scholwalter. The old woman lived in a back room of Mrs. Sampson's boarding house. When Victor entered her room in response to her curt, shouted summons, she was sitting by her window in an oak rocker, wearing a black dress with a bit of frayed lace around the collar.

When Victor had paid her almost half the money needed to buy the farm on Grant Creek, she looked at the bills lying in her lap, then stared at Victor. Pointing at him with one bent forefinger, she squinted and rubbed her snuff-stained lips together before she said, "If you'll agree to preach my fun'ral sermon when need be, I'll forgit what you owe."

Victor sat on the edge of her bed. "But, Ma'am, I'm not a preacher."

She leaned toward him with her forefinger still pointed, and she squinted harder. "You're Susan Walker's boy, Fluty, ain't you?"

"Yes, Ma'am," Victor said.

She drew back and nodded, twitching her withered lips. "You'll *be* a preacher," she stated, rocking.

Victor stood and took up a long stamped-and-ribboned piece of paper from the bureau. "No one else needs to sign this—not your—"

"*I* own that land free an' clear!" Mrs. Scholwalter snapped. "An' all you've got to do is take care of it—'specially the elm tree by the baptizin' pool in the creek. Me an' all my family was baptized in that pool." She squinted and pointed at him. "So you take care of the tree, you hear?"

"Yes, Ma'am, I hear," Victor said, going to kiss her forehead.

After he left the boarding house and was walking up Main

Street, he met Lon Casteel. Lon stopped, pushed back his hat, and grinned. "You sure don't look like no prince on a white horse. But I reckon you must be."

"Why's that?" Victor asked, reaching out to shake his hand.

Lon pumped it once, then again. " 'Cause you blew me clean out of the saddle without even being in town." He laughed. "Congratulations! I heard you're going to marry Miss Lucy."

"I hope to," Victor said. "But I didn't realize that you—"

Lon waved his words away. "I never had a chance, not once she'd set her sights on you. I wish you the best," he said, shaking Victor's hand again and walking on.

Victor rode straight back to the Smith farm. He dismounted, unsaddled the chocolate brown, shiny-coated mare, and rubbed her down with a gunnysack. He took the bridle over her small, pointed ears and turned her into the horse pen by the barn. Leaning against the fence, he watched her frolic around the perimeter of the fence, flicking her feet, then nicker at the other horses before she lay down for a roll in the dust. Victor grinned and went to the house to show Mr. Smith and Lucy the deed to the Grant Creek farm.

The summer passed quickly. At harvesttime Victor worked in the fields with the Smith and Hall men, driving a header machine to cut the wheat or helping operate the noisy, smelly, steam-powered threshing machine. The broad fields also produced hay— timothy and red clover—and Victor helped the other men run the bull rake that came along after the surrey rakes. Stacking the hay at the edges of the fields was hot work, pitching huge forksful on top of the stacks that eventually rose far above a man's head. Laying it right so rain wouldn't penetrate the stack and ruin it was a specific skill that Victor's father had taken care to teach him, and the other men watched what he did, then imitated him.

When the Smith harvest was finished, the threshing crew moved on up to the Hall farm, then the Jewell farm. And each day, no matter where they were working, Lucy Smith was among the women who brought the men their dinners in covered baskets and sat with them in the shade of the machinery while they ate. And Victor noted that, unlike his mother, Lucy never once said anything about the way he smelled or about how dirty he was. In fact, he caught her several times looking at his bare chest with half-concealed interest. When he looked at her, she looked away, blushing and wiping strands of glossy brown hair from her forehead. Thereafter he wore a shirt under his overalls despite how the other men gently teased him.

One Sunday afternoon after the crops were in, Mr. Smith took Victor into the parlor. He sat down in his chair by the organ and motioned almost formally for Victor to sit near him. For a while he looked at the fading photograph of his father above the organ, then cleared his throat. "You haven't asked me if I was going to pay you for working."

"No, Sir," Victor said. "Mr. Cox pays me enough to live on and save from. So I really hadn't thought—"

"Think about it now," Mr. Smith interrupted. "You know we can't afford two hired men."

"No, Sir, I know that," Victor said.

"So, what I'd like to do," Mr. Smith said with the tone that men use when they have reached the end of bargaining, "is give you something. But you've got to promise beforehand that you'll take it." He gave Victor a serious look, but his eyes were sparkling.

"All right. I promise," Victor said, wondering....

"Belle is yours."

"Your Arabian mare?" Victor asked incredulously.

"With her saddle, bridle, Pendleton blanket, and halter."

"But she's only three; she's in her prime," Victor protested. "I didn't earn but maybe—"

Mr. Smith raised one hand, palm outward. "You promised."

Victor swallowed and nodded, looking at the floor. Softly he said, "Did you know how much I—"

"A man who doesn't think highly of something," Mr. Smith said chuckling, "doesn't stand around watching it."

"But still—" Victor objected, knowing the worth of the animal.

Mr. Smith stiffened. "Son, this also is my wedding present to you." He stood, holding out his right hand. "Now we can go to work on your house. With Bill and me working with you, we'll have your house *and* barn finished in a few weeks."

Victor stood, inwardly struggling to accept Mr. Smith's generosity and to believe that such a long-term dream finally had come true. He shook hands with Mr. Smith, then watched as he took a piece of paper from his shirt pocket, unfolded it, and handed it to him. Victor read, "Bill of sale, one Arabian mare, paid in full."

On the first Monday of September, school started. Each weekday after that, Lucy walked Sammy and Catherine into Ravanna to school, then stopped by Mr. Cox's store to see Victor if he was there and not over working on the new house. But for days and days after President William McKinley was assassinated, the store was full of people talking about the assassin and about the new president, Theodore Roosevelt. His name being mentioned invariably brought up the Spanish-American War and the Rough Riders; and if Hardy McClary—Mr. Thogmorton's renter who had fought with the Rough Riders—happened to be in the store, an argument invariably broke out between him and the Hall, Ruth, and Smith men, who had not served in the war because of religious reasons. The other kind of argument that went on almost daily concerned the age of the new president, who, at 42, was the youngest president the country ever had had.

"He'll send us into a worse depression than the '90's!" Amos Hall declared. "He has *no* understanding of anything but foreign conquest!"

"He couldn't mess things up much worse than they are now," Robert McCargue grumbled, "what with crop prices bein' so low."

The group's mood changed as the men looked "slaunchwise" or sideways at Robert, who was known to have unusual ways of paying off his debts. Someone couldn't resist saying, "Got debts...and a new barn, have you?"

Mr. McCargue reddened and—stomping his boots on the floorboards—left the store. Just before he was out of hearing range, Abe Ruth slowly and loudly said, "I'd sure hate to sell that man insurance."

" 'Specially *fire* insurance," Amos Hall whooped.

The men laughed. Victor straightened when he saw Lucy stop in front of the door, then hurriedly go on, unwilling to come inside and brave the plaguing of the men. Victor slumped, wishing the men would congregate somewhere else so he could resume his visits with Lucy. But he knew they wouldn't. Now that the crops were in, the pressures of note payments and bills were off them, and they had topics of conversation. So Victor bided his time.

The women of Otterbein church held a quilting bee for Lucy, setting up their quilting frames in the church and stitching together the lining, batting, and carefully pieced-together tops while they talked. The patterns were mainly like the tolework and barn decorations of the Pennsylvania Dutch: roosters in red and blue; yellow tulips with green leaves; turkeys in gold and brown; and various geometric designs, each rich with traditional meanings. As the women talked, they questioned Lucy—Miss Lucy—about the items in her hope chest. Had she made enough dresses? Had she made enough gowns, towels, and pillowcases? What was her wedding dress like? When would Victor finish moving her things into the new house, which they'd heard was finished? When a man dared stick his head into the church to summon his wife, he was driven away with loud cries that he was "disturbing the peace!" Most men fled at once, but Victor stood for a long time in the doorway, watching Lucy at work beside her mother, letting her mother answer most of the questions. Even from a distance he could see what tiny stitches Lucy made. He smiled, thinking of his mother's work.

It snowed in late September and snowed harder as October progressed. By the 20th, the day Victor and Lucy had settled on for their wedding, the ground was almost entirely blanketed in gentle white, sweeping in sparkling crystals over the rounded hills and across the broad fields. Victor's father, sisters, and brother arrived two days before the wedding, and Smith relatives began arriving from as far away as Kansas and Ohio. Frequent complaints were heard about the "winter wedding," but otherwise a feeling of festivity budded as though the season were spring. The Smith house became absolutely crammed with people, and Victor was kept busy trying to remember all the names of Smith cousins, aunts, uncles, great-aunts, great-uncles....

To no one's great surprise, old Reverend Turnbull of the First Baptist Church of Princeton drove out to conduct the ceremony. He spoke genially to the members of the Brethren churches, shaking hands as he bowed from the waist, his back stiff even while stooping. Soon he went to the end of the parlor and motioned for Gertrude Jewell to pump the organ and begin playing. The crowd that was gathered in the parlor, in the hall, and across in the dining room respectfully quieted, even the small children.

Gertrude began to play as Victor took his place, Matt beside him, both stiff and solemn in new blue serge suits and starched white shirts with celluloid collars and blue ties. Wagner's "Wedding March" poured forth into the waiting stillness, and before long the crowd began to turn to look toward the stairway. Victor smiled when he saw little Clara shyly pacing through the crowd in an ankle-length, frilly white dress, scattering paper rose petals in her path from a basket.

Behind her came Sammy, glancing aside at uncles and aunts and cousins, looking very manly as he carried a velvet cushion on which lay the golden rings. He placed his feet carefully, knowing full well what would befall him if he tripped on the rug. Behind him demurely came Midge Hall, Lizzy Casteel, and Catherine Smith, Lucy's bridesmaids. Then, as Gertrude pumped harder and the music swelled from the organ, Mr. Smith appeared with Lucy beside him, their arms interlocked. Mr. Smith pressed his daughter's arm against his side, raised his head to look toward the minister, and proudly led Lucy to the "altar." Her white organdy, satin, and lace dress was so long that May, carrying the train, was four feet behind her sister. As Victor memorized this vision of loveliness, he caught a glimpse of Lucy's shining eyes behind the veil, and he winked at her.

Reverend Turnbull's words were "by the book" for most of what he said; but when he closed his little book, he looked solemnly at the couple and said, "You have exchanged your vows, forming a bond that neither time nor human can break. You have pledged your love and all you have and will have, all that you are and will be. I hope you understand that God Himself has called you to this union. I am thankful that you have obeyed His will!" He looked penetratingly first at Lucy, then at Victor, who noticed that the old man's eyes misted over, glistening. Reverend Turnbull bowed his head, spread his hands toward the crowd, and loudly prayed a lengthy blessing on the couple. Then, quietly, he said, "Victor, you may kiss your bride."

Gently, Victor turned to her and held his left hand beside hers as they looked down at the golden rings. Slowly he raised her veil, and they came together for their very first kiss. Oddly enough, there were no muffled cries of "Whooo-ee" from the men or boys. There was only a waiting silence, and it was not broken until the kiss ended and the couple turned, beaming, toward their families and friends. Then began the festivities.

The following day, three families drove to the Grant Creek farm. Victor helped his bride down from the new spring wagon that Judge Jewell had presented them the evening before. The families gathered beside the wagon and the two buggies, looking at the tidy house—at the freshly painted white walls, the gray-painted porch, the black-painted trim and gutters, and the square sharpness of the roof lines. Forty or so yards behind it, the old house had been painted barn-red, and a winter-furred Jersey cow and her large calf stood in a pen looking over a board fence at the people.

Victor suddenly scooped his bride into his arms and carried her across the blanket of glistening white snow, up the steps, and across the porch to the door. He opened it, then swung around as Lucy clung to him with her arms around his neck. Radiant, he called, "Come on in, folks! Welcome to our home!"

5

Settin' Up

That night after everyone had gone, leaving the couple alone in their new home, Lucy found herself standing in the middle of the living room. One kerosene lamp burned on the shiny dark-oak table near her, and another lamp dimly lit the kitchen. Victor had gone outside to tend to the cow, and the house was utterly silent. Lucy could not seem to stop the trembling in the muscles of her upper chest and along her arms. She wrapped her arms around herself and turned toward the new Acme cannon stove; she moved toward its radiating heat, but knew that her trembling was not caused by a chill. She smelled the freshly painted walls and floors, the new wood, the faint scent of hickory logs burning. She looked at the few pieces of furniture: the square table with its massive center pedestal and four chairs, a Mission rocker with black leatherette upholstery, a davenport couch covered in figured velour. She took the lamp from the table and walked into their bedroom. She stared at the wooden bed, the mirrored chiffonier, the double-doored oak wardrobe closet...then looked back at the bed. She hurried out of the room and into the kitchen.

A Puritan ice chest-refrigerator faced her against the far wall. Against the right-hand wall stood an Acme Charm six-hole steel range with an attached hot water tank. Closer to her against that wall was the largest piece of furniture in the house: a three-level kitchen cabinet. In the top level, she knew, would be dishes and spices. The middle level was a work surface. The bottom level contained drawers for utensils, bins for flour and sugar, and a cupboard for pans.

On the other side of the kitchen were a separator, a churn, a Curtis washing machine and wringer, and a large zinc sink with a pump at one end. Broad shelves had been built along that wall, and from hooks under the shelves hung various utensils; on top of the shelves stood empty canning jars, large pots, and spare lamps, already filled.

"Mine...my house," Lucy thought experimentally. True, Victor had obtained most of the furniture and fixtures. And relatives or friends had contributed most of the utensils, the dishes, and much of the rest of what was in the house. But...it was *her* kitchen...*their* house.

The idea staggered her, and she associated it with her trembling. Her house. *Her* and her *husband's home*...not house. No longer would she "go home." She *was* home...and if she wanted her mother and father, sisters and brother to be with her, she would have to invite them. She gently tucked her lower lip between her teeth and looked toward the front door and the darkness beyond the lacy-curtained window. She was alone...alone with a man...alone on a farm two or so miles from the nearest neighbor and at least 17 miles from her own home...her *old* home...her childhood home. Her throat tightened suddenly and tears swam in her eyes as she looked almost frantically about herself. The back door opened, startling her into whirling around. A gust of frigid air reached her at the same moment she saw Victor come onto the back porch; he gave her a quick smile before he blew out the lantern he was carrying. He pulled an empty nail keg to himself and sat to begin tugging off his muddy, snowy boots. She ran to him.

With a grunt he dislodged one boot and almost hit her with it as he jerked backward. In that moment his head came up and he saw her face. He stood immediately. "Lucy, dear, what's wrong?" He didn't seem to know what to do, and he stood stiffly, holding his boot.

"I..." she began, spreading her arms and gesturing at all the newness, the strangeness...and she looked at him with the same expression; he too was strange, suddenly alien. "I don't know what's wrong." She laughed, wiping her tear-streaked cheeks with the backs of her hands.

Thoughtfully he sat down and, with a grunt, jerked off his other boot.

She clasped her hands in front of herself. "I should've done that," she said lamely.

He smiled up at her, his large hands cradling the boot, his kind eyes twinkling with deep, rich blue. He set the boot down, wiped his hands on his overalls, and laughed. Seizing one of her hands so quickly that she flinched with surprise, he stood and led her into the living room, taking one lamp from the kitchen with him. Her surprise grew as he let go of her hand and knelt in the middle of the floor; grinning at her, he set the lamp nearby. Uncertainly, she knelt beside him.

He took her hand again and scooted around facing her, then took her other hand. Bowing his head, he firmly said, "Lord, we're new here, but You're not. We've already given ourselves, our lives, to You, and now we give You this house, our home. We ask that You consecrate it to Your uses, that You protect it against the Adversary, and that You bless it and us as You see fit." He squeezed Lucy's hands, and when she looked at him, she saw that his eyes were shining with tears. He drew her into the circle of his arms and held her close against his body until her trembling ceased.

As he held her, he buried his face in her hair, smelling its freshness, feeling the softness of her gentle curls. Her body felt slight and young against him, and he reminded himself how eternally gentle he would have to be. The feel and smell of her rushed within him, healing with softness and light the two throbbing aches inside his being—one for Alex and the other for his mother. He had not realized—nor admitted to himself—how deep was the hurt, the emptiness, the loneliness he had harbored, the loss he lived with, until he felt Lucy's hair, the side of her face, her chest against him and her arms around him, pulling him to her. Her slim hands began ranging over his back, his shoulders, his neck, feeling the muscles as if trying to identify him. He waited, sensing that she was *learning* him, that she had been nearly panic-stricken with changes, with newness...with him. He waited, holding her tightly but not so tightly that she would sense his franticness for contact, for *filling*—and feel threatened.

When she became uncomfortable in her kneeling position, she released him and stood slowly, pulling him upward with both hands. They stood gazing into each other's eyes, and Victor watched Lucy's gaze rove to and fro; she then stared wide-eyed into his eyes and looked at his features as if seeing him for the first time. He let her look, and he looked back...and discovered that in a way it was the first time *he* had seen *her*. Always before, someone either had been with them or had been nearby, preventing him from really *seeing* her. He began to smile, and his smile grew until it became a laugh. Her face clouded instantly, and she stiffened.

"No...no!" he said. "I like what I see...I *love* what I see. I've just never really *looked* at you before! You...you're absolutely beautiful! It's like Alex said: You're an angel." His last words were spoken with such tenderness that her concerned expression melted.

She lowered her gaze, blushing and edging closer to him. "I was afraid...." She glanced up and briefly tightened her lips. "I was afraid you didn't like what you saw...that you were sorry...."

"Oh...*no!*" he said, laughing again. This time she identified his laughter as delight, and she too was delighted. He approved her, she realized, and she boldly looked up at his face. His smile, the twinkle in his eyes, and the set of his mouth became questioning, teasing, and he tilted his head slightly to one side as if posing.

"Yes," she said definitely, "I like you, too." she grinned shyly. "You're...handsome." Quickly she added, "I never realized that. I...*knew* you were to be mine...but...." She paused in confusion, looking around the lamplit house. "But now everything I dreamed about and tried to imagine is *real.*" She laughed nervously, holding her hands tighter and shaking them as she looked into his eyes. "And you're everything I thought you were...but you're something else...something more. You're a *man.* And I'm *married* to you." She leaned against him, bowing her head against his chest so her face was hidden. She murmured, "I've never seen a man undressed...and I've never been....Not even Sammy has *seen* me."

He put his arms around her and gently drew her against him. "Are you afraid I won't like what I see?"

Without revealing her face, she nodded.

"I've thought the same thing," he whispered.

She quickly looked up at him. "You have? But you're...."

"Older?" he asked. She nodded. He smiled and shrugged faintly. "I never even thought much about girls—no, don't you laugh at me!—until I started thinking about you. I may be older, but I have very little idea what women are like. We...we'll have to learn together."

She sighed, softening, and turned her face sideways against his chest. Bending slowly so as not to lose contact with her, he picked up the lamp and went toward the bedroom. She hung back slightly, hesitatingly, and he waited for her; when she went forward, he went with her.

He set the lamp on the chiffonier and went back into the kitchen to blow out the other lamp. Lucy stared at the bedroom lamp's reflection in the mirror and watched the soft yellow-golden glow cast shadows around the strange new room. She looked for a pitcher and washstand, and she was puzzled by their absence.

She felt of the quilt on top of the bed and pushed on the feather mattress. She heard Victor open the stove in the living room and add a log, then adjust the flue. When he came back into the bedroom, she was standing stiffly, her hands clasped before herself. He went to a door at the far side of the room, opened it, and went into a smaller room. She heard him washing up, and she thought it was very odd that he would put the pitcher and basin in a small side room.

When he returned to her, she tremulously asked, "Are we safe?"

"Perfectly. We have neither dogs in the yard nor locks on the doors, but we are far safer than those who do. The Lord is our Guardian, and I am yours...even," he added quietly, "as you are the guardian of my heart and spirit."

He blew out the lamp, and she listened to quiet rustlings as he undressed. Slowly, with a return of her trembling, she did the same. She heard him open the wardrobe, take out a hanger, and arrange his clothes on it. She realized then how essentially neat he was, and that realization gave her assurance. As she unbuttoned the long row of buttons on her dress, she added up other facts: He had not made one demand upon her; he had not clumped into the house in his boots, leaving tracks for her to clean up; he *never* had said one loud or unruly word to her; and he had turned to the Lord at each step of the way, gently taking her with him. She sighed, loosing the tension in her abdomen.

She tensed slightly when she heard him turn back the covers on the bed and climb in. Quickly she took off her lace-trimmed union suit, dropped it onto the floor, and climbed into the bed. She shivered as the chilly cotton inner blanket touched her skin, and she moved toward Victor, seeking his warmth, seeking the touch of his skin. The excitement of newness rushed upon her, and she savored each moment as that excitement filled her.

•　　•　　•

Lucy awoke slowly with a delicious feeling of luxurious comfort. She stretched under the thick layer of warm quilts, and for a while she thought that she was back in her parents' home. Then she remembered where she was...and stretched again, smiling and snuggling under the comforts in her warm nest. But suddenly she sat bolt upright; the bed beside her was empty, her man had gone, and she—wife!—had duty to do! She was out of bed in a jiffy, and the touch of the ice-cold floor against the soles of her feet brought her fully awake.

Resisting a desire to remain unclothed and warm in memory

for a while longer, she took a long, lace-trimmed gown from the wardrobe closet and slipped it on as she looked all around for a chamber pot. Puzzled that there was not one, she remembered the small room into which Victor had gone the night before. She went to the door and almost cautiously opened it. To her amazement, it hid a bathroom—a real bathroom just like the city folks had! She silently clapped her hands as she ventured in to explore the astounding, unfamiliar territory.

She looked with fascination at the porcelain sink in one corner, with faucets of porcelain and brass and pipes below it. Above it was a cabinet with a mirrored door, which she cautiously opened. She next stared at the eagle-claw-footed, rolled edge bathtub and saw that it also had faucets and pipes. Across the room from the tub were shelves on which towels and washcloths were stacked. Finally—wonder of wonders!—she stared at the water closet, remembering how in her parents' home—indeed, in all the farmhouses she had been in—they had had to use chamber pots or the outside privy, to which a trip in winter was a dreaded expedition. She looked out the small bathroom window, wondering where the running water came from, and she saw the thick stone wall of a large, above-ground cistern.

As she turned on one faucet of the bathtub, she wondered fancifully if hot water would come out. After a few minutes the water began to steam in the chilly air of the rather long, narrow room, and she again clapped her hands silently. Hot running water! The house had seemed such a small, simple house, squarish with a higher roof in back above the upstairs bedroom. Now it seemed not small but comfortable, not simple but complete. She hastened to bathe, noticing that the bar of soap she had found in the mirror-doored cabinet (next to Victor's bowl of shaving soap, his straight razor, and some talcum powder) was Castile soap, not lye! She luxuriated in her bath, thinking how strange it was to find her things with *his* things and to find things he had bought and placed here and there obviously for her benefit alone...and how many details of *their home* he had thought out with her in mind. But from where, she wondered, did the hot water come.

As she sat in the tub, bathing herself with customary fastidiousness, she saw that the back of the room was stepped— the underside of the stairway leading to the upstairs bedroom, she reasoned. Hurriedly she finished bathing, wondering where Victor had gone...and wondering what the upstairs bedroom looked like. When she had brushed her hair and pinned it up for the day, she chose a housedress from among those Victor had brought over days earlier and unpacked. She then stood undecided about whether to go to the kitchen and do what she was supposed to do...or go upstairs. She ran to the corner of the bedroom opposite their bed and hurried up the stairway.

The room's ceiling was slanted on the front side where the roof sloped down toward the eastward-facing front porch. There were no windows there or to her left, in the northern wall, but two windows were on the south and two opened toward the west—the latter two overlooking the backyard between their house and the old house that had been transformed into a barn. She looked out those windows at the white expanse of pristine snow surrounding the buildings, and she saw three sets of tracks between the barn and the house. But Victor was nowhere in sight. Lucy turned and looked around the room, noticing for the first time that the walls were papered...and the wallpaper had tiny yellow flowers on its ivory background. *"He's made a baby's room!"* she thought excitedly, noticing a walnut crib against the western wall. She also saw her hope chest. She ran to kneel beside it. Caressing the lid that her father so patiently had carved, she thought about the design: two doves, two rings, and a heart.

Nearby stood a treadle sewing machine, a Singer, in a carved oak cabinet. Where had he gotten it? she wondered. Was it supposed to have been a surprise? It, like the crib, she felt he had been saving as surprises, since he had said nothing about getting them. *"Those things—our baby's crib, my sewing machine, my hope chest,"* she thought as tears of joy and realized-longing swam in her eyes, *"are as much signs of my womanhood as our union last night!"* Oh, she wanted to run and shout, to sing and dance, and she whirled and raced down the stairs as fast as she could. When she burst out of the stairway, she ran smack into Victor. He caught her up and swung her around, grinning proudly. She looked at him, speechless with joy.

"You saw?" he asked, holding her tightly in his arms.

She wiped her eyes, laughing and nodding. She saw that his cheeks were cold-reddened, and she felt the deep coldness of his hands as he held her. "The sewing machine?" she managed to ask breathlessly.

"My mother's," he said, setting her on her feet.

"And the crib?"

"Alex's, then Matt's, then mine, Ella's, and Nanny's. And before us it was my mother's, and before her it was grandfather Hall's, and before him...." He laughed, watching her nod at each person's name. "It was made in the 1700's. Twelve generations have used it."

"You...your family...?" she stammered, sensing a depth of history, a continuity that she never before had even guessed at.

"Well, Lucy Smith Walker, did you think your husband's people were just Johnny-come-latelies?" he asked lightly, his eyes twinkling.

"No," she said quickly, "I mean, I never thought...."

He laughed and put one arm around her shoulders as he led her toward the kitchen. "I'm sorry; I shouldn't tease you so early in the morning...or maybe not at all." He looked questioningly at her.

She suddenly clapped her hands and danced away from him, whirling around and around into the living room. "And the bathroom! The hot water! We're just like rich city folks! Oh, Fluty, where does the hot water come from?"

"From a wood-fired boiler set into the cistern wall—the cistern we must hope won't freeze," he said with a hint of concern about his innovations working properly—innovations he had carefully kept secret from everyone lest he be thought trying to be "better than he was." "And next summer we'll have ice from the ice house I built like your father's. And the pump in the kitchen sink is hooked to a well that taps springwater—not groundwater." He watched her dance in three more circles, the hem of her dress whirling out like the petals of a flower. Suddenly he cocked up his right arm, set his left fist on his waist, and danced a quick-stepping Scottish jig in his own circle before her. She became motionless in amazement and delight, staring open-mouthed at his feet, then looking at his eyes. He stopped dancing, slightly embarrassed.

"I didn't know you could do that!" she exclaimed, running to hug against him and kiss his lips.

He kissed her back...then kissed her long and deeply. When she sighed and laid her cheek against his chest, he whispered, "No one else knows either—not even Daddy."

She looked up at him, realizing he was sharing secrets. She whispered, "But where did you learn...?"

He winked in the same way he did when he performed one of his little magic tricks. "Promise you won't tell?"

Eagerly she nodded.

"Walkers are Scotsmen, from clan MacGregor." He rolled his "r's." "My grandfather, Henderson Walker, was taught by his grandfather to play the pipes and dance jigs and the fling, and he taught me...but not even my parents knew. *They* said we were English in our beginnings—as good as any Rouths or Smiths or Jewells." He winked at her and bowed his head toward her to whisper in a conspiratorial manner, "But just between you an' me, I'm as stubborn as any Irishman, as penny-pinching as any Scotsman, and have none of the patience of the English!" He laughed broadly, his eyes bright and twinkling. "And I can talk the arm off any Yankee peddler!"

"Can you?" she asked, truly curious. When he drew back and stared at her as if chiding her disbelief, she added, "But usually you don't say any more than what's necessary."

"Ah, when you're around stones, you speak as stones do," he confided. "I have *no* desire to be plagued for rattlin' on all the time!"

She relaxed and clasped her hands before herself, staring seriously at him. The solemnity returned to her blue-gray eyes, and only the tendrils of chestnut-brown hair curling around her white, smooth face betrayed her youthful joyousness. "So you do have the gift of speaking, don't you?"

His expression became as solemn as hers. "Yes," he said.

"Why do you hide it?"

He shrugged. "I've been the youngest of three brothers and a dutiful son of my father. Only *now*," he said, raising one eyebrow and regaining some of the bright twinkle in his eyes, "have I begun to come into my own."

"Because of me?" she asked hopefully.

"Ex-actly!" he rejoiced. Turning his face toward the ceiling and raising his hands, he cried, "And I do thank You, Lord!"

She stared, open-mouthed again; never had she seen him so demonstrative, so open and unrestrained. She began to blush, realizing the reason for his flowering.

He caught her up into his arms with a sweeping motion that made her shriek playfully. "And now, heartmate, to the breakfast of our start in life together—which I prepared for you before tending our beasts, in case you awoke ravenous!" He carried her into the kitchen.

"But I was supposed to—" she started to protest, until she saw the biscuits on the warming tray at the edge of the stove, the platter of fried eggs and bacon, and the bowl of buttered grits—and smelled the aroma of fresh coffee.

When he set her down and started to serve the plates, she stepped in front of him and took the long-handled spoon. She bumped him out of the way with one hip and snorted. "Up before dawn," she muttered, "rummaging around in *my* kitchen!" She turned on him with grinning fierceness. "And I suppose you've already milked the cow!"

"Milk's in the separator," he said meekly, holding out one hand to take a plate.

She swung it away from him and marched into the living room. She set the plates on the table, on placemats that were finely crocheted—by his mother, she supposed, judging from the quality of the work. She went back into the kitchen and took a towel away from him before he could take hold of the coffeepot handle. She poured his cup full and poured herself half a cup. Suddenly uncertain, she looked at him. "Cream or sugar?"

He shook his head. "Like Uncle Matt says, 'Coffee's not coffee with anything else in it!' But," he added in a quieter tone, "if Aunt Nervy comes, you'd best have cream and sugar in *china*." He laughed and followed her into the living room...and pulled out her chair, then seated her. She nodded graciously to him and watched him seat himself. He clasped his hands, said grace, and began to eat voraciously, while she frequently glanced at him, estimating how much food she would need to cook for each meal.

After they had eaten, he helped her wash and dry the dishes, despite her protests. Thereafter he showed her around the kitchen, proudly naming each utensil he had acquired and explaining the operation and care of each appliance. He started to tell her how to build a fire in the stove—how to lay the kindling wood atop the shavings—and when he looked at her, he saw that she was silently crying.

He stood quickly, frowning questioningly, and put his hands on her arms. "Now what've I done?"

Pouting, she slowly shook her head, "I know how to do *some* things," she said in a hurt tone.

"I'm sorry," he said sincerely, bending down so he could look into her downcast eyes. "Really, I am. It's just that I'm used to—"

"Well, you've got to let me *learn*...Papa!" she said with mild vehemence. Her expression softened. "Papa," she repeated, tilting her head slightly and looking at him with a return of her joyousness. "That fits you." She snuggled against his chest, discovering that she could press her thighs against his with pleasure.

"I love you," he whispered, caressing her hair...and feeling the pain of tragedies recede further and further from his heart.

"And I love you," she murmured, holding him more tightly. Thoughts of her parents, of Chloe and her baby's deaths, of her "abandonment" of responsibilities for her younger brother and sisters, all seemed far in the distance. At the moment there were simply and purely Victor and Lucy. Shyly she glanced up at him. "Would it be all right...I mean, could we—"

He grinned. "Go back into the bedroom?"

She nodded slightly, smiling with all the joyousness of the morning.

He led the way, holding her by one hand, and she quickly followed.

•　•　•

They lay in bed talking for a long time; Victor told Lucy where each item in their home had come from, how much it had cost, and where the money had come from. He told her how much money he had left and what the situation with his father and the Spickard grocery store was, and he explained what he thought best to do with the Grant Creek farm. In fact, he told her everything he could think of to tell her, and he let her be the judge of whether she needed to know any given fact. She remained silent, lying on her right side, a quilt pulled up and tucked under her left arm.

She watched his eyes as he talked, wondering that they could be so open and show such depths—an openness and depth she never before had seen him reveal. She looked at his lips, wondering that they could be so tender in private and so closed and unrevealing in public. She kept silent mainly because never before had any man, relative or otherwise, taken her into his confidence; furthermore, as far as she knew, Victor was telling her far, far more of his business than most men told their wives—sharing, even as he had shared his secrets, in a way that not even her father had shared with her mother. Lucy hardly knew how to react. In one part of her being she felt very much a child because of her ignorance; in another part of her being she felt herself growing minute by minute, expanding, learning not as she had learned in school—by rote and dull memorization—but by a deep desire not to fail this man, not to displease him. She flinched when he stopped speaking and reached across to stroke the line of her jaw.

"Please don't look at me like that," he said gently. She blinked, puzzled. He explained, "Don't feel that you have to remember everything I'm telling you *or* that you have to be perfect. God knows *I'm* not!"

She nodded, not having realized he was watching her so closely or was able to understand her so well. She smiled and lay down with her head on her right arm. "Thank you," she murmured.

"Lucy," he asked, still in a gentle tone, "what are your dreams?"

Again she was puzzled; no one except Midge and Trudy had ever asked her that, and they had talked only of childhood dreams and hopes. She had never thought what her adult dreams might be.

"If God would grant your greatest wish, what would it be?" he asked encouragingly. "He will, you know—if you want it badly enough and if it's within His will."

She turned onto her back and smiled as she stared at the ceiling. Half-formed thoughts drifted through her mind, coalescing, beginning to radiate a light of which she realized she had been vaguely aware all her life. She murmured, "I want to be the best wife...the best mother I can be." She turned and looked at him. "I want to stand beside you no matter what happens, and when I die, I want our children to be a credit to us and to remember me and say, 'She was a good mother.' "

He delicately kissed her lips.

As he leaned back, she smoothed down strands of his hair. "Fluty, can I ask you the same thing?"

He crossed his hands under his head and lay back; she lay down beside him with her right cheek to his chest. She felt his heart beat strongly and listened to his breathing, then to the vibrations of his voice. "Matt thinks I'm crazy, and Alex just listened to me in silence, but I have only one dream." He stroked the left side of her face and tenderly uncurled the hair over her ear. "Promise you won't think I...never mind. My dream is, '...seek ye first the kingdom of God.' "

She moved up and lay halfway on top of him, her face six or so inches from his chin. "So you won't be a farmer all you life," she said decisively.

He smoothed back the hair from either side of her face, looking at its oval grace and the delicacy of her bone structure. "You and Mrs. Scholwalter," he murmured.

"Mrs. Scholwalter?" she asked, moving slightly on his body.

"She said I didn't have to pay the other half of the farm's purchase price if I'd preach her funeral."

Lucy tickled the bottom of one of his feet with her toes. "You

will," she stated, laying her left cheek against his chest and caressing his right side.

"I will?"

She nodded, and he thrilled to the sliding of her long, lightly
curling brown hair against him.

"Do you know something I don't?"

"Maybe."

"When you pray, do you feel answered...do you receive the
Counselor?"

She nodded, again thrilling him with the sliding of her long hair
against his skin.

"Is that how you knew we were right for each other?"

She nodded.

Hesitantly, almost dreading to bring up the subject, he asked,
"Did you know that Alex wasn't the one?"

After a moment she said, "I knew that he would lead me to
something for which I was to wait."

Victor was awed; here was the certainty his mother had had;
here was a faith such as he struggled for, gained and lost, gained
and lost. "Oh, how I love you," he murmured.

They arose later to prepare dinner, and as Victor was helping
Lucy wash the dishes, they found themselves touching almost
continually—not getting into each other's way but simply main-
taining a contact that rapidly and startlingly was filling a void in
both their lives.

He became curious about the void, wondering if what she was
feeling—as she brushed against him, let her hands slip to him
briefly, picked lint from his shirt, and groomed his hair in
passing—was like what he was feeling. "Did your parents love
on you much?"

She looked at him and assessed his tone of voice, then said, "No.
Never. You know how people are—taking joy in children but
scared half to death that if they love them too much, something
bad will happen."

Victor nodded. "It's like they're afraid of worshiping the child
instead of the Creator, and thereby bringing wrath upon
themselves."

She nodded, uncertain as to what he was thinking.

"So your father never kissed you?"

"Goodness, no!"

"Not even when he went off on trips?"

"Oh, maybe then," she said, beginning to see what he was mentally putting together. "Was your mother affectionate...is your father?"

He shook his head ruefully. "When I was growing up, I used to think they didn't love me. I've always *known* that God loved me, and when I learned more about Jesus, I knew He did, too. But I used to wonder about my parents." He raised his curved, dark-auburn eyebrows. "Alex and I used to lie in bed late at night...listening, you know, to find out if they loved each other." He grinned bashfully. "They did. But somehow nothing got carried over to us kids...nothing physical, that is. I've...yearned for that. For touch." He took Lucy in his arms and drew her against him.

"Me too," she murmured. "A lot more than I knew." She looked up at him, her eyes darting from side to side and swimming with tears. "Poor Park," she said, trying to keep her lips from trembling.

Victor nodded. "Daddy, too."

She put her lower lip between her teeth, refusing to cry, then said, "I used to grieve for Alex and Chloe...but I kept being told, 'Grieve not of the dead in Christ, for they are eternally *in* love.' "

"You were *told?*"

She nodded. "And after I saw you at Chloe's wedding, I realized that what the message meant was that I had to love you, not worry about Alex. We...we're *here*, in this life, to do physically what the Spirit does spiritually, aren't we? We're supposed to *show* God's love for others."

His eyes widened slightly. "I...I've never thought of that," he said quietly.

"Well, it's true," she said certainly, going to the cabinet to finish putting away the dishes and pans. When she had closed the cupboard doors, she turned and sighed, clasping her hands before herself. "What shall we do this afternoon? Is there work to be done?"

"He laughed. "No, my bride. Why do you suppose I wanted to get married in winter? This is our honeymoon. We're building our nest, settin' up. Do you want to get cold and wet?"

She saw the merriment in his eyes and trusted him despite his teasing. "Surely."

"Then let's bundle up and take a walk around *our* farm. A foreigner like you from the flatland of the English needs a good introduction to Lower Tennessee."

"You!" she said, trying to tickle him as he sprinted toward the bedroom. Hurriedly they put on their woolen winter garments.

The sun was bright yellow southward in the western sky. Its glare scattered across the rolling, snow-covered hills and fields, making millions of tiny points of diamond light. The chilling air was still, crisp, pure. The coldness penetrated their clothes, but the least exertion drove away numbness, and they walked quickly to the old house-barn.

A large double doorway had been made where the old front door had been; a low ramp led up to the doorway. Victor pushed open one of the doors and ushered Lucy inside. She inhaled the smell of the cow, her big-eyed calf, and the pair of horses, and she heard the low clucking of chickens. "Oh, good," she said, going toward the pen where the chickens were scratching in straw. "I was wondering what we'd do for eggs."

"Ed Kauffman made me take back my daddy's Rhode Island Red hens and a rooster as soon as he knew the barn was finished. He also gave me back my little Red-Cornish-cross hen." He pointed to the dapper little hen, scratching by herself for bits of corn among the straw. "She's our setting hen; her Cornish banty blood will make her spread herself over a good-sized clutch of eggs and stand off even us if we try to touch them." He laughed, watching the dainty claw movements of the hen.

"Sixteen," Lucy said after counting the flock. She hid her mouth with one hand and pointed to the rooster watching her out of one eye, his head cocked to one side, his golden hackle feathers ruffling. "Does he think we're about to take one of his hens for the stewpot?"

Victor snorted. "Roosters 'think' about only one thing."

"He seems so protective, though."

"Let a dog or fox get in here, and he'll be the first one to fly for the rafters."

She looked at Victor. "So men really aren't like roosters?"
He gave her a peculiar look. "Some are, I suppose."

She looked back at the chickens. "Men...no, *you* aren't like a rooster or a bull or a stallion."

He figured she was confirming some thought or belief, so he bit back the teasing reply that first had come to mind. Seriously he said, "No, I'm not." He saw her lips tighten as she nodded slightly.

"And women don't have babies like cows have calves, do they?" she asked, still looking thoughtfully at the hens clustered in their pen, methodically scratching around and around.

"No," Victor said. "Animals have an easier time usually—unless something goes wrong—because they don't think about it. And because they don't think about it, they don't fight it. It just happens. But women having babies can be the same—if they don't let fear get hold of them, if they remember to breathe, and if they have good help."

She turned quickly to him. "You know how to deliver a baby?"

He nodded. "Jane George happened to be at our place with just Mama and me when Olin decided to be born." He laughed. "Maybe that's why he's so wild: He was born on-the-go, you might say."

Lucy came closer to him. "You'll stay with me?" She reached toward him, and he took her hands, feeling their slim softness.

"Every minute," he assured her.

"Is it messy?" she asked with what Victor thought was an odd note of excitement in her voice—which he realized might be long-suppressed curiosity.

"Yes, it's messy, but the messy part is taken care of easily enough. Do you want me to tell you what happens from start to finish?"

She nodded, hooking her right arm through his left arm as they walked out of the barn. While he talked, they passed Belle and Mack, who were holding their heads out of their stalls into the aisle. Victor absently stroked their faces and muzzles as he went toward the door.

The couple walked to the west, toward Grant Creek. To their right, northward, lay the undulating, shadowy gray-black, almost looming mass of the virgin forest. To their left, southward, ran the clay road, disappearing and reappearing among the folds of the hills. Their feet broke the crust of the snow and they sank four or so inches with each step, deeper in drifts near the ditch that ran diagonally from the northeast to the creek. Victor carried Lucy across the ditch, then arm-in-arm they climbed a long, low hill. On the other side they stopped, looking down at the tall bottomland forest along the creek. Rising taller than the other trees soared the massive, bare, gray-brown branches of the elm that Mrs. Scholwalter had told Victor to guard. It stood on the far side of the creek near the road, and it seemed the patriarch of all the surrounding trees, standing fully 120 feet tall.

They turned and worked their way down the ridge of the long, low hill to the creek. Along the bottom, near the edge of the meandering edge of the forest, the snow was much deeper. The couple had to force their way forward, with Victor breaking trail and Lucy stepping high to keep in his footprints and not get bogged down in the soft snow that covered and clung to her legs.

He stopped and looked at her to see how tired she was becoming. "Cold?" he asked.

She sniffed her reddened nose and patted her red-pink cheeks, smiling stiffly. "Yess!"

"The baptizing pool is over yonder," he said, pointing through the trees to the creek. "The big elm is at its foot. There used to be a rope hung high up in it so the kids 'round here could swing out and dive."

They waded through the thick snow under the trees, stooping and trying to avoid the snow-laden branches. Frequently, though, they brushed a branch and were showered with whiteness. Soon their heads, shoulders, and backs were mantled. Shaking themselves, they came to the creekbank.

The pool was solidly iced over with snow drifted around its edges; it was perhaps 30 feet across and 50 feet long, and in the center of the pool, green depths showed faintly through the wind-swept ice.

"Are there fish here?" Lucy asked, shivering against Victor.

"Catfish, perch, bluegills," he replied, looking down at the ice. "Bullfrogs, too. Ever eat froglegs?"

She shuddered, grimacing. "No! I heard they jerk all over the skillet while they're fried...and sometimes when they're served."

"Better'n fried chicken," he suggested teasingly.

She looked around him, downstream. "Is that the road?" she asked, pointing through bare, gray, thin branches toward the faintly visible, red-rusted iron spans of a bridge.

"Yes, and across the road and west of the creek is the Bohring farm—Ira and Grace, you know. Dad Bohring can tell more about gardening than a person could learn in a lifetime. And south of his place, about three miles from here, is Pleasant Ridge Church,

where the road south to Princeton jogs. South of it is Ed Kauffman's place.'' He pointed westward. ''On down this road about
two miles is the Sparks' farm. North and west is the Gentry place.
North and east of us is the Lewises' farm—or dairy, I should say.
Mott Lewis is weaving rugs, I've heard.''

''Is she nice?''

''She's one of our neighbors,'' Victor said. ''And yes, she's
nice...but you may have to get used to her.''

Lucy frowned slightly, looking up at him. ''Why?''

''Well...the Lewises...and the Sparks may not be what you're
used to having as friends and neighbors.''

She shoved him. ''Say, I'm not some high-falutin' debutante!''

He was grinning. ''Oh?''

She snatched up a handful of snow, packed it between her
hands—while he backed away, doing the same—and threw it at
him with an accuracy that left his face snow-covered, his eyes
blinking as he gave a startled laugh.

''Oh ho! A baseball player!'' he hooted, arching his snowball
at her.

She ducked, grabbing another handful of snow. Before she could
pack it, he chased her and tackled her. They fell together into the
snow. Shrieking with delight, she tried to rub her snowball in his
face, but he got her first. Sputtering, she cried, ''You...you!'' and
flung snow at him. They wrestled, and she wound up on top, strad-
dling his waist, pinning his shoulders to the ground in the impression in the snow he made.

Laughing, he cried, ''Uncle...uncle. I give!''

''You won't call me a high-falutin' debutante?'' she demanded
playfully, pushing on his shoulders.

He became serious, searching her eyes with his gaze. ''Lucy,''
he said, almost pleadingly, ''don't you know how fine, how
ladylike I think you are?''

Surprised, pleased, she relaxed her pressure against his
shoulders.

''I admire you,'' he said softly. ''I respect you...for your fineness,
for the fact that you *are* a lady.''

She smiled at him. ''I never thought of myself—''

''I have...and I do,'' he said, reaching up to put his fingertips
to her face. ''You're the finest thing that *ever* has come into my
life, except my mother. And you and she are quite a lot alike.''

She was stunned by the comparison, for she knew what the entire county thought of Mrs. Walker, how so many women held up her memory as an ideal. Tears came to Lucy's eyes as she lay down against Victor, digging her hands into the snow to wrap her arms around his neck. "That's the nicest thing you could have said to me," she murmured.

He gently pushed back her head and kissed her tenderly.

Times and Seasons

Halloween came and went unnoticed by Victor and Lucy. Winter deepened its gripping cloak over the land. But the season that for Lucy once meant days of boredom broken by taking younger sisters and brother off Mother's hands was now a season of growth, deepening and being enriched below the surface. The surface was what Lucy identified as the girl her parents had known, the good student at school, the playful friend of Midge and Trudy. She felt distinctly that that part of her life was like the land outside: It was there, but it was quiet, inactive, unchanging though becoming fainter. Beneath that surface, she felt roots going down, twining with the roots of Victor's inner being, finding and drawing upon sources of sustenance and strength that she never had imagined in all her attempts to envision the "adult life."

She watched her man continually, observing, filing bits of information, correlating facts when something she previously had wondered about suddenly matched some new piece of information—information he willingly but in his own good time revealed to her about himself. He was not guarded, exactly, and she quickly learned she could tease or play him out of whatever guardedness he showed. But, she also was learning, he was layered with depths that he himself was perhaps not aware of, was perhaps slightly aware of but either avoided or chose not to bring up, or was perhaps afraid to reveal too quickly. It was not that he did not trust her; she knew beyond a shadow of a doubt that he trusted her with what was most essential to him—his spirit, even as she trusted her spirit with him. But reticence was ingrained in him, as it was in everyone she knew except those folks generally considered to be blabbering fools. Victor's reticence, however, was different.

The other men who had been around as she was growing up said little to avoid being thought foolish. When Ed Kauffman and his wife had come calling in early November, Ed had remarked, "Better keep your mouth shut and let everyone think you're a fool than open your mouth and prove it." Lucy had laughed, remembering how her father and even Judge William Jewell had said essentially the same thing. But Victor's reticence, she had observed, was not that kind of unwillingness to say something onto which the "plaguers" and "bla'garders" could latch and make a topic of teasing for years and years. Victor had an easy way with such people—the Albert Trasks and Amos Halls of the world; they did not intimidate him, and he slid from under their thrusts even when most other men would have been rankled and galled into rebuttal.

As November progressed and Thanksgiving approached, Victor worked in the upstairs room near Lucy. He was making a high chair, and she was sewing shirts for him. They usually worked in silence; Victor's plane curled shavings of walnut from the legs and chair arms he was shaping, and Lucy's feet treadled steadily as she fed neatly cut pieces of fabric through her machine. Occasionally she asked him to stand and hold out his arms for a fitting, and occasionally he asked her what she thought of some idea or another—ideas that when she added them up gave her, she thought, the conclusive correlation that explained his reticence: He was very smart, and he had a fear of letting anyone know it. When she realized that fact, she stopped sewing and sat back to stare at him, watching the muscles in his forearms flex below the rolled-up sleeves of his flannel shirt, watching how intent his eyes were upon making the rich brown walnut he had cut and dried himself as straight and smooth as glass.

"Victor?"

He was silent until he had finished squaring the slender rung he was working on and had unclamped it from the padded jaws of the vise he had placed on the worktable he had built first. He looked at her.

"Why don't you want anyone to know how smart you are?" she asked.

His gaze quickly dropped, and he brushed shavings from the table into a pile on the floor. "Maybe if I were smart, I'd have something to let people know."

She smiled; it was exactly the answer she had expected. "Where do all your ideas come from?" she asked, pursuing him patiently.

He glanced at her. "Oh, I don't have so many ideas."

"Let's see," she said, holding up her fingers so she could count on them, "first there was this house—nothing special, nothing that would make folks talk, but just as neat as a pin. Then there was the water system; then there was—"

"You're just as smart as I am," he said reassuringly.

"I know that," she said sweetly. "But that's not what I meant. What does the Word mean when it says not to light a candle and put it under a bushel?"

He straightened, gazing steadily at her, and realized that she had been watching and listening to him more closely than he had been aware. He also realized that she was more perceptive and better able to reason than he had been aware; he then saw that he had assumed that women could not reason...and he felt ashamed for having underrated his wife, even though she had misinterpreted his motives. "Is hiding a candle under a bushel the same thing as 'To everything there is a season, and a time to every purpose under heaven'?"

She leaned forward and placed her elbows on either side of her machine on the polished oak cabinet. "Oh," she said softly at last, smiling as she felt a chill run faintly up her back and neck. "Oh...you're waiting."

Tightening his lips, he nodded solemnly.

Her expression was equally solemn, and she felt humbled that she had too hastily judged her man. She knew immediately that there were levels of him yet beyond her vision. He came to her purposefully.

Taking her hands and feeling the smoothness of her skin, he said, "Thank you for understanding me. No one else *ever* has seen me the way you already do." He suddenly laughed. "Just think what we'll be like after 20 or 50 years of marriage, how the years will ripen, how...." He broke off, and she sensed that he was reluctant to predict, as though predicting would ruin the prospect.

For Thanksgiving, they went to Lucy's parents' home the last Thursday in November and stayed for three days. It was Lucy's first visit home since her marriage, and she was surrounded and overwhelmed by the reception her family gave her and Victor. She was beseiged with questions from Catherine, Sammy, May... and Clara climbed onto her lap whenever she sat down. As the older children pumped her for every detail about her and Victor's new home and farm, Clara leaned against her chest, sucking her thumb and looking triumphantly at the other children whenever one of them happened to look at her. Mr. Smith, meanwhile, drew Victor into the parlor while the finishing touches were being put on the Thanksgiving dinner in the kitchen and on the long table in the dining room.

Mr. Smith was beaming. "So, son, how's Belle?"

"Fat and sleek," Victor said, settling down to wait until the serious questioning finally began.

"Ed Kauffman sold you back that workhorse of your father's?"

"Yes, Sir, and I'll buy a teammate come spring; figure on going to Ed...or Henry George. What d'you think?"

Mr. Smith nodded judiciously, reflectively. "Ed does have some fine horses. You might also see Bill Hall. 'Course, his draft animals might be too strong for yours; he's pretty old, isn't he?"

"Twelve. You think Mr. Hall might let me pay him when crops are in?" He folded his arms, watching the older man think.

"I dunno. He's pretty sharp. What'd Ed tell you?"

"Twenty dollars for a six-year-old and payment in hay next fall."

Mr. Smith blinked at Victor's forthrightness in disclosing money matters. "I'd take that, if I was you," he said with equal forthrightness. He began to smile slightly. "By the way, have you seen Henry's little girl, Margie? She's a year old, Jane said. We saw them in town when they were buying the girl a birthday present. You know what a fine person Jane is? Well, young Margie already is just as graceful and calm—not a bit like Olin."

"How's Cliff?" Victor asked casually, knowing the five-year-old never had been expected to live long.

Mr. Smith shook his head. "Shame that boy was born a boy. Got eyes like a Jersey cow; soft brown hair like his mother's, soft-spoken, slender. He looked healthy enough, though. But that Margie! My...." His bright, happy look held for a moment, then slid toward pensive sadness. "If Chloe's baby had lived...." He tightened his expression and jerked upright. Slowly his happy look returned, and he gave Victor an assessing, almost teasing look. "Any news for us?" Mr. Smith inquired innocently.

Victor played the game. "Oh, we're gettin' along just fine."

"Anything comin' for that upstairs room?"

"Well, yeah, I've set up a woodshop there. Been makin' furniture."

"Don't say?"

"Yep," Victor allowed, watching Mr. Smith's breathing become more and more shallow. In the older man's expression, somewhere behind his eyes, Victor saw the basis for Mr. Smith's expectancy: his dream of a son, which ended in tragedy; his dream of a grandchild, which ended in tragedy, and the further tragedy of Chloe's death. What Victor saw was like a faint glimmering hope that was afraid to emerge lest something else happen to damage it. He softened considerably toward Mr. Smith.

Mr. Smith let out his breath...and a bit of his patience. "Any prospects of a grandchild...you scamp?" He grinned broadly, acknowledging what he thought was the fact that Victor had outplayed him in the patience business.

"No," Victor said with a twinge of regret that he couldn't give life to his father-in-law's flickering hope. He dodged mentally into the teasing way of handling sensitive matters. "But you might ask Lucy what she has in mind."

"What she...ask Lucy?" Mr. Smith stammered, completely thrown off track. Victor's growing smile made him burst into laughter. "Son, you had me going there for a while!"

"Dinner!" sang the cheery voice of Mrs. Smith.

When he joined Lucy at the table, Victor saw that she looked flustered and harried. He figured that the peacefulness of their past five weeks of isolation had been shattered forcefully. He took her hand and held it while Mr. Smith said grace.

After they had begun eating, Mrs. Smith straightened slightly, looking at Lucy, and said, "But you will tell me as soon as you know."

It sounded to Victor as if she were continuing an earlier conversation with her daughter, whom he noticed was reddening up her neck.

"Mother!" Lucy said almost sharply. "I told you you'd be the second person to know *anything.*" She stared at her plate and dabbled at her food.

Her mother huffed quietly, "Well, I just love you, that's all, and I worry about you, after...well, you know what I mean." She glanced toward the empty chair at the table...a small void all of them had been avoiding noticing, despite their continual awareness of it.

"Yes, Mother," Lucy said without raising her head. "I know what you mean." Victor took her hand when it dropped into her lap, and she squeezed it hard.

Lucy huddled under the embroidered lap robe against Victor during the cold drive back to their farm, and she was silent all the way. But once they were inside their home, she quietly exploded.

"First they delay and delay telling me anything about being a married adult, then they can't stop *rushing* me into being a mother!" She forcefully shut the wardrobe door and turned to face Victor. "I *know* how important grandchildren are to them, but you'd think they'd realize how important children are to me...and how pushing me makes me feel...inadequate." Her shoulders sagged as her head drooped forward. "Oh, Victor, you don't think...."

He came to her, taking his long scarf from around his neck and dropping it onto the bed before enfolding her in his arms. "Do I think anything's wrong with you...or me?" She leaned her forehead against his chest and nodded. "No, love, I definitely do not. 'To everything there is a season.' "

She looked at him, her eyes filmy with tears. "Oh, Fluty, I hope I'm not going to have to be like Abraham's Sarah...or Chloe."

He took her firmly by the shoulders and braced her, looking intently into her eyes. "We've been praying since the beginning." A slight twinkle invaded his blue eyes. "And we've certainly been doing our part." Her lips spread with a smile. "The rest is up to the Lord. His timing certainly isn't ours."

"No," she quietly admitted, "it's usually a lot better."

He nodded, running one forefinger across her lips in a way that made her smile broaden. She softened against him.

Later in the day, the sound of buggy wheels and a horse whickering at their own horses made both of them spring out of bed, hurriedly dress, and hasten to the front windows. Victor moved aside the curtains and peered out. "Mott and Luther Lewis," he said, grinning in a bemused way as he looked at Lucy. "Our neighbors have come calling. Guess they want to see the debutante."

"You...!" Lucy said with mock threat. She followed him outside.

The buggy that had stopped near the house swayed heavily first one way—as the ample figure of Mott climbed down with an "Ooof!"—then swayed the other way as the equally stalwart figure of her husband climbed down. The pair made the buggy and horse seem small, and Victor glanced at Lucy and smiled as he saw her eyes widening. She edged around behind him with a solemn expression. *Mott may eventually see the real Lucy,* Victor thought, *but Luther never will!*

Luther heaved his bulk onto the porch, his jolly red face beaming as he assessed first the house, then what he could see of the "bride." His close-cropped, sandy-red hair was uncovered despite the cold, and he clapped his huge, thick red hands together to loosen them of their stiffness from holding the lines, then shook hands with Victor.

"Nice place you built, Victor," he declared in a voice that could not conceivably have quieted. He pumped Victor's hand...and Lucy edged further behind her husband. Mott had gotten a long, heavy bundle from the back of their buggy, heaved it up across one shoulder, and was lugging it across the snowy yard to the house. She plopped it down on the boards of the porch and set her fists on her hips.

Smiling widely, her features as thick and broad as her husband's but greatly softer and more pleasant, she gave Lucy a kindly look. "Brought you something. Housewarming," she said.

"Well, come inside," Victor said, turning so quickly that he bumped into Lucy, who was immobilized behind him. She moved quickly, glancing behind herself with an expression as if a cow and a bull were about to invade her home. Victor shooed her on.

The fragrance of brewing coffee soon pervaded the living room as the four sat—Luther and Mott crowded on the davenport, Lucy and Victor on chairs from the dining table. Mott had been smiling hopefully, encouragingly at Lucy—who had not spoken a word.

Mott looked at Victor. "Little bit of a thing, ain't she?"

Victor looked proudly, affectionately at his wife. "She'll do."

"Oh, I reckon she will," Mott said, booming with laughter. "If you picked her, I'm sure she's the best of a litter some'eres."

"How's your cows, Luther?" Victor asked, crossing his legs and settling in for an afternoon's conversation.

"Um, most o' them's carryin'. When they calve an' come fresh, them Holsteins'll be good milkers," Luther said, crossing his pillarlike legs with a wheezing sigh. "But I wisht I had a dozen like that Jersey in yor back lot. Bet you get a right smart lot o' butter off'n her."

" 'Nough to sell," Victor said, "or trade." He looked at the bundle Mott had lugged inside the house.

She raised both hands and slapped her thighs resoundingly. "Oh me, that's not for tradin'!" She laughed. "That's my gift to our new neighbors." She leaned forward and winked benignly at Lucy. "Bare feets gets cold paddin' 'round hardwood floors of a mornin'."

Lucy, wide-eyed, nodded slightly, trying to smile.

Mott heaved herself upright. "Gimme yor knife, Luth," she said, holding out one thick hand.

Grumbling, he dug in one pocket of his overalls and produced a three-inch blade. Mott took it and went to cut the twine binding the bundle. She grabbed one edge of the undone roll and flung out three rugs, each woven of rags in brown, beige, and red tones. Proudly beaming, she looked at Victor and Lucy, folding the knife blade into the staghorn handle and tossing it back to her husband.

Victor, amazed, stood and went to kneel by the rugs. "Mott, we can't accept these! Why, this must be more'n a month's work."

"Naw," she said easily, squinching her face and waving his objection away with one hand. "First efforts." She looked quickly at Lucy. "Not that anythin's wrong with 'em. They're right enough...but I'd rather give 'em away than try to sell 'em. They're a bit thick and just a tiny bit loose." Seeing that Lucy was staring at the rugs with a perplexed look, Mott went toward her. "Hon', what you do is throw 'em down until they get dirty. Then you just rip 'em up in strips an' wash 'em. Bastin' stitches put 'em together again. The strips won't come unwove or nothin', you can rest assured." She unfolded her arms under her bosom and looked defiantly at her husband. "Luther don't think much of 'em, but he'll change his tune when they bring in more'n that herd o' black an' whites o' his." She sniffed the air, turning toward the kitchen. Bending and reaching tentatively toward Lucy, she gently said, "Hon', I think yor coffee's done."

"Oh," Lucy said as if awakening. She looked at Mott...and slowly smiled. Mott softened noticeably, her broad, rounded shoulders slumping as she straightened with a pleased look. She turned toward Victor as Lucy hurried into the kitchen. "Bit shy, ain't she?" Before Victor could answer—and Mott acted as if she didn't really expect him to—she followed Lucy into the kitchen.

Victor took the top rug, shook it out, and dragged it into the bedroom. It perfectly fit the space between the footboard of the bed and the bathroom. The second rug he dragged into the kitchen, smiling as he saw that Mott was close beside Lucy, one large hand lightly resting on the young woman's shoulders as if gentling her to her touch. The third rug he spread between the dining table and the stove in the house-width living room; then he went back into the kitchen. He hugged Mott and said, "Thank you very much—for your work and for your thoughtfulness."

She swiped at her eyes and nose, smiling broadly in a close-lipped way. Hastily she took a cup of coffee from Lucy and carried it into the living room for Luther. Victor followed her with his own cup and sat to resume his conversation with the dairyman, while Mott returned to the kitchen; there, Lucy was still standing by the stove.

Lucy watched as Mott sat on a chair at the worktable that Victor had made, and realized how well Victor made chairs, too, because the chair creaked but did not tilt or sag. Lucy blinked and noticed that Mott was watching her with a gently probing gaze. Lucy heard the men talking unhurriedly in the living room, so she sat near Mott and tried to think of something to say. She took a deep breath, watching Mott sip her steaming coffee, and ventured, "Your real name is Martha?"

Mott leaned toward her. "Hon', will you pray for me?

Lucy frowned slightly, drawing back. She saw honesty and sincerity—and a deep concern—in the woman's bright, black eyes. Yes...of course. But what—"

As casually as breathing, Mott said, "You see, me an' Luther been married eight years. We ain't had no children, not even a stillborn. I been prayin' 'bout it as reg'lar as the sun comin' an' goin', an' the other Mrs. Walker was prayin' for me. But now, she's gone...and now, there's you. You've got the Spirit too, you know."

Lucy could only stare, her lips parted, as Mott put one hand to her braided, up-pinned black hair in which a few gray strands showed.

Mott waved her hand, smiling affably. "Hon', I know you're frightened of me, jist walkin' in an' treatin' you like you was kin. But you gotta understand a couple of things." She leaned forward a few inches and whispered, "First yor man is godly, but mine ain't. Second, you an' Victor'll have the kids you want—oh, yes, I can see plain as day that you want 'em—'cause the Lord's on yor side. But me and Luth?" She drew back as her shoulders hunched upward, a sad, questioning expression on her broad-featured face.

Lucy's lips closed quickly as they began trembling. "Oh, Mott, I'm so sorry," she murmured, clasping her hands tightly in her lap.

Mott leaned forward and patted Lucy's hands with one of her own callous hands. "You...sorry?" she whispered. "*I* oughta be sorry—upsettin' a sweet thing like you. All I meant to say was, you gotta pray for me. You're for that, you know."

"I am?" Lucy asked, puzzled and hesitant.

Mott's head tilted to one side, and she gave Lucy another gently probing gaze. "Child, why do you s'pose the Lord brought you together with Victor? You can't cook, can you? An' I'll wager you never touched the teats of a cow or hoed a garden." Seeing Lucy's budding defensiveness, Mott laughed and held her hands in the air as if to dampen Lucy's rightful feelings. "Don't get me wrong; the Lord must've never meant you to do such things; folks like me, yes. But you can *pray*. You can talk to *Him*, an' when you join yor prayers with Victor's....That's why I come. I knowed you an' him together...." Tears swam in her eyes, and she swiped at them. "The Lord'll listen to you two, an' He'll open me up...'cause I want kids to hold an' nurse an' love, same as you do." She stiffened, sitting erectly with her head back, her lips firm. "An' I'll raise mine same as you will—to seek first the kingdom!"

It did not occur to Lucy to argue with or deny what Mott had said, but she wondered rather anxiously why so many people seemed to have to show her things about herself—things she had sensed but never would have put into words until someone else did. Quietly she managed to say, "I'll pray for you and for Luther. Victor and I both will." She nodded, holding her lips firm.

Tears brimmed over Mott's lower lids and ran down her broad cheeks as she took Lucy's hands and gently squeezed them. "I knew you would. I took one look at you an' knowed right off."

Lucy smiled, feeling a warmth spread within her that she could tell was the Spirit's affirmation. Strangely, the warmth made her feel weakened and strengthened at the same time.

Victor finally followed the Lewises outside to their buggy, and Lucy waited in the middle of the living room. When he rejoined her, he was smiling; but when he noticed Lucy's expression, he became solemn. He held her hands, and they stood gazing at each other in silence for a minute or so.

To make sure she knew that he understood—though she really was sure without asking—she inquired, "Do you know what Mott told me?"

"Sort of."

"Could you have told me the same things—that...that my purpose with you is to be...." She faltered, thinking that to say it might somehow be bragging.

"My spiritual partner, my prayer partner, my co-worker in the Lord."

She felt borne up...and somehow weakened. Her childhood lack of awareness had been sundered; from within the pieces were emerging...."You knew?" she wondered aloud.

He nodded.

"Is that why you moved so...so deliberately?"

"The time had come 'round."

"Oh, Fluty, what if I fail...what if I'm not good enough?"

"You *aren't*, but *He* is," he said, arching one curved, richly auburn eyebrow.

"Oh," she murmured, softening and moving closer to him. Quickly, though—despite what she knew that she knew—she looked at him, frowning. "But I feel so inadequate...so immature...so...."

He did not stop her words, and when they trailed off, he continued staring into her soft, blue-gray eyes until certainty came back into them.

As Christmas approached, Lucy and Victor began working on gifts. Victor took a quiet, special delight in sitting in the sunspot that poured through the western windows and carving toys—locomotives, trucks, steam engines—for Lucy's brother and younger sisters. She, watching him occasionally, refined her skills at working scalloped embroidery on the nightgowns she had sewn for her sisters...and on tiny garments that Victor looked fondly at but did not say one word about.

Christmas was only a week away when the couple heard the sounds of heavy wheels, several horses, and thick harness popping. Victor and Lucy went onto the porch in the frosty morning and saw a hauler's wagon coming up the drive. By the house, the four-horse team stopped, blowing white plumy breaths as they shook their collars and harness loose from their steaming, dark-brown hides. Mel Hickman jumped down from the high seat, looking glumly at Victor.

"Mornin', Mel," Victor called as he went toward the wagon. "What'cha got?"

"Bad news, first off," the drayman said, pulling off his thick, bullhide gloves to shake Victor's hand, "Preacher Turnbull died last week. Didn't ya hear?"

"No," Victor said in a low voice, frowning...remembering... "Peacefully?"

"Reckon so," Mel said, spitting a stream of tobacco juice onto the snow. "Come on, hep me unload."

"Unload what?" Victor asked, shivering from a premonition more that from the cold.

"Combination bookcase an' a couple o' crates o' books," Mel said stolidly, putting on his gloves and going to the tailgate of the wagon.

"From Reverend Turnbull?" Victor asked, feeling a swimming dizziness near his eyes.

"He willed the stuff to you. His boy—Drake, from St. Lou, ya know—paid me to haul it out here." He gave Victor a frowning, black-eyed look and spat another jet of juice. "Why would Preacher will you anythin'?"

"Beats me," Victor said evasively, looking toward the wagon bed.

The combination bookcase they placed against the short wall between the bedroom door and the kitchen doorway, opposite the davenport. The crates they set on the living room rug. Lucy brought the hauler a cup of steaming coffee as Victor went upstairs to get a claw hammer. Mel drank his coffee and watched Victor pry open the crates...then fold himself cross-legged on the rug as he stared at the backs of the top layer of books. Without turning, Victor said to Lucy, "Guess what kind of books they are."

Though Mel looked at her for her answer, she simply smiled.

When the hauler had gone, Victor opened the barrel-glass door of the left-hand, bookcase half of the head-tall, varnished oak piece of furniture. The right half was topped by a cabinet door inset with a rectangular, bevel-edged mirror. Below that cabinet was an inward slanting, large lid that let down to become two-thirds of a desk top. Revealed by the lowering of the lid were two small drawers, a compartment in the center behind a small, square door with an enameled pull, and three vertical slots for letters on each side of the center compartment, as well as round-grooved trays for pens. The desk top and pen grooves were stained blue-black from ink, and Victor reverently touched the stains, realizing that at this desk Reverend Turnbull had written his sermons. Below the desk section was a round-fronted drawer with a keyhole. In that drawer, tied in a neat bundle were three wooden-handled, steel-pointed pens, a stoppered bottle of ink, and a packet of paper sheets. Beneath the drawer was a large, doored compartment with shelves.

While Lucy handed him books from a crate, Victor placed them side by side on the bookshelves. "Church history...Greek dictionary...Hebrew dictionary...Spurgeon's sermons...Matthew Henry's commentaries," he murmured. "History...economics...biology...government." He turned when Lucy held onto one book to make him look at her as he read the back; he laughed. "*Flaxie Frizzle!* What on earth?"

"Reverend Turnbull must've had a sense of humor...or a granddaughter," she said, kneeling beside her husband and placing her hands around his as he held the book.

He sighed, looking toward the book-filled shelves. "Yes," he said in answer to her silent question. "I know what it means." He gazed at Lucy's eyes, and she thought she saw fear in his. "Heartmate, it's my turn to feel inadequate...immature...and certainly not good enough." He looked at the books. "There's more learning—and calling—there than a man could deal with in a lifetime."

Her hands tightened against his, and he looked at her. She said, "That's what it'll be, you know."

He frowned slightly, tensing his wide lips. Her hands clenched his again, and he sighed. "But who am I?" he muttered, shaking his head almost disconsolately.

She jerked gently on his hands, forcing him to look at her. "The man He wants, that's who."

•   •   •

The Sunday before Christmas day, Victor saddled Belle, and he and Lucy rode double down to the Pleasant Ridge Church. The snow was deepening—almost to the tops of the fenceposts in most places—so buggy travel from their farm would have been difficult at best. But Belle stepped smartly through the drifts and carried them safely to the church by midmorning. To their surprise, there were ten or so buggies in the churchyard and several more across the road in the schoolyard. The sound of "Joy to the World" was ringing from the church as Victor led Lucy inside.

The interior was packed; the benches had been pushed against one wall, and perhaps 40 people filled the space between. They were gathered around a large cedar tree whose tip almost touched the ceiling. On the cedar boughs were bright paper and glass ornaments, strings of popcorn and bright red berries, and lighted candles in tin holders. The faces of the singing people were lit by the soft candlelight, reddened by the cold, and merry with the season. When the song ended, they turned and shouted greetings to Victor and Lucy.

The circle melted apart as the people came to shake Victor's hand and admire Lucy's dress as Victor helped her remove her wraps. Dad Bohring and his wife Deborah were first, followed by Grace Bohring and Ed Ash. Ed and Libbie Kauffman came next, followed by Pearl, Bill and his wife and children, and the Kauffman beauty, Jamie. Mott Lewis somehow had managed to persuade Luther to come, and their greetings boomed as they made their way to the Walkers. Otto and Wilma Sparks—who, like the Lewises, were a childless couple—came to solemnly shake Victor's hand and inspect Lucy, or "Mrs. Walker" as Wilma, though older, kept saying. Victor's sister Ella appeared from near the platform, where she had been rehearsing the children for their performance, and she dragged her husband, Fred Wilcox, to her brother. She looked at Victor for a moment, then embraced and clung to him; after a while she released one arm to reach out and pull Lucy into the embrace. Fred coughed uncomfortably, and when Ella looked at him, he nodded, frowning, toward the onlookers as if he were ashamed that his wife was making a display of herself.

Several other families from the area were present, and Victor introduced himself to those he did not know or knew only slightly. He even sought out the children and solemnly shook their hands, repeating their names in a mischievous fashion:

"Willard Tatum, is it?"

"Yessir," the red-haired boy said, obviously uncomfortable in his suit and tie, uncomfortable talking to a strange adult, and probably anxious about his upcoming program.

"Sure that's not 'Tater'?"

"No, Sir...I mean, yessir, I'm sure it's not."

"Not 'Tattle' either, I suppose."

The boy gave Victor a squint-eyed look, realizing he was being plagued. "Not 'Tattle' neither," he assserted.

" 'Cause if it was 'Tattle' you'd have to have a tail, and I can plainly see you've not got no tail...least not one you can tell," Victor said, his eyes twinkling merrily.

Young Willard grinned from ear to ear and ran off to tell one of his friends what the funny man had said. As he and the other boys whispered, looking at Victor, Victor make his ears wiggle back and forth. The boys convulsed with laughter.

"Now, Flute," said Ella, coming to him with an exasperated look, "I've spent an hour trying to get them organized, so don't you go and—"

Victor put out one hand and touched her pale, dull-brown hair. "Don't worry, sister; they'll march pretty as you please, 'specially now that they've relaxed a bit from a good laugh." He winked and went back to find Lucy—to rescue her, he saw, noting that the womenfolk had clustered around her.

Lucy was speechless, standing stiffly with her hands clasped before herself. Victor came beside her and wrapped one arm around her shoulders. She leaned against him and up under his arm, looking from one of the farm wives to another as they discussed the depth of the snow, the program, and the visits from relatives they had had—and asked her any number of "How're you doin'?" questions.

"Uncle Charley" Hickman had come down to preach that day, and he found Victor as soon as the organist began to play "Jingle Bells." Mr. Hickman leaned close to Victor and Lucy and in his genteel way said, "I surely am glad to have a Mr. and Mrs. Walker with us again; place wasn't right without *that*." He nodded emphatically toward Lucy, who looked proudly at Victor.

They all sang "Up on the Housetop" next, and then the program began. Ella shooed the first group of children onto the platform at the front of the church, motioned the beat of the drill to the organist, and pointed to the children who would lead out. Looking at their parents, grinning bashfully at friends, encased in their new suits and woolen dresses, the children marched through several drill routines. They formed squares, crosses, diamonds, and crossing patterns on the platform, giggling slightly when one happened to bump another.

When the younger children stepped back to the rear of the platform, the older girls came up. They did a pantomime in unison, their gloved hands making gestures to suggest birds flying, snow falling, and wind blowing, all to varying accompaniment by the organ. Finally three young women and one young man came onto the platform. One by one the young women each said a piece—the first, a poem; the second, an essay she had written on faith; and the third, a humorous narration. The young man spoke his piece last, on "What Christmas Means to Me," and he bowed to applause when he finished. With that, the children were released to flee the platform while the adults dragged the benches back into place.

Reverend Hickman preached a short sermon on Christ the Redeemer and how the dead of winter was a good time to look forward to the promise of rebirth which the Redeemer had brought humankind. At one place in his sermon he pointed sharply toward the decorated cedar tree. "While the purity of white death surrounds us outside and deadens our land," he declared, "it is well to think of the green of life and the red of *His* blood, without which we would be no better than the stubble that is plowed under the ground!" The men "amened" and the women looked at one another and nodded, while the children by and large fidgeted until someone either pinched or nudged them to make them sit still. And though the preaching was long to the children, a few adults grumbled slightly when Mr. Hickman finished in less than an hour and announced, "Let's eat!"

Baskets were brought from along the walls, and Lucy looked quickly at Victor. "You didn't tell me I should've—" she began. He hushed her with one upraised finger and pointed toward Mr. Hickman. The preacher had gone to stand by the tree, and he spread his arms and shouted to get the crowd's attention.

"This here's not just a Christmas celebration; it's a celebration for our newly married couples, Mel and Madge Goin and Victor and Lucy Walker. Some folks set on infares for newlyweds; well, this is *our* infare! Let's have at it!"

By Christmas Eve, Lucy and Victor again were ensconced at the Smith farmhouse. Victor's father had come up from Spickard, but he had come alone; Matt had married a Spickard girl whom, apparently, he had no desire to show off to the family, and Nanny had gone with Tom McClary to his family's celebration. James Walker seemed so solemn and sad that Lucy hardly recognized him, and Victor and he spent several hours talking together in one of the bedrooms. When they came out, Lucy saw that Victor had been crying. When she could get him alone, she simply held him; all he would say was, "Things have gone from bad to worse."

For the remainder of the winter, Victor spent his time sawing ice blocks and stacking them in the icehouse, covering each layer with sawdust from the sacks of it he had gathered while sawing wood to take into Princeton and sell for cash money. When he wasn't cutting ice or wood or tending the livestock, he spent long hours reading the books that Reverend Turnbull had willed him. Each night at the supper table he would explain to Lucy what he had read. She listened patiently but did not pay much attention to what he said—not because she wasn't interested or didn't understand it, but because she knew he was telling her so he himself would remember better.

Thaws began in February, but the snow covering the land did not begin to vanish until late March. Then Victor acquired another plowhorse from Ed Kauffman and went down south for a few days to hire out to Henry George. Lucy went with him, and while the men were plowing, Lucy earned daily wages by helping Jane George cook for the hands. She quickly began to love Mrs. George, and they talked quietly in the evenings as they alternated reading the Bible with mending clothes. Lucy also grew to love Jane's children, especially Cliff, who was as graceful and soft-spoken as his mother; but one of the other children—Olin—was, as they said, a pistol, and Lucy had to keep her eye on him constantly lest he put straws in her shoes or a dead rat in the bed in which she and Victor slept.

One night Victor came in from plowing with the other men, took his turn in the bathtub, then led Lucy off by herself. He was exhausted, but she could see the familiar twinkle in his blue eyes that told her something was up. "What day's today?" he asked casually.

"April fifth," she said, holding her breath.

"You're gettin' to be an old lady, you know?" he said, tisking as he dug in one lower bib pocket. "Eighteen, isn't it?"

"You remembered!" she cried, hugging him.

"I can count," he said, grinning as he dangled a glimmering golden necklace before her. He held it away from her until she stopped reaching for it, then slipped it carefully over her upswept, pinned hair and settled it around her slim white neck. He was kissing her when he felt something tugging on his pantleg. He and Lucy looked down...and saw the toddler, Margie, wonderingly staring up at them. Lucy laughed and picked up the child to show her the necklace. As Margie cooed at the bright strand, Lucy gazed at Victor with longing in her eyes.

By the first of May, Victor and Lucy returned home so he could plow their own land. She made various attempts to help him, but she had neither the strength nor the skill, and he had no patience for her. He put her in the freshly plowed garden and gave her gloves and a hoe and told her to work until he could get Dad Bohring to come and tell her what to plant where. A bit hurt, she watched Victor work from dawn until full dark—13 or more hours a day, and she rubbed his shoulder and neck muscles at night as he lay soaking in the tub. It was then that she realized, with an ironic smile, that he had not gone to all the trouble of installing the unheard-of rural luxury of indoor plumbing for her benefit alone! She rubbed harder.

After plowing, he disked and harrowed the fields, then began planting corn. When that was done, he went into town for hayseed, and Lucy went with him—her first oportunity to go shopping since her marriage. She followed Victor closely from store to store, almost in his shadow, and she nodded to those to whom he spoke, standing silently when he engaged someone in conversation. She broke away from him only when she saw Lizzy Casteel and Midge Hall, the latter of whom, Lucy quickly learned, was in town for a fitting of her wedding dress. When the Walkers' wagon was loaded with supplies, they returned to the country, and Lucy tried hard not to cry from the realization of how isolated they really were.

Later in May, Victor took time out from his work to drive Lucy over to the Otterbein Brethren Church cemetery for Decoration Day. They had gathered upspringing wild flowers—violets, Dutchman's-breeches, columbines, lady slippers, and sweet Williams—and went to the cemetery to decorate the graves of Glen Smith, Chloe Smith Robinson, and the unnamed baby buried beside her. There, for the first time in many months, they met Park, who had remained single and who still seemed to be in mourning. Victor and he talked for a long time as Lucy knelt at the graveside.

After visiting Lucy's family and eating dinner, Victor and Lucy drove back across the county to the Pleasant Ridge Church cemetery. The sun was setting, a golden band lay along the western horizon, and nightbirds were calling as the couple placed the remainder of their flowers on the graves of Alex and Mrs. Susan Routh Walker...and once again memories flooded back. Lucy and Victor talked quietly of those memories as they stood by the graves, glancing at a few other latecomers at nearby graves. As they rode home in the darkness, Lucy was surprised to feel that it had not been a sad day, as she had expected; she and Victor had talked about their loved ones "over there" and what they were doing, and that series of images actually had given them more joy than driving past the greening fields and budding trees and smelling the warming air and the scent of plum blossoms on the breeze.

Once again began the unending rounds of work, day by day, night by night. The rounds were not broken except by Sundays; then, unlike most other farmers, Victor refused to do any labor except what was absolutely necessary. Their cow had calved again, a heifer, and she had to be fed after the cow was milked. There also were three hogs to be fed, and Lucy had acquired a number of turkeys, geese, and ducks to add to the chickens in her flock of fowl. Taking care of the animals was for both Lucy and Victor a relaxing time interspersed with pieces of conversation. Otherwise, however, the routine of labor was not interrupted until the celebration, parade, and band-playing on the town square lawn in Princeton on the Fourth of July.

After the fireworks and celebration, Victor took Lucy down to Spickard on the train, and both of them were depressed by a visit with Daddy Walker. The grocery store had degenerated, as James himself had, and Victor was unable to find anyone who would work in it—as he likewise was unable to find either Matt or Nanny.

When the crops were in and the hay promised in payment for the second workhorse was delivered to Ed Kauffman, Victor slowly began to lose some of his persistent, driving fervor for work. The first frost came hard in September, and he and Otto Sparks helped each other and their wives with hog-killing. For Lucy it was the most awful time of the year, and she could not bear to hear the hogs squealing or watch their throats being cut, their lengths slit open as they hung from hooks in a tree, the blood running, the intestines spilling into tubs, and so on. She helped knead sage, pepper, and salt into tubs of sausage that Victor and Otto ground; she helped render caldrons of lard to be poured into stone jars to cool so fried meat could be thrust down into it to keep fresh; she helped salt slabs of bacon in wooden boxes, hang hams and shoulders in the smokehouse that Victor had built between the icehouse and the barn; she helped make head cheese from the meat on the hogs' heads, and finally sat down over at the Sparks' place to enjoy a much-looked-forward-to supper of pork loin. Both families ate together with Mrs. Sparks' sister, Maude Fister, who was staying with the Sparks during one of the "off again" stages of her romance with John Henry Meim.

"He tried to kill her this time," Mrs. Sparks whispered to Lucy as they carried dishes into the kitchen after the meal.

Lucy paused, staring at the back of Mrs. Sparks' pear-shaped body. She hurried to catch her. "He did what?"

Mrs. Sparks stacked the dishes in the sink of gray, soapy water at the back of her kitchen and wiped a strand of sweaty, straw-colored hair from her forehead. "They were out ridin', an' he got mad at her," she whispered quickly, hoping that Maude would stay in the dining room until she had shared her anxiety with Lucy. "He whipped up his team, careened around a curve, and tried to push her out of the buggy! Who would've believed such a thing! Maude had to hang on for dear life while John Henry lashed at the horses and shoved on her until he lost the edge of his temper. 'Course then he stopped before the horses became a runaway, and he tried to make up. But she was cryin' so hard, she said, that all she could tell him was to take her here." She looked toward the dining room. "Poor thing," she murmured. "I've plumb forgot my own troubles—wantin' kids an' all—just worryin' over her."

Lucy was dumbfounded. "I didn't know people acted like that," she muttered, beginning to wash the dishes almost mechanically.

"Oh lands, child!" Mrs. Sparks said, taking plates from her and rinsing them. "People'll do most anythin' when they're mad—and John Henry's not as bad as some. We used to laugh about him and his brother bein' named John Henry and Henry John, and that's the way they usually are—funny and polite. But you take some'un like Carl Hauk; he cut up two men the other night down at the 'Shorts' because they *looked* at that whore, Half-Millie, while she was walkin' home with Carl."

"Cut them up?" Lucy asked, trying to correlate the words with the images she was trying hard to forget of the hogs being cut up.

"Sure, you know, slashed them with a corn knife." Mrs. Sparks gave Lucy a peculiar look, then drew back and tucked her double chin down against her neck. Her whole attitude seemed to change. "Oh, child, I *am* sorry. I didn't mean to be upsettin' you. You ain't never been around no-good folks, have you?"

Lucy shook her head, scrubbing grease from a plate.

Mrs. Sparks put one sturdy hand around her shoulders and gave her a firm hug. "Well, you be glad you're married to a man like Victor Walker. An' I'll tell the men hereabouts to take particular care o' you—watch their mouths an' see you don't come to no harm."

"Thank you," Lucy said slowly, carefully, "but I'm not—"

"Oh, I know, child; you can carry your load. I don't mean that. But I ain't seen till now that you...you're special. Like Fluty. Like them first flowers that come up in spring an' make the rest of us folks sit up right proud an' smile 'cause the flowers tell us winter's 'most over." When Lucy looked at her, Mrs. Sparks smiled hugely.

Mrs. Sparks, true to her word, spoke with Victor before he left and told him how the hog-killing and any kind of news of violence had affected his wife, and she sternly told Victor that she was *not* being critical—that she simply thought he should know. She folded her arms and waited for his reaction to her intrusiveness. He grinned and nodded solemnly.

September passed, as did almost three weeks of October. On the twentieth, Lucy was preparing supper and realized that she hadn't seen Victor since dinner. She was beginning to worry when she heard Belle whicker at Mack and the new horse, General, as the mare trotted up the drive. Lucy put on a coat and took a lamp outside to light Victor's way from the barn. When he came he looked as solemn as ever, but as lamplight flicked across his face Lucy caught a glimpse of a mischievous gleam in his eyes. The gleam grew during the meal, but Lucy decided to outwait him.

When he went to the combination bookcase and took out a book to read, she finished doing the dishes, then got out the scraps of cloth she was cutting into pieces for a quilt top. She took her work and one of her Great-grandmother Hall's quilt patterns to a chair near the living room stove and sat down with an audible sigh.

Victor turned, his eyes twinkling in the light of the lamp he had set on the desktop near his open book. "Something wrong?" he asked blandly.

"Oh...no," Lucy said, unfolding the age-browned pattern and assiduously studying it.

"By the way, do you happen to recollect what day this is?"

"The twentieth."

"Um."

She turned and stared at his profile; he was writing notes on his reading, carefully blotting each line. She sighed audibly again and turned back to her work.

In a while he asked, "Heard your daddy was puttin' in a telephone over at his place."

She jerked around. "Really? They're running wires to the farms now? Where can you call?"

"They've got a central switchboard in Princeton. I heard if you wait long enough you can call pretty far away—Kansas City even."

She sank back dreamily. "Just think, talking to someone miles and miles away...someone you can't even see."

"Might come in handy here, too—if you don't mind everybody on the party line knowing what you're saying—in case we ever have a baby and need to call the doc out in a hurry."

She glared at him. "Don't you start in on me, too. My mother, Mrs. Kauffman, and the other women around here are bad enough." She mimicked, " 'Course you *are* young.' " She continued to glare at him.

He suddenly snapped two fingers. "Oh, by the way, what d'you think this might be?" He came to her, digging a piece of metal from one pocket and handing it to her.

She took it and saw that it was about three inches long with opposite-turning right angles bent into it, a flattened ball turning at one end, a notch at the other end. "Looks like a crank," she finally said.

He knelt by her chair, his arms on its arm. "What d'you suppose it might crank?"

It dawned on her what he had been getting around to. She quickly put her material on the floor, jumped up, and, as he stood, she embraced him. "Oh, Fluty, you're getting us a telephone!"

He grinned and waggled his ears.

"Now I can *call* my parents instead of having to spend almost a day....Oh Fluty, that's *wonderful!*" She kissed him three times, pecking each of his cheeks and his lips. "Is that our anniversary present?"

"Anniversary? Of what?" he inquired, blinking.

She pushed him hard in his abdomen, and he staggered backward with an "Oooff!" He recovered and began digging in his pants pockets as if he had lost something therein.

"Found this, too," he said, as if not knowing what it was either. He held out one closed first. "What'll you give me?"

"A kiss and a peck," she said, reaching for his hand, which he snatched away.

He shook his head.

"Cinnamon rolls for breakfast."

He shook his head.

"Cross my heart and hope to die, I 'll love you and never lie."

He grinned and nodded, opening his fist.

Hesitantly, delicately, she picked it up. "Ohh," she murmured, "a cameo brooch!" She looked closely at the finely carved face in profile of a lady with upswept hair. "Is it real?"

"From Italy," he said. "Looks like you. Mounting's 14-karat gold." He took it from her so he could hang it on the chain he had given her for her birthday. She hurried to the mirrored cabinet door of the bookcase and held out the cameo on its chain to stare at it. "You think it looks like me?" she asked, flattered.

He nodded.

She frowned slightly. "Can we afford this?"

Solemnly he took her hands. "It's worth it to give up a few necessities to enjoy a few luxuries. And don't you ever look at the thing without knowing how much I love you."

The year had come round, completed. For renters, a year was "March first to March first"; for children it was "first Monday in September to first Monday in September," when school began; but for Lucy and Victor Walker, a year was from anniversary to anniversary...as time ran golden.

7

Giving Birth

As if to start the new century off right, a number of other marriages and a number of births took place during the years 1900-1903, beginning the new generation of Mercer County residents. In 1902, among the weddings in the county was that of Lizzy Casteel and Ray Bearden; their union seemed to sew up the ownership of one entire side of the Princeton square in one family, for Ray took his bride to live above his father's photography studio and oversee two stores next to the Casteel Drug Store and the Casteel Clothing/Dry Goods Store. Lizzy continued working for her father, and Ray worked for his father. As if not to be outdone, Lon Casteel married Midge Hall and opened the first appliance store in the town, selling the newfangled electric appliances that many of the townspeople had begun asking for. Lucy and Victor Walker attended both those weddings, as well as the wedding of Grace Bohring and Ed Ash. Ed had bought a farm west of the Walkers' Grant Creek farm, and after Ed and his bride were installed there, Grace and Lucy began to grow closer and closer.

Tom Fairly married the wild, red-haired Celia McCargue soon after her brother Jim married a Clark girl. That set off a spate of marriages among the younger Fairly, McCargue, and Clark clans that seemed to promise the disappearance of the "Fairly Gang." Anvil Fairly divided his large holdings among his sons, and for the first three years of the century all the carpenters, stone masons, and painters in the county were kept busy with the new construction of houses and barns.

Quincy Thogmorton and his wife, Lorna Routh Thogmorton, proclaimed an heir to the Thogmorton bank and land holdings with the birth of Quincy Orville in 1903. And his birth was as celebrated in town as another birth was celebrated in Lower Tennessee; it was the birth of Maude Lucy Lewis, born to Mott and Luther in the spring of 1903. Also in that year, Kelly Combs opened the first automobile dealership in Mercer County and began selling Buicks and Oldsmobiles from one side of his livery stable. He installed a hand-cranked gasoline pump in front of the stable, and for a while perceptive folks could *see* the main change that marked the new century: horses tied near a gasoline pump.

The sound, sight, and smell of automobiles putt-putting around town and along the highway north and south were outright annoyances and hazards to most people and their teams of horses, but they were a prophetic symbol to a few other people.

Among those few, a trend toward mechanization began, for the farmers were becoming more wealthy as farm prices rose. As their age-old drive for self-preservation gradually changed to a drive for ways to relieve the man- and animal-killing labor of farming, the wise and capitaled city people brought in the machines to meet the farmers' needs. While women still yearned for the Gibson Girl image, their menfolk increasingly began to yearn for more credit in the new John Deere store, where the new plows, harvesters, and tractors were appearing. Then, as if to crown the new century's beginning, Fred Ash married Trudy Jewell.

Few of the Mercer County residents would forget the haunting, romantic beauty of Fred and Trudy's wedding and the song Robbie McCargue played for them on his silver flute—"Beautiful Dreamer." If most folks in the county were becoming devoted to John Deere plows, at least some covertly clung to the romantic vision in the flute's voice drifting "Beautiful Dreamer" on the warm evening air—a vision, embodied by Trudy Jewell, of the young Gibson Girl with pompadoured hairdo, large hat, tiny waist tightly corseted, bustle, elegant lace and satin gown, and devastating beauty...and a vision embodied by Fred Ash of a handsome, merry, talented, and very romantic lover.

The run of weddings and births had a twofold effect on Victor and Lucy Walker. The first effect was to increase their joy in their own marriage, to affirm the growth of the intimacy between them that had become nearly invisible to people who chanced to observe them; superficially, they had become "just another farmer and his wife," but underneath was a current of understanding and trust that knew no limits and that was strengthened as they watched their friends becoming united in the same kind of bond. But the second effect of the weddings and births was that a new current began between them. The year 1903 ended, and 1904 began with a current of expectancy, of unspoken prolonged hope between the husband and wife. Victor continued his studies in Reverend Turnbull's books as the winter of the new year maintained its grip upon the land, and Lucy continued her sewing...but frequently they shared a look of sparkling secrecy. Both she and Victor, without a word being said on the subject, began counting weeks on the Cardui calendar. The only verbal sharing on the matter came during their prayer times, for the child was consecrated even before it began to move in its mother's womb, and each night before they slept, Victor and Lucy would place their hands on her abdomen and pray, dedicating what was to be.

In March the farm work began in earnest. Victor plowed the garden, then went off to hire out to Henry George. Instead of going with him, as she had in the past years, Lucy remained at home, and Grace Ash came to stay with her. Grace's father, Dad Bohring, also came to the Walker farm occasionally.

He was a small, compact man with pure white, wispy hair and a full white beard. He seemed frail, but he hoed in the garden beside Grace and Lucy with springy strength. Lucy quickly observed that he said nothing aimlessly, that each of his terse comments was something she should remember. She connected two facts: first, that the other, more burly and "masculine" farmers teased the older man unmercifully; second, that Mr. Bohring was terse in the extreme; and she correlated these facts with Victor's own reticence. She concluded that Dad Bohring also was very intelligent and also made a habit of hiding that fact. But despite his taciturnity around the other farmers, he spoke kindly to Lucy, and he treated her as he did his own daughter—with gentle friendliness and openness. He already had planted much of his own garden, and, without saying anything about it, seemed glad to respond to what Lucy was sure had been Victor's request that he come and help her learn more about gardening.

"I'm afraid I haven't been very good at this," she explained ruefully.

His gray eyes softened as he looked from his hoeing to her face. "The ground's just this year getting properly 'seasoned,' " he said easily. "It takes a while for newly plowed earth to soften, for mulch to decay into 'made-dirt,' and for earthworms to get properly settled in." He used his hoe blade to turn up one of the wriggling red crawlers, then covered the worm carefully. "You'll do better this year."

"The manure wasn't rotted that first year, Victor said," Lucy added.

He reached ahead with his hoe blade and raked some of the freshly spread, well-rotted manure back and forth until it disappeared into the rich brown soil. "Victor also said pests had gotten in pretty bad." When Lucy nodded, he seemed to feel free to say more. "We'll plant onions around the perimeter. They keep out a lot of pesky things. And we'll plant pole beans in rows of corn so the nitrogen of the bean roots will help feed the corn. But when the ears come on, you'll have to search each one every morning for worms. Picking them off corn and tomatoes and bugs off the potato plants is a job for kids, though." He gave her a look that she thought was a smile, but his mouth was hidden behind his beard. She smiled at him, wondering if he knew....

He looked over at Grace, who was taller than Lucy and larger but very feminine, almost voluptuous. Her skin—covered nearly completely by her long-sleeved dress, her gloves, and her starched bonnet with its tail—was honey brown. Her eyes were dark walnut brown and carried a softly sensual expression. Her hair was the glossy brown of her mother's, who was said to be Cherokee; where her hair had escaped her bonnet and hung in the sunlight, golden highlights gleamed. She was as silent as her husband, Ed, unless she was alone with Lucy; then her voice and laughter delighted Lucy with their throaty fluidness and melodious quality; why she did not sing in public was something Lucy could understand only because she realized that both she and Grace shared an intense shyness in public and felt truly comfortable only with their husbands and with each other.

Mr. Bohring continued explaining various things as the three of them worked toward the end of the garden. He made comments about beneficial insects, about which crops to plant early for early harvest, what to plant in harvested rows, and what to plant late in the summer—such as turnips and chard—for autumn harvest. Lucy was listening carefully and hoeing rhythmically when she suddenly stopped and straightened. Mr. Bohring and Grace took no notice as she removed her gloves, leaned on the hoe with her left hand, and placed her right hand on her abdomen. Yes, there it was again—small but definitely noticeable.

"Grace!" she called. "Come feel."

Grace hurried toward her, pulling off her gloves. Lucy placed Grace's extended hand on her rounding abdomen and held it there until her friend smiled and nodded.

"She's waking up," Lucy whispered as if afraid to disturb the baby.

"It's the first time you've felt her move?" Grace asked, low and melodiously.

Lucy nodded. "Oh, I can't wait for Victor to come home!" she said, while through her thoughts ran the refrain, *"Thank You, Lord...thank You, Lord!"*

She was only mildly surprised when Victor came riding up to the house late that afternoon astride Mack. The horse was wearing his team bridle, and Victor was sitting on a saddle blanket; he slid to the ground, let Mack wander loose to nip the upspringing bluegrass, and hurried to the porch where Lucy was waiting. Without saying a word, he put his arms around her thickened waist and leaned the side of his head against her abdomen. When he felt the baby move, he looked up at Lucy, and she saw that tears sprang to his eyes. He placed the side of his head against her again as she put her hands on his shoulders, sensing his excitement grow.

"I knew I had to come home," Victor said at last, going with her into the house.

"I wasn't sure you'd leave work," she said, wrapping one arm around his waist. She grinned at him. "But I cooked supper for two...three."

"Grace went home?"

Lucy nodded. "I told her I thought you'd be here before dark."

He laughed broadly. "Say, maybe we don't need that telephone after all!" He jerked one thumb toward the tall, white oak box on the wall just inside the living room from the kitchen; its black mouthpiece, earpiece, and crank were still shiny new.

Lucy's eyes lit brightly. She went to the telephone and, as if picking up a fish, she took down the earpiece and jiggled the hook, then whirled the crank vigorously. In a few moments she shouted, "Hello, Central! Would you ring me Mr. Walter Smith over at....Yes, all right!"

"You don't have to yell," Victor whispered in her ear. "Electricity carries your voice over the wires; it's not like you were standing on a hilltop, having to—"

"Hello, Papa? Yessir, it's me." She smiled at Victor, who went into the kitchen to begin serving their plates from the pots on the stovelids. "Yessir, I'm *fine!*" she shouted, unable to convince herself that the telephone didn't need her help. "More than fine. Let me speak to Mother, will you please?" She turned toward the wall, her head bowed, until she said, "Mommie? Guess what!" She grinned at Victor, then added, "Yes...yes, we are!" She laughed, then laughed again. "Yes, Ma'am, I'm sure. I waited until I was sure before I called you. I felt her move today!...Well, I just know it's a her, that's how....No, Ma'am, I didn't dangle a needle on a thread over my tummy to see which way it'd spin," she stated with faint sarcasm. She soon answered, "We figure sometime in September....Yes, Ma'am, we'll call you in plenty of time." She stared into the kitchen at Victor, who was watching her from in front of the stove. "Mommie," she added urgently, "you don't have *anything* to worry about. No...just please believe me!"

In the months that followed, Lucy's world shrank to the space bounded by the house and the barn, and it was all the world she needed or wanted. Victor came and went, leaving her in the company of the house and its needs, of the garden and its needs, and of the animals and their needs. There were three cows now and a new, curly haired, liquid-eyed, yellow-brown calf. There was Belle's new colt, a stallion that Victor planned not to geld. There were 30 or so chickens—give or take a few depending on what Victor happened to buy from other farms because he thought the additions would please Lucy, and depending on the "tithe" taken by foxes and raccoons. There were geese whose feathers would help fill the bag of down they were accumulating for a new mattress and pillows. And there were the hogs—the fattening young ones that Lucy continually pitied as she fed them and the huge red sow she continually feared and avoided. The sow seemed to know the purpose for which her piglets were being reared, for she would growl and click her long teeth at any human—including Lucy—who came near her. Only Victor could enter her pen, and he did so only because he could place a well-aimed kick on the end of the sow's snout when she charged him growling.

But the garden was the "county" of Lucy's "world" that came to please her the most. Mr. Bohring continued to come by occasionally, bringing her things such as apple tree saplings, asparagus roots, herb seeds, and most precious of all, the distillations of years of experience—advice which he seemed eager, in his restrained way, to share with somebody who needed him. And Lucy definitely needed and appreciated him, and he knew she did and came by as often as he could. On many days she would go outside and find him already at work. It occurred to Lucy that everyone else she knew, including her father and probably Victor, would have resented Mr. Bohring's "intrusions" as an implication that they did not know what they were doing, that their self-sufficiency was defective. But Lucy knew better. She knew that Mr. Bohring *never* "intruded" on anyone else's farm or garden because, if for no other reason, he had ample work of his own to do, with no one to help him except the occasionally available Ira.

One morning she joined Mr. Bohring in picking green beans from the pole-twined vines, and they worked for an hour or so near each other without speaking. Finally Mr. Bohring took off his broad straw hat, mopped his face with a bandana, and smiled at her. "Morning, Lucy," he said. "Hope you don't mind that I got a bucket from the smokehouse without askin'." He looked at her for reassurance, then commented, "Beans came along nice; no rust or blight."

"I tore down the vines that showed the least sign of anything wrong with them. Burned them."

He nodded. "Wish there was some other way. Sulfur helps some things, but no matter what we do, an awful lot just goes to waste."

They worked a while longer in silence, until Lucy decided that Victor was right about her needing more gumption at times. She took a deep breath and hesitantly ventured, "Ira home?"

Mr. Bohring shrugged without looking at her. "Now and then. He has his own ways, you know. To his credit, he *does* usually show up when I need him. I think he's grateful."

"Grateful?"

Mr. Bohring nodded and said nothing further.

When the two varieties of cucumbers began to ripen, Lucy called her mother and wrote down two recipes for pickles, and got a suggestion from a woman who was listening on the party line to tie the spices in cheesecloth. The first recipe was for "bread-and-butter" pickles; the other was for "million-dollar" pickles. When Victor came in that night from cultivating the ten-acre corn-field, he found his wife busily engaged in tying spices in small bags of cheesecloth. She greeted him with, "We're 'bout out of jars."

He looked at the determined expression on her face, at her sweaty hair, and at her rounded tummy. Smiling with satisfaction, he went to take his bath.

As the crops farther south began to ripen, Victor went away to hire out again. He was gone for days at a stretch, and Grace Ash again came to stay with Lucy—this time with news bursting from her as soon as she and Lucy sat at the kitchen table, their hands around cups of tea. "Did you know Wilma Sparks is going to have a baby, too?"

Lucy sighed, smiling, then asked, "Does she feel like she can carry this one full term?"

Grace nodded. "And she told me the same thing Mott did: It's all because of Lucy and Victor's prayers." She squared her shoulder and leaned forward as her shy grin widened. "Plus, I think I might be—"

"Really? That's *wonderful!*" Lucy cried, leaning close to Grace as they shared a secretive, deeply pleased smile. Then she straightened, wiping sweat from her forehead and wishing the stuffy air in the kitchen would move somewhere. "Mott came by the other day; it was pretty obvious she's working on her second, thank goodness." She stood and led Grace onto the back porch, which wasn't yet filled with sunlight that made her drowsy each afternoon and sent her napping like the lazy cats that had come to live with them. She sat beside Grace on the deacon's pew that Victor had made the previous winter. In front of them on low shelves were the pots and cans of houseplants that Lucy had begun growing from sprigs and leaves which various neighboring women had contributed during their passing visits. They gazed out the screened back of the porch at the flock of chickens, geese, and ducks pecking and grazing through the garden and yard.

Lucy fanned her face with the end of her apron and shyly looked over at Grace, admiring her smooth skin and richly brown hair and voluptuousness. She hoped childbearing wouldn't ruin her. "When do you think yours will come?"

"If I counted right, sometime early next year."

Lucy silently clapped her hands. "Oh, good! Now my girl will have playmates all around."

Grace looked at her, and her expression became cautious. "Are you scared?"

Lucy's eyebrows flicked up and she blinked. "Some. But I feel *right*. I've never been more healthy."

Grace's smile briefly crossed her sensuous lips. "I can tell. You've bloomed."

Lucy looked out at the patiently scratching chickens, whose idle cluckings comforted her. "That's what Victor keeps saying. But still, it makes me almost uncomfortable how heavy I'm becoming." She shifted on the bench, putting her hands on its edges and pressing them downward. "And sometimes the baby puts one foot right up into my lungs like she's saying, 'Hey, don't forget about me!' " She laughed.

"You haven't been sick or anything, have you?"

Lucy looked at her. "Not after the first. It's getting hard to find a sleeping position, though."

Grace gazed silently at her for a time, then in a low voice asked, "Are you scared of what may happen after she's born?"

Lucy looked at her, and Grace saw the fear. Lucy quickly looked away. "So many die, don't they?" Grace reached over and took Lucy's hand and briefly squeezed it, wishing she hadn't brought up anything unpleasant. She was surprised when Lucy quickly brightened and said, "But this one will live. She was promised."

Grace did not argue with her; whenever Lucy Walker said something like that, no one argued with her...and although her remarks of that kind were rare and usually made as if to herself, everyone became silent when she said something like that, feeling that their own faith had been strengthened. "You do so much for me," Grace murmured, patting Lucy's hand.

"Do I?" Lucy asked, staring at her with a surprised expression.

Grace laughed musically. "Goodness, yes! And the nicest part is that you don't intend to; it just comes from you...from Him."

"Oh, don't say things like that. It makes me uncomfortable...almost afraid."

"Why? Because you don't think you're good enough?"

"Yes. And I don't want the idea to get started in my head that I'm anything special. I'm not."

Grace smiled to herself.

The storm cellar-"cave" that Victor and Otto Sparks had dug on the north side of Victor's house, under the shade of a maple tree and near the thick stone walls of the cistern, became lined with the canned goods that Lucy put up. With deep, almost grim satisfaction, she stood one day in early September staring at the jars lining the shelves. She counted the jars of green beans, of pie cherries, of corn, and so on. She counted the crocks of sauerkraut, the boxes of dried apples and apricots, and the other visible signs of her providence with God's providence.

She climbed the steps out of the cellar and swung the heavy wooden door shut upon its slanted frame. Pressing her hands on the small of her aching back, she went toward the house. She knew that soon it would be hog-killing time again, for already she could feel the high, light, and chilly air of autumn. She knew she would hate the hurry, the squealing, and the blood and smells, but the addition of pork, as well as the beef from the yearling steer they planned to slaughter, would complete their larder—and to that completion she looked forward almost as much as she looked forward to the birth of her baby. Wearily she climbed the steps onto the back porch and closed the screen door behind her.

She was alone: Grace was at her own home, and Victor had gone to take a wagonload of wheat into town, having waited until the glut was off the market and the prices had gone up slightly. It had been a good year; they had money in the bank, and they were debt-free. But as Lucy walked through the house, she noticed how silent it was. She often had been aware of the silence, and during those times she had yearned for the clamor of her younger sisters and brother. She felt mildly guilty for regretting even one part of her life when so many parts of it were being so richly blessed... and yet.... She smiled slightly, looking forward to the sounds of her baby playing and running...or even crying for its mother. With Victor gone so much, she had come to need someone else to love and to need her. Even with the incessant work of the farm and her satisfaction in providing her share of fruits, she did not like the silence of the house, except for the fact that it made her look forward to her baby's coming more and more. She was ready.

But even as she had had to wait and wait before she became pregnant, she also had to wait what seemed an interminable time before the baby decided to be born. It—she, as Lucy persisted in calling it—was moving almost continuously, making her distended abdomen protrude here and there as knees and elbows exercised, beginning to seek freedom. Lucy did almost nothing to help with the hog-killing activity, and the franticness of it swarmed around her as if she were in the eye of one of the tornadoes that had passed within sight of the farm during the spring—a sight she had involuntarily turned away from lest it somehow "mark" her baby.

Lucy virtually ignored Victor, as well as Otto Sparks and the others who came to help with the hog-killing. She cooked and served and moved in general as if in her own world—which, indeed, in her readiness she was. It seemed to her that she and the baby alone existed in a shrinking sphere in which they and the Lord communed steadily, without words or even distinct thoughts—all in preparation. She knew that Victor was becoming impatient and annoyed with her, but his attitude did not faze her. When she saw his looks, she went to him and kissed him if she felt like it, and if not, then she simply prayed that he would remember all that had been before, be patient, and understand.

On the seventeenth was a full moon, and on the twenty-first came the first good snowfall. The storm moved through massively and the snow fell heavily, but the wind was nothing like that of the blizzards that would come later. Victor and Lucy woke to a world clad in white, and they looked out the westward-facing windows to watch the young animals pawing the white covering in wonderment at their first experience with the strange stuff. Victor snorted and climbed out of bed to begin dressing, but Lucy caught him by one hand. Her look told him what he had been waiting so impatiently to know. He grinned broadly as he carefully hugged her. He went straight to the telephone, and in a while Lucy heard him say, "Yes, Mrs. Smith, it's time. Would you come now, please?"

By the following afternoon her mother and father had arrived—Sammy and his sisters having been lodged with Grandpa Smith south of Ravanna. Lucy's labor had begun, and her mother pronounced that it was real. Mrs. Smith tried to shoo Victor out of the bedroom, but he refused to go and Lucy gave her mother a stern look that made the older woman's eyes widen, and made her say nothing further about Victor going anywhere.

Mr. and Mrs. Smith and Victor had barely finished eating supper when Lucy called to Victor and her mother. Her contractions were closely spaced now, and her breathing was fast and hard,

Mrs. Smith noted before hurrying back to the kitchen. Victor sat on the bedside and took Lucy's right hand. She gripped it so hard that he was surprised and almost hurt. He stared at her sweating face, her sweat-soaked and matted hair, and barely kept from wincing as she squeezed his hand when the next contraction swept down her abdomen. *"Oh Lord, what have I done to her?"* he wondered, trying to force down the fear and uncertainty he felt swelling sickeningly through his body. *"Was it fair, right, to put her through this?"* "Breathe, honey," he whispered, wishing desperately there was something more he could do, some way he could take her pain. He turned when Mrs. Smith came back into the bedroom with a pan of water and a washcloth. She looked seriously at him, and he wondered if she were accusing him of causing her daughter this pain. But she wet the cloth in the water, wrung it out, and gave it to him with a smile of reassurance: It was right, it was normal.

He spread the cloth over Lucy's forehead, then wiped her face and her dry lips, which she repeatedly moistened with her tongue-tip as she pressed back her head. Each time she pressed her head into the pillow and bit her lower lip to keep from crying out as a contraction rolled down her body, Victor felt tears creep into his eyes; he could not keep from remembering how his mother had died, arching her back in agony until she had cried out and died. Victor dipped the cloth in the pan that Mrs. Smith had set on the floor beside him, half wrung it out, and held it to Lucy's mouth to let the water dribble in. She flashed him a hurried smile, then thrust back and down, squeezing his hand so hard that his joints popped. *"Where does she get that strength?"* Victor wondered, amazed.

"It's coming," Mrs. Smith said, scurrying off to bring the sterilized sheets she had prepared before supper. When she returned she also was carrying a large pan with some warm, barely soapy water in it. Victor gently lifted Lucy's lower body as her mother slipped the sheets under her.

Victor then smoothed Lucy's darkly sweaty hair from the fringes of her face, but she shook her head almost violently. He was puzzled. "Breathe," he whispered forcefully to her, and she nodded. That, he realized, was the kind of help she needed—his participation, not his fussing. He gripped her hand, moving closer beside her on the bed as he concentrated on becoming attuned to the rhythm of her birthing. As the next contraction came, he gripped her hand again, willing his strength into her. "Come on, honey; you're almost there...she's almost out!"

When the next contraction came, Mrs. Smith sharply cried, "Push!"

Lucy strained, setting her jaw, squeezing her eyes shut and clenching Victor's hand hard. He spoke his encouragement tersely, telling her to breathe deeply after the contraction had passed. The next one came almost immediately, almost before she could catch her breath...and Victor again was amazed at the strength and endurance in his young wife's body, at how she did not look pleadingly or fearfully at him...and at how she did not cry out, not even once.

"Push!" Mrs. Smith again commanded as Lucy's abdomen rippled visibly with a powerful contraction. "Push her to us!" Victor watched Mrs. Smith bend, take hold of the baby's head, and ease her out. Quickly Mrs. Smith pulled scissors from her apron pocket, cut the umbilical cord, tied and iodined it, then washed the baby's eyes and nose, took up a small bottle of weakened silver nitrate and carefully placed drops in the tiny eyes she forced open, took a bulb syringe and cleaned mucus from the little girl's nostrils, then held her up by her blood-streaked heels and slapped her soundly on her tiny pink buttocks. The startled baby sucked in air, breathed, then let out a wail. Victor grinned and cried at the same time, turning to Lucy as she raised up and wrapped weak, trembling arms around his neck. "She's alive?" Lucy asked, trying to focus her eyes on the child.

"Yes!" Victor all but shouted. He disengaged himself and ran into the living room. As Mr. Smith stood expectantly, Victor cried, "She's a girl, and she's alive!" Then back to the baby he ran, watching Mrs. Smith holding her gently in the warm water, bathing her. Mrs. Smith looked proudly at Lucy, then Victor, and nodded as she wrapped the baby in soft flannel and brought her to her parents. As if in answer to Lucy and Victor's unspoken question, Mrs. Smith said, "She's all here; not a blemish on her."

Victor looked at Lucy and heard her sigh deeply as she lay back on the pillow with her eyes closed and a smile of satisfaction on her lips. He began caressing her and whispering to her as Mrs. Smith took a needle and sterile thread from her apron and went to work on her daughter. Victor and Lucy, meanwhile, stared at the baby in the soft, yellow-golden lamplight. Lucy winced as her mother stitched her, but still she did not cry out, and her tears had stopped, for she wanted a clear view of the precious, precious being lying beside her. The baby's eyes were squinched shut, and one tiny pink-red fist wavered toward her puckering mouth.

"Is she hungry?" Victor asked.

"Not yet," Mrs. Smith said, standing away from Lucy. Victor gazed at Mrs. Smith...and saw the effort the birthing had cost her; he understood why most women preferred to use a midwife rather than a relative. But the look quickly faded from the older woman's eyes, and she smiled at her son-in-law, then removed the sheets from under Lucy. With her head held high and her jaw set, she folded the pads upon themselves so her husband wouldn't see the afterbirth as she went into the kitchen.

When she returned to the bedroom, Mr. Smith was following her. Lucy raised herself, and, with Victor's help, she scooted up against the headboard. With trembling arms, she held out the baby. When Mr. Smith hurried around to her side of the bed, Lucy—with tears running down her flushed cheeks—said, "Papa, your first grandchild."

Mr. Smith's face was stiff with his effort not to cry; he stared at the baby, then at his daughter. He half-raised his hands, then held them out when Lucy nodded for him to take the baby.

The tiny bundle looked even more tiny in his arms, and he held her as if she were the most fragile, precious thing in the entire world. His eyes filmed with tears as he looked back at Lucy, then Victor. "What's her name to be?" he asked softly, as if afraid to disturb the peaceful child.

Victor and Lucy exchanged looks, and Victor replied, "Mary Susan Walker."

Mr. Smith looked proudly at his wife, Mary, then down at the baby in his arms. "September twenty-second, 1904," he pronounced.

Victor grinned at the Smiths and Lucy, holding out his hands. "Come on, you three. Let's make a circle around her." They gathered on Lucy's side of the bed, and Mr. Smith and Victor each placed a hand on the baby's head. Victor's voice rose so strongly that Mr. Smith no longer could keep from crying, and as the prayer of thanksgiving ended, he quickly handed little Mary Susan back to her mother and left the room...as a knock sounded on the front door. They heard Mr. Smith open it, and they heard Dr. Powell's greeting cheerily and loudly pervade the house. He came into the bedroom alone, beaming.

"So, you're delivered without my help, are you?" he asked Lucy, coming to the bedside and setting down his bag. He took the baby from Lucy and examined her, waking her into a spate of crying. When he gave Mary Susan back to her mother, he said, "She's fit as a fiddle. Weighs more than Mrs. Sparks' baby did."

Lucy leaned upright. "She had hers, too?"

" 'Bout as long ago as it took me to get done and over here,"
Dr. Powell said. "They named her Opal Lucy."

Lucy looked at Victor with a surprised, pleased expression. "So
now I'm godmother to *two* of Mary Susan's future playmates,"
she said, lying back against the headboard with a contented smile.

Mrs. Smith looked from Lucy to Dr. Powell. "Who's the other
one?"

"Mott Lewis's Maude Lucy," he answered.

Mrs. Smith stared at him, perplexed, "Why would they...?"

"They said Lucy was the main cause of their being able to have
a good, healthy child."

Mrs. Smith's perplexed look deepened, and she turned toward
Victor and Lucy. "But...how?"

Victor looked fondly at his wife and replied, "Because she's been
praying for them for years, that's why."

Mrs. Smith stared at her daughter as if seeing her in an entirely
new light. Lucy gazed back peacefully and with a soft glow of
satisfaction. Unaccountably, Mrs. Smith began to cry and hurried
from the room with her hands to her face. Dr. Powell motioned
for Victor to leave also, so he could examine Lucy to make sure
everything was well.

When he came out of the room, Victor immediately rejoined
his wife and daughter...and Dr. Powell, smiling to himself,
closed the bedroom door on his way out.

Victor gently lay beside Lucy, and for a long while they remained very still, watching Mary Susan sleeping between them.
Lucy abruptly flinched, turned, and asked, "Fluty, are you sorry
she wasn't a boy?"

"There's time yet for a boy to come," he said, lightly stroking
the baby's wrinkled forehead with the tip of one finger.

"She'll smoothe out," Lucy said absently. "But are you sorry—"

He stopped her words with his look. "I'm just glad she's alive
and normal and you're all right. What more on earth could I ask
for?"

Lucy remained silent, knowing his desire...and his capacity for
patience when patience was called for. She sighed, deeply tired
and beginning to feel it fully. She slid down on the bed, and Victor moved quickly to bring the covers from the floor up and over
her. He tucked them around her and the baby until only their
heads showed. Then, listening to the sounds of Lucy's regular
breathing as she slipped into sleep and to the quick, fragile breaths
the baby drew, he set his spirit free to soar into the realms of
gratitude and love. *"All is well...all is well!"*

Growth

Proud Papa Walker was stern Papa...as well as loving, playful, and frequently absent Papa. He watched his blue-eyed, brown-haired daughter nurse, cuddled against her mother's breast, and they smiled at each other. He held his daughter while she slept and he read. He changed his daughter's diapers, and when she was old enough to begin eating semisolid foods he fed her. But when she was past a year old and stood one day in a store on tottering legs and wailed to be picked up, he ignored her until she stopped crying and sat down to investigate the cracks between the floorboards. And when she was 18 months old and would not stop crying as she strained to reach something he had twice told her she could not have, he spanked her little bottom. She gave him a hurt, bewildered look of total surprise that violence existed in her world of adults who hurried to her demands, but he looked steadily back at her with no sign of remorse that she could learn to manipulate into guilt and into getting her way. So, when she was around Papa, she obeyed and she obeyed quickly.

However, more often than not, Mary Susan was alone in the house with her mother while her father worked in the fields. Early, she learned not to touch the stove, for her mother had restrained herself as the baby reached tentatively toward the hot oven and learned instantly what "hot!" meant; she had wailed, and her mother had run to pick her up, but she never touched the stove or anything on it again. Also early, she learned not to climb down the stairs by herself. That piece of information no one had had to teach her; the forbidding chasm of steps leading down to darkness had triggered an instinct that made her draw back, even when she had a tight grip on her mother's forefinger and was led slowly downward a step at a time with her mother bending down beside her to reassure her. By her second birthday, though, the stairs had been conquered coming and going, and she moved on to bigger and better things—in the great world outside.

The Great World Outside was indeed marvelous—full of the sounds of life that the house itself lacked, being so still most of the time. The outside world had chickens clucking, calves that butted her when she was allowed to feed them, and— terrifyingly!—the great grunting red sow and the honking geese. The great red sow stared balefully at her as she peered between the lower two boards of the hogpen to watch the piglets coiling their tails as they squealed and chased one another—all 12 of them. And the geese—the "watchdogs" of the farm—generally tolerated her presence, moving away from her grubby, greasy fingers that so loved to clutch their feathers. If she came too close, the gander would rush at her, his wing knobs pummeling her as she turned and hid her face, his serrated bill snatching a hold on her dress and jerking in a way that made her run screaming to where her mother was thinning carrots in the garden or hanging wet clothes on the lines. Her mother, sounding almost as stern as her papa, would bend down and point to the gander, who was huffily honking away in triumph, and tell her, "Pick up a stick! Don't let that silly thing bluff you."

But the Great World Outside had other marvels besides the proud geese with their high-held heads and the sullen red sow. There were the horses—vast, overtowering creatures who became motionless as she toddled under their enormous bellies to pick a feather from the straw while her father milked by lanternlight. She loved the furry smell of the old cow, whose youngest off- spring bawled from a nearby pen to get to the distended udder which Victor milked. He noticed Mary watching him, tickling her nose with the feather she had found, and he beckoned to her. When she came near him, he aimed a teat at her and squeezed it between his bent thumb and forefinger; the jet of milk splashed against her mouth, and reflexively she opened it and closed her eyes. She had seen Papa hit the cats that way, often scaring them into fits of face-washing and licking, and she was tickled that he was grinning at her and shooting the milk her way. He chuckled and set the jets of milk alternately hissing into the pail, which he let Mary help him carry back into the house. She was glad to be with Papa, walking in the circle of lanternlight that he held down for her small feet to see by, for the night around them was vast and deep, and she knew not what might be "out there."

She burst into the house. "Mama...Mama! Papa washed my face with milk!"

Lucy gave Victor a disapproving glance and continued serving the plates for supper.

He did...and it tasted *good*!"

"Well, go wash your face like a good kitten and come eat," her mother said mildly.

By the time she was three, Mary was feeding the chickens—fighting them off with Papa's sternness so they wouldn't knock the pan of scratch from her hands. She could help Mama pick beans, too; "This one, Mama? This one, Mama? How 'bout this one, Mama?" And she had learned a very useful, very marvelous question—a question that guaranteed her far more attention from any adult, especially Grandpa Smith, than any other. "But *why* can't I pick the radishes when they're *this* small?" "*Why* can't I sleep with a kitten? *She* wants to." "*Why* are you too tired to read me another story, Papa?" "Why do I have to get scrubbed to go to church?"

It was in her third year that Papa did a very exciting thing. He took her and the horses and met a lot of other men and went a long way away and brought a house—a whole house!—back on wagon beds hooked up to several teams of horses. The house was ghosty empty, but her Papa put her in the doorway and told her to watch to make sure the horses didn't run away with the house, for it was to be her Grandpa Walker's new home. She was tremendously impressed with the size and scope of her responsibility, and she sat very still in the front door, wondering how sad old Daddy Walker was going to live in a house on wheels...until she became bored and figured out that the horses weren't going anywhere in a hurry. So she carefully crawled through the house as it swayed and bounced along the rutted clay roads. She found a spool, a hairpin, and a length of faded red ribbon. She became so engrossed in playing with her newfound toys that she was completely startled when the house lurched up an embankment through a cut fence of the Grant Creek farm. She recovered herself, put her toys into the pocket of her gingham dress, and tottered to the door. She saw that they were approaching a clear piece of ground on a slight rise near the creek.

The house was jacked up, the wagon beds were pulled out, and stone foundation piers were built beneath the old structure that Ed Ash had wanted removed from his place, five miles east. The men were met by their wives, who had come from the Walker farmhouse, a quarter-mile away, and Papa came to take Mary Susan down from the old house. He carried her close against himself in both arms to the shade of a nearby black walnut tree and set her on the quilt that her mother had spread on the grass.

Her mother was laying out platters of fried chicken and roasting ears, and she smiled at her daughter. "Have a good ride?"

"Look at what I found!" Mary said, ceremoniously producing the spool, the hairpin, and the length of faded red ribbon. Her mother carefully looked at each item.

"Those are very nice, I'm sure," she said in her solemn way. "They will fit nicely with your other treasures in your dollhouse."

Grandpa Smith had built her a perfect miniature of a farmhouse, with one side open so she could move the dolls he had carved and could rearrange the numerous pieces of furniture he had made just like big people's furniture. She thought to herself, *"No, I won't put the things I found today in the dollhouse; I'll put them in the cookie box in the barn loft,"* for in that painted metal box were her *real* treasures—a glass marble that Cliff George had given her, a few pieces of broken china she had found that had bits of flowery blue designs on them, and various other oddments she had collected here and there, including a feather from one of the pigeons that roosted way up in the cupola of the barn.

Her father tapped her on one shoulder, and she turned to see that he was showing her a hard-boiled egg. As she stared at him, he held the egg between two fingertips, put it to his mouth, and moved his hand very quickly to pop the whole egg into his mouth. His cheeks bulged as she stared at them, and he waggled his ears as if he were having a hard time swallowing the egg whole. But then he hit himself on the back of the head and appeared to cough forward, to one side of her. She looked, trying to see where the egg had gone. He tapped her on the shoulder again, and when she looked at him, he was pointing to her hair. She felt of her long brown curls, but he shook his head. Seeming to lose patience, he reached for her hair at the back of her head...and pulled out the hard-boiled egg! She stared at it, incredulous, and immediately kneeled in front of him. "Do it again! Do it again!" He did...a second and a third time, and she never once saw how that egg got from inside his mouth to the underside of her hair! "Oh, Papa, you're wonderful!" she said, laughing as she hugged his neck. The men sitting around with their wives in the shade chuckled and winked at their womenfolk. To top it all, Papa gave her the egg to eat while he made a small show of enjoying Mama's million-dollar pickles and coleslaw.

During harvesttime, Mary once got to ride on top of the haywagon, held around the waist by Bill Kauffman, Ed's son and a farmer of his own land, who had begun helping Victor and Ed

Ash. Bill kept her secure as the hayload swayed back and forth, sweet-smelling and springy and a long, *long* way from the horses' backs and the ground slowly passing below them. Bill showed her how to suck the honey from the red clover blossoms. The men let her stay in the hayloft as they pitched forksful of hay up and packed it. She waited until they were through working, then she asked Bill if he would hold her up to where the pigeons roosted. He grinned tiredly and did so, but she was disappointed to find that the nests were empty. When he lowered her, he said, "That's what happens. The baby birds grow up and fly away so next year there can be more babies."

Soon it was the time of year that Mary and her mother dreaded: hog-killing time. Mary hated the hogs' squealing, and she pressed her hands to her ears to try to shut out the awful sounds. But it did no good. She looked out from the porch as Papa killed a hog that had been born two years earlier, one that Mary had named despite Papa's strict admonition not to give any animal a name. She watched as Bristles was hung up, gutted, and lowered into a vat of boiling water. Then she ran through the house and upstairs and threw herself onto the bed that her Papa had made when she learned to climb out of her crib. She was sleeping when, late that night, he climbed slowly up the stairs and awoke her.

She took one wakeful look at him and screamed, "I hate you! You killed Bristles! I hate you!"

An angry look flared across his face and he rolled her onto his lap, bottom up, and spanked her soundly. Then he set her on the bed beside him and waited until she cried herself out. Slowly, holding her chin so she could not avoid his gaze, he told her, "Animals come and animals go. But my love for you won't stop, no matter what you say or think." With that, he took up the lamp he had brought and left the room. Guilt overwhelmed her, but she could not make herself creep downstairs and apologize to him for her words...and ask for her supper.

She lay on her bed, her bottom stinging, her mind in a turmoil of regret, of feeling that the words she had screamed at him were the worst, most disgusting thing in the whole world. The darkness around her seemed to agree with her mood, and it helped her guilt deepen. A dark chill crept into the room and surrounded her; she huddled on the bed with her knees drawn up to her chin, her arms around her knees, and it seemed to her that in an odd way—a way that was entirely new and which did not at all make her feel comfortable—she belonged in the darkness. If her mother had come up then with a plate and a lamp—an interference that Victor had discouraged with a frown—Mary would have shrunk from the light, knowing herself to be bad and awful. When the gloomy chill around her seemed about to pull her entirely into it, she lay down and jerked the covers over her body, vowing to please her father the next day and never again to make him angry with her.

Soon thereafter came her fourth birthday, and her mother baked an angel food cake and covered it with lemon icing. Mary was staring in amazement at the cake when people began arriving. In from the snow came Maude and Hazel Lewis, followed soon by Opal Sparks. Mary hurried to them and wished Opal a happy birthday as Opal said the same words to her, their voices rushing to beat each other and rising to a squeal of delight that several adults hushed as they came inside. Later, Grace came with little Debby, and Ella Walker Wilcox brought her young son, Veech. Grandpa Smith and his wife and children came next, followed by so many other people that Mary Susan was quite overwhelmed. But of all the presents that adults and children laid in her lap as she sat ripping off wrapping paper in the new Morris chair, she best remembered the stunning sight of the gold ring her father presented her. On it were three pieces of turquoise with a tiny red stone between each of them. Mary, open-mouthed, sat turning it around and around, then jumped up and leaped into her father's arms as he reached down for her. "Oh, Papa," she said, kissing his slightly stubbly face and smelling a residue of his shaving soap, "I'll treasure it *forever,* more'n *anything!*"

"You'll keep it in my purse, too," her mother said in passing.

In his spare time during the next few months, Victor remodeled the old house on the rise near the creek, and in March, Daddy Walker came to live in it. Mary silently watched Papa carry the old man's furniture and belongings from a wagon into the house, and she silently obeyed her mother's commands about helping. She puzzled over words she picked up from the adults' conversations: "debts," "foreclosures," "wasted credit." She remembered Daddy Walker from only one time before, and that was a very vague memory. She had been very young, and she remembered being handed to an old man who didn't smell good. She recalled that her Papa had told the old man, "Like I promised, here is your future!" Her Papa had been smiling proudly, but the strange-smelling old man had not seemed very happy, and Mary remembered being afraid of him. She still was, and she noticed that her mother said not one word to him that wasn't necessary.

She watched her mother carefully as they arranged Daddy Walker's belongings, and she saw that her mother was not unfriendly or resentful but was just her usual quietly solemn self. When Daddy Walker sat down with a sigh in his broad-armed rocking chair and patted his lap for Mary to come sit with him, she did so, but it was with a sense of duty and not pleasure. He rocked her as Papa carried in the pieces of a bed and set it up in the best bedroom—the one closest to the old cannon stove he had installed after bringing a new one for his own house. Mary looked up at her grandpa's face, thinking that everything about him was like that stove—old, worn out, cast off.

Soon thereafter, Mary Susan began to notice that something was different about her mother. She wasn't picking her up as often as she had; she was moving more slowly, especially when she climbed the stairs to the upper bedroom. And then one afternoon after Papa and Grandpa had finished plowing, her mother and father took her for a walk.

They went north, toward the looming wall of the greening forest. Mary Susan somehow had thought that the forest was the edge of the world, for it blocked all view further northward and extended west and east over as many hills as she could see from the swing that Papa had hung from a sturdy branch in the maple tree beside the storm cellar. As they neared the forest, Papa took one of her hands and Mama took her other hand, and she felt safer as they entered the dark realm of the giant trees. She heard phrases she didn't quite understand: "girdling them," "lot of cash money," "land for more corn now that...." Papa's words seemed often to trail off into whispers that Mama caught but Mary couldn't. But it didn't matter. She was engrossed in the almost-overwhelming vision of wild splendor around her.

Her parents walked slowly, occasionally holding Mary up so she could swing between them as they walked. The girl looked at the trees rising from thick trunks to spread their branches far, far overhead. She almost lost her balance craning her neck back to try to see the tops of the trees, and Papa had to pull her upright, tugging on her hand to make her "walk right." She climbed over fallen branches and peered into the shadowy depths of the forest. There hid plants and flowers she had never seen before and only later would unravel the mysteries of: ferns, wood violets, adder's tongues, columbines, creepers. She saw toadstools and, around the shed bark of a dying elm tree, strange, crinkly-headed things.

Each was about as long as one of her fingers, and each had a whitish stem and tall brown cap that was disgustingly like the waviness of animal brains.

"Morels!" Papa cried, going to the crinkly things. He broke several from their stems. Mary wrinkled her mouth in distaste when her mother put the things into her dress pockets.

"I'll wash them and fry them in butter for you," she bent down and told Mary.

"No!" Mary said, backing up a step.

"Oh, there's nothing better in these woods than morels!" her papa said, laughing down at her.

She knew better than to argue with him. After all, from this forest, she knew, he brought them tiny strawberries, walnuts, hickory nuts, and "haws" or hawthorn berries from the thickets along the forest's fringes. From these woods he also brought a number of plants and berries and roots that he made into medicines according to recipes that Mrs. Sparks had inherited from her grandmother and he from his. Mary especially remembered the bright red "bittersweet" vine berries he brought home from the woods, then crushed from their red hulls to leave sticky orange balls that he mixed with tallow to make a burn medicine; it had healed her without leaving a scar when she had scalded herself trying to pour tea for her mother. So she hurried ahead of her parents, looking everywhere for the morels her father quite obviously treasured. But even where she had just searched, he stooped and picked them, and she blinked in amazement, wondering how he had seen them when she had not. She redoubled her efforts, scrambling over branches and almost rooting across the leaf-littered ground until her mother sharply called her back with a warning about snakes. She did, however, manage to find a grand total of six morels, for which she was rewarded by one of Papa's grandest, proudest smiles. Her heart swelled, and she walked beside him as his hand rested lovingly on her head, occasionally stroking her hair.

When they reached the boundary of Walker land, they turned back. By then Mary was tired, and she ran in front of Mama and pleaded to be picked up and carried. Her mother smiled sadly and placed her hands on her tummy, which for the first time Mary noticed had grown amazingly large. As she was staring at her mother's tummy, Mama said, "I can't carry you anymore, honey; Mama's gotten too big."

Papa picked her up and, as she squealed in delighted fright, swung her high into the air and settled her onto his shoulders. She wrapped her hands around his forehead and felt secure as his big hands gripped her ankles. As they meandered back through the darkening forest, Mary looked at the deepening shadows as the words echoed through her mind, *"too big...too big."* Was something wrong with Mama? Mary wondered.

Her father suddenly stopped, stepped in front of his wife, and set Mary on the ground beside her. A man appeared from the gloom of the forest, and Mary, peering around her father's legs, saw that the man seemed as dark as the forest itself. He stopped, facing Papa, and she saw that in one hand he was carrying a long gun; in his other hand he carried a brace of dead rabbits.

"Evening, Ira," Victor said in a low voice, intently watching the man.

"Evenin', Victor," replied the other. "Want a rabbit?" he asked, coming a step closer to the family. "After all, they was shot off'n yor place. Don't mind, do you?"

"I'd rather you'd asked first," Victor said pleasantly, letting his shoulders slump to one side as he shifted his weight to one foot.

Ira held out the rabbits, his eyes as shadowy as the pools of darkness under the trees.

"No," Victor said, shrugging. "You're welcome to whatever you need. How's Dad Bohring?"

"Fine. Said he'd be over to help your wife again pretty soon."

"How's your mother?"

Ira shrugged faintly.

Victor raised one hand, and Ira went on in the direction he had been going. Mary tried to follow him with her stare as she clung to her mother's left hand, but the man was quickly swallowed by the shadows.

That summer Mary learned the meaning of work. Her mother had her beside her constantly, whether they were working in the house or outside in the garden. Frequently her mother would have to go into the shade and sit down and rest, and Mary quickly learned that it pleased her mother greatly if she volunteered to fetch things or would simply continue to work. In the kitchen, she stood on a chair and helped her mother can and put up their winter supply of food, and she watched carefully how everything was done. When her mother burned herself boiling jars and lids before putting lima beans into them, Mary ran and got the bittersweet salve. When her mother moaned once trying to set jars on the top shelf in the cellar, Mary dragged over a stool and climbed up to put the jars into place as her mother gratefully handed them to her. And Mary delighted in scrambling into the places where the chickens who would not sit in the nest boxes laid their eggs. She even learned to tell her mother which chickens were laying, for her mother did not seem to be paying as much attention to such things as she usually did; she almost had Victor kill one chicken that Mary liked especially well, until Mary assured her that the hen was laying her eggs in one corner of the cowpen.

Sunday afternoons Mary learned to love the best. Yes, she had to sit very still while Uncle Charley Hickman preached...and preached. But the organist, Jane George, often let her sit beside her on the bench and turn pages for her. Mary loved Mrs. George almost as much as she loved Grace Ash and her own mother. Later, while the adults gathered outside after the service, Mrs. George would let her sit on her lap and play while she pedaled. After they all had eaten dinner under the shady hickory trees in back of the church, Mary was allowed to run off and play across the road in the schoolyard with Maude, Hazel, Debby, Opal, and a number of the other children from the area. She avoided the boys, such as Veech, her cousin, and Olin George. Olin loved to tell the younger children how bears lived in the woods along the creek, just waiting to gobble them up. Maude and Hazel squealed in delicious fright at his stories, but Mary simply didn't like him *or* his stories.

One Sunday afternoon late that summer as they were going home from church, her mother hugged Mary close and happily said, "You be proud of your papa! The men just picked him to be the new Sunday school superintendent. That's quite an honor."

Mary saw that her mother was looking both fondly and appreciatively at her papa, and she did the same—not knowing what a "superintendent" was but knowing that whatever it was, it was important. And she was proud of her papa anyhow, so she stood up on the jouncing seat and kissed his cheek as he put one arm around her waist to keep her from falling. "You sit down now," he said, giving her a warning look in which she saw the twinkle of his blue eyes.

The leaves were turning brown, yellow, golden, and red, and before long a cold wind blew from the northwest that sent showers of the leaves chasing one another in scurrying, faintly rattling waves across their yard. Mary chased the leaves, laughing with delight, then sat down in a mound of them to select as many dif-

ferent kinds and colors as she could. She was arranging a bunch
of them in her lap when the wind gusted strongly, stealing her
leaves and sending them spinning and whirling into other waves
of them, waves that were becoming drifts against the house and
along the fences and hedgerows. She frowned, set her mouth in
a determined tightness, and stood to begin assembling another
collection. But her endeavor was interrupted by a cry that froze
her and made her heart pound. "Mary! Mary, girl, where are you?
Tell Papa it's time!"

Not knowing what might be wrong and fearing the worst, Mary
ran off toward the back of the barn where Daddy Walker and Papa
were sawing wood. They had been cutting, splitting, and stacking cords and cords of firewood to sell in Princeton during the
winter, and she found them working with their shirts off and the
bibs of their overalls down as the two-handled bucksaw whirred
back and forth through the oak log set on a sawhorse.

"Papa...Papa!" she screamed breathlessly. "Something's wrong
with Mama! She said it's time!" He was running past her even
before she could finish. She started after him and was startled
when Daddy Walker laid one hand on her head.

He knelt and with surprising gentleness said, "It's all right, girl.
You Mama's just going to have a baby." He put on his shirt and
hooked up his overall straps, watching her.

She was staring open-mouthed at him. "A...baby?"

"Sure. That's one thing mamas do better'n papas," he said, grinning and taking one of her hands. "Come on; let's go see if we
can help—or just stay out of the way. Can you cook supper for
us men?"

She was so staggered by what he had told her that she could
hardly answer; she then remembered what Bill Kauffman had told
her about how baby birds had to grow up and fly away so there
could be more babies. Would she have to "fly away" somewhere?
she wondered. Finally, with all of her almost five-year-old dignity, she said, "Yes, I can cook supper. Mama taught me." She
then stared up at the graying, wrinkled old man. "Granddaddy,
will Mama be all right?"

He knelt in front of her and placed his heavy, callous hands
on her shoulders. "There's only One who can keep her right. Do
you know Him yet, honey?"

Lowering her face, afraid that she would cry, Mary whispered,
"Jesus?"

Daddy Walker nodded, and Mary was surprised to see tears

begin to line the edge of his lower lids. He said, "My Suzie went away, but your mama won't."

Mary blinked, trying to swallow the lump in her throat. "Granddaddy," she asked hesitantly, "*I* won't have to go away anywhere, will I?"

Daddy Walker stared at her, then abruptly laughed. He hugged her against him. "No, darling. But...pray for your mama, honey. Pray hard."

Mary and Daddy Walker—the first more than the latter—set about preparing a meal, and Granddaddy would not let her stop working long enough to go toward the bedroom or even to get worried. Before long Mrs. Sparks arrived, and soon after nightfall Dr. Powell came from town. The tall, dignified, and gray-haired old doctor smiled briefly at Mary's inquiry if he wanted supper, then disappeared into the bedroom with Mrs. Sparks. In another hour or so Mr. and Mrs. Smith arrived, and Mary was greatly relieved to have the company—and reassurances—of Catherine, whom she considered the finest young woman she knew. Catherine sat with her, May, and Clara in the kitchen. They all became motionless as through the silence of the farmhouse came a tiny, fragile-seeming cry...then another, a more prolonged wail that soon hushed. Mary bounced off her aunt's lap and led a small procession to the bedroom door, which soon opened.

Dr. Powell came out, coatless and with his glasses low on his nose. He peered down at Mary, wiping his hands on a towel. He shifted his shoulders to adjust his suspenders over his white shirt, then learned toward her. "Well, young lady, you have a fine, healthy baby sister. Bigger'n you were, but just as right."

Mary suddenly experienced an emotion entirely new to her. She wrinkled her nose and dropped her gaze. "I don't want a baby sister," she muttered.

"Like it or not, you've got one," Dr. Powell said, going to put on his black coat.

Catherine, May, and Clara hurried into the bedroom past Mary, who reluctantly went toward the bed—on which, leaning against the headboard, were her mother and father. Her mother was holding up a wrapped bundle for Grandpa and Grandma Smith to admire. Grandma took the bundle and rocked it back and forth, counting fingers and toes. "Oh, she's beautiful," she crooned, "just beautiful."

Mary's new emotion grew, seeming to shrink her vision as if she were becoming dizzy. She shuffled to the bed with her head down and stared at the knees of her papa's overalls. Suddenly he picked her up and set her beside him. "Isn't it wonderful, Mary? You've got a baby sister, and your mama's *fine!*" He reached across and patted his wife on one leg; she placed one of her hands on his, and Mary stared at them as they smiled at each other. Then her mother saw the look on her face.

"What's wrong with you?" she asked.

"Why're you all sweaty and...and tired-looking?" Mary asked pertly, almost angrily...having some idea that the baby was the cause of it all.

The adults laughed, and her mama said, "Because having a baby is hard work, honey. Do you want to hold her?"

"No!" Mary said almost fiercely.

Her father slapped her legs, glaring at her. Tears swam in her eyes as she glared back at him, and he slapped her legs again. "You get that jealousy right out of you girl, before I spank you good!" he declared, boring into her with his look.

She hung her head, her lower lip trembling.

"You'll step on that lip someday," he said, pulling her closer to him and holding her chin between two fingers to force her to look at the baby that Grandma had given back to her mama. She looked unwillingly.

"She's ugly...like a dried beet," Mary stated.

The adults again laughed and the girls giggled while her mama patiently explained, "Honey, she'll smoothe out. She's frowning now because she's come from a warm, safe place into the cold, awfully frightening world of big people. Don't you ever get scared?"

There was silence in the room as Mary considered the question. Slowly she looked again at the baby. Her tiny fists were clenched as tightly as her eyes; she seemed stiff and not at all sure she wanted to be where she was. Mary leaned closer to her. "Will she cry a lot?"

Behind her, Daddy Walker snorted as her papa said, "Probably. You did."

Mary looked quickly at him. "I did?"

"Yes, for a while. Mama had to nurse you every hour or so, you were so hungry to grow up."

"I'm not grown up," Mary protested, snuggling against her father.

"Baby...baby," May twittered, nudging Clara.

"Hush," Grandpa Smith sternly told them. They became stiff

and silent. Mary was so stung by their words that she never forgave them.

Mary's dark mood was almost like the time she had hated her papa for killing Bristles. She lay in her room that night and during the nights that followed, wishing deeply that little Mildred Elizabeth never had been born. Her papa and mama spent *all* their time either in the bedroom fussing over her or in the kitchen fussing over her. And she could not stand to watch her mother nurse Mildred; something about that sight shocked and offended her. So she usually stayed in her room, playing with her dolls and dollhouse and reading to herself from the book of Bible poems she had memorized as her papa *used* to read them to her. She played like he still read them to her, and she was careful to read each word correctly, since he had questioned her closely to see if she really was reading or was just repeating what she had memorized. When he had ascertained that she indeed could read, he had run off to tell Mama, and both of them had come to kneel before her as she proudly and with great gusto read to them. Now, maybe...just maybe if she read and got better and better at it, they would notice her again; after all, Papa read a lot, so maybe she could get his attention back that way.

But for the time being, all her parents' approval of her was gone. Gone with the coming of the *ba-by*. Mary pronounced the word with distaste, and she flopped down in the darkness of her room to go over the entire situation again and again in her mind. And each time she went over it, the dark chill around her seeped more deeply into her.

When the crib was cleaned and set up in her room again, she realized that it no longer was *her* room. Something else had been taken away from her, and her resentment hardened when her papa took her sternly by the shoulders and told her, "You will watch Mildred, and if she just needs changing or rocking, you do it. But if she's hungry or *really* cries—like she's in pain—you come get me or Mama. Do you understand?"

Mary nodded numbly, her gaze on the rug.

"You're partly responsible for her from now on, just as she and you will be responsible for the next baby."

Mary's stare shot to his face, but the sternness of his gaze broke her look. She began to cry.

He held her, but she could tell that he was angry with her. The warmth, the tender closeness seemed to have gone, and she hated Mildred for having made it go away. Victor, for his part, saw the jealousy and resentment in Mary's attitude and prepared to do long battle against it.

In a few weeks Mildred was moved from her parents' bedroom to the crib in Mary's...in the upstairs bedroom. Mary was shown how to change her diapers, how to put them into the pail of water and baking soda, how to keep small or sharp objects away from her, how to.... Mary dutifully learned, and she dutifully did everything she was told, exactly the way she was told. Well, almost exactly.

She soon figured out that she could wait a few minutes after Mildred started crying before calling her parents and before they would hear her and come to investigate. So she would lean against the bars of the crib, her hands gripping the rail, and watch Mildred cry harder and harder, and she took small satisfaction when the baby's face turned redder and redder. But one day she failed to hear Papa come silently up the stairs; she did not even sense his presence until the belt whistled and smacked her soundly across her hips. Shocked and surprised, she whirled, and he grabbed her hands away from her buttocks and whacked her again.

"You are never...*never* to be cruel!" he shouted down at her.

Holding her stinging buttocks, she glared at him, feeling a rise of the dark chill of resentment that crept within her during the nights.

His eyes widened, and he glanced warningly at Mama, who had come to pick up Mildred and was looking pleadingly at her husband. His wide-eyed stare went down to Mary, and he pulled her over to the bed and set her down. He sat beside her and turned to face her. "You get that mean look out of your eyes." Mary swallowed hard and tried to relax her look. He pulled her chin up and jerked on her to make her look at him. He studied her eyes and shook her again. She pulled back slightly, blinking to get rid of the look she knew he still could see. "Get it out of you, Mary! That's Satan, our mortal enemy, who's trying to get you to hate your sister and me."

Mary felt as if she had been stabbed. Putting that awful name to the chill of resentment and jealousy she had been brooding sent something fleeing into the dark corners of her mind.

Her father closed his eyes and tilted back his head as Mary stared in awed silence. "Lord God, protect my daughter by the precious blood of Jesus Christ and let no harm reach her from our Adversary!"

From then on, each night after she had snuggled under the

covers and after enough time had passed so that she ought to have been asleep, she was aware that her parents came silently into the bedroom and stood beside her bed. She had no doubt what they were doing; she *felt* their prayers descending over her, around her, warming her in a blanket of love. She waited for that blanket to descend upon her each night, for then she could go to sleep quickly, sleep dreamlessly, and wake up in the mornings to willingly help tend Mildred—whom she discovered was learning to focus on her face and coo in recognition. Love was born.

Mary would change her diaper and talk to her constantly, then tickle her rounded cheeks and chin and let her grip her forefinger. As Mildred cooed and drooled and blew bubbles, Mary leaned over her and cooed back, letting the baby take her down-swinging curls and clutch them to feel their softness. When Millie—as Mary began calling her, much to the silent displeasure of her mama— began to eat solid food, Mary was relieved that the nursing was less frequent; she was so relieved that she willingly fed the baby as she sat in Mary's old high chair. And with those changes came another—one that was crucial to Mary's happiness. Her father's attitude gradually softened toward her; he no longer gave her hard stares when she was around the baby.

As Mary's sixth birthday came and went and Christmas approached—with its trek to the warm, well-lighted chaos of the bustling Smith household—Mary saw that her father gradually came to trust her again, although she well knew that he was ready to pounce upon the least sign of rebelliousness or bitterness she betrayed. He trusted her again, but he also watched her, looking behind her eyes and silent mouth.

Because he watched her, she learned to keep her "silly thoughts" to herself—thoughts about such things as naming ducklings and piglets and collecting leaves and feathers. And all the while, she depended on being blanketed by the love and prayers of her parents, knowing that the dark chill that had crept upon her was kept at bay by her parents' strength of spirit and by the power of the Lord Jesus. Thus there developed four buttresses of Mary Susan's life: her father's trust, her parents' love and prayers, her own private thoughts, and the companionship and protection of Jesus Christ.

Winter of Learning & Loss

When Mildred was two years old, in 1910, the earth passed through the tail of Halley's Comet. As the event approached, uncertainty and dread arose among the people as they wondered whether the earth would be destroyed. The old men grumbled and worried among themselves that the End, Judgment Day, was upon them. Mary heard parts of such conversations when she went with Papa into Princeton. He seemed to delight in showing her off, in taking her from store to store as he made purchases—including lemon drops for her, with a reminder, of course, to save some to take home to Millie and Mama. But as the tail of the comet became more and more visible in the nighttime sky, their trips into town took on a somber note. And at night the entire family would stand out in the yard, staring up at the heavens.

During those times, Daddy Walker stood with his hands shoved down into his overalls pockets and muttered things incompletely, like, "I wonder..." and "D'you suppose...." Later each night the family gathered in the "main house" around the dining table while Papa read from the big family Bible. The rest of the family listened intently, even Mildred, as he read the words of the Prophet Isaiah...and he always ended by reading a passage from chapters 53, 54, or 55.

" 'Incline your ear, and come unto me: hear, and your soul shall live; and I will make an everlasting covenant with you....' " Papa looked at Mary. "A covenant is a deep, two-way agreement." When she nodded understandingly, he resumed reading, and from his deep, steady voice as much as from the words he read, Mary drew comfort.

Her mother became pregnant again, and Mary began to overhear Daddy Walker plaguing Papa: "You ever gonna throw a son, boy?"

Papa never said anything in rebuttal, but Mary knew how deeply hurt he was by such barbed comments—though she also understood that Daddy Walker said them because he sorely needed something of which to be proud, something to cling to in his landless old age of depending on his son for even daily sustenance. Mary pitied him, even as she had pitied him at Christmas when he had taken no joy in the occasion because, as he glumly had said, his Suzie wasn't there to share it.

Since Christmas, Mary had watched Daddy Walker carefully, trying to figure him out. Once she asked him why he hadn't gone to live with his daughters, Nanny McClary and Ella Wilcox. " 'Cause," he stated sourly, "they don't do my shirts right; your mama does...and she's patient with me. Cooks good, too," he added with a grin, taking Mary onto his lap and rocking her for a long while in silence.

As the spring came and her mother grew larger, Mary noticed that Mott Lewis stopped coming to the Pleasant Ridge Church. On Mary's next trip into town with her father, they happened to see Luther Lewis with Maude, Hazel, their five-year-old son Luther, Jr., and the other three children. Mott herself was in Casteel's Dry Goods Store buying fabric, so Luther had time to talk, but seemed reluctant to do so. Victor, holding Mary's hand, finally gave up talking about cows and the comet whose tail was still visible at night, fading off into the distance, and asked Luther bluntly, "Goin' to church some'eres else?"

Luther slightly squirmed his vast bulk. "That comet thing scared me pretty bad," he admitted, glancing at the upturned faces of his brood. "So, when Preacher Biggs an' the tent meetin' set up down on the river, me an' the missus started goin'."

"You're going to the Holy Rollers?" Victor blurted.

Luther frowned and doggedly shook his head. "Don't you say nothin' bad 'bout Preacher Biggs." He squirmed more noticeably. "I'll say straight out that fallin' in the sawdust in a fit an' speakin' in tongues ain't exactly my idea o' relig'n, but...." His large, florid face took on a childlike expression of wonderment. "But Mr. Biggs explained how that comet was a warnin' from the Lord God about the kinda hellfire an' damnation that'd come to us if we didn't repent. So I repented."

Victor slowly smiled and reached out to shake the huge man's hand. "Well, I praise God, Luther, that you finally came home." He said nothing further about Luther's church affiliation, and they soon parted company.

Mary had seen the light in Luther's eyes when he had spoken about being saved, so she began to wonder several things—such as that apparently there was more than one way to worship the Lord God. She resolved to ask Grace Ash about the matter, since Grace did not become upset with her "silly ideas" as her mama and papa did. In fact, Grace did not seem to be upset by anything—not even the antics of Eddie, her unruly five-year-old son.

But when Mary got an opportunity to ask Grace about other ways of worshiping, Grace was silent for a while, gazing at Mary with soft, dark eyes. She finally said, "Love, you need to talk with Anna Gentry. Do you know her?"

Mary had seen her several times alone at the Pleasant Ridge Church services—a matronly woman with an absolutely radiant face—so she nodded.

"Well, talk to her when you get a chance," Grace said cautiously, then added, "but please don't mention to your papa that I said so." She smiled and touched Mary's cheek with her fingertips.

Mary, however, did not see Anna Gentry for a long while, and something far more important began that first Monday in September of 1911. She started to school.

She knew how to get to the school: You walked west along the road, crossed the creek at the bridge, passed the Bohring farm, and soon turned south at the crossroads. A mile-and-a-half down that road you made an eastward turn and went a hundred yards or so to the school that was across the road from the church. And of course she knew most of the children and young people who went to school there. For two or so years she had realized she would have to go to school, and she was glad that her father already had taught her much about reading and arithmetic. So she was eager to begin formally "gettin' educated," as folks said. But on that first day the old conflict between what her parents told her and what she herself thought came to the fore.

They sent her off, lunch sack in hand, knowing she was ready and eager...but they did not reckon on her secret thoughts.

She set off walking early in the morning that Monday, and everything went as planned...until she crossed the creek. There she saw that a fascinating thing had happened. Sandbars had built up below the bridge and extended some distance along the creek bottom. The sand was pale yellow and perfectly smooth, and Mary could not resist the temptation to climb down from the road and touch—just touch—that smooth sand. She soon discovered that its surface was perfect for drawing pictures on, and then she decided to practice making her letters of the alphabet, just in case Miss Pearl, the teacher, asked her to. She practiced...and practiced...until finally she remembered that she was supposed to be doing something else. She brushed herself and her new, lace-trimmed, cotton dress and climbed back up to the road. The sun was warmer upon the land now, and she began walking faster.

Dad Bohring waved to her from his large garden, and she turned aside to talk with him—until he frowned and asked if she were on her way to school. She waved to Mrs. Bohring, who was sweeping the front porch of her neat, scroll-decorated, two-story white house, and went on...but saw some blackberry bushes near the crossroads and just had to see if any berries were ripe. And then it was another and another fascinating thing to investigate; after all, she rarely was sent off on her own, except for the great adventure of going to the mailbox up near the Lewises' place. This walk was something like those adventures, and somehow she had the idea that her goal was the same—to go and return at her own pace.

When she finally arrived at the school, she noticed a strange stillness. She had expected children to be playing tag and chase in the schoolyard and hide-and-seek along the paths among the haw trees west of the school. But there was no one in sight. She wondered if school had been called off. She went slowly to the closed doors of the white frame building, trying to decide what to do. She finally clenched her lips determinedly and did what her papa had taught her to do when she encountered a closed door; she knocked.

There was such a silence within that Mary had about decided that indeed there was no one there—when the right-hand door opened. Miss Pearl looked out, then stared down. She opened the door wide as Mary walked inside...and suddenly froze.

Before her, with the older youths in the back and the youngest children at the front, there was a shaded slope of faces in wide rows—all of them looking at her and most of them either grinning or beginning to giggle. Miss Pearl made a slight movement with one hand, and the giggling stopped as all the faces snapped back around and bent over slates and open books.

"I'm late, aren't I?" Mary whispered, feeling her face and neck burning with shame.

Miss Pearl nodded, smiling patiently, and gently but firmly placed one hand on the girl's back. She guided Mary to an empty desk on the front row, gave her chalk and a slate, and told her to write her alphabet so she could see where to begin teaching her. Nearby, Veech Wilcox and his sister Alma, Mary's cousins, sneered openly at her—until Miss Pearl tapped a ruler on her desk.

Grade by grade after dinner, Miss Pearl heard the recitations of the lessons which the older students had learned that morning. As she listened, she added coal to the huge stove in one corner of the single large room, for the schoolhouse had become chilly. Then, grade by grade, she began listening to the younger children read. As each was called upon, she or he stood self-consciously and cleared his or her throat assiduously before reading in a halting voice, glancing often at Miss Pearl for help with the words they did not know. Gently but firmly Miss Pearl corrected mistakes and supplied words—and there were many. As it came closer to Mary's turn, she determined not to make any mistakes and to impress Miss Pearl. She had been following along in her copy of *McGuffey's Eclectic Primer* (for "Little Children," she read on the title page with disdain), and she rapidly figured out where her turn to read would fall.

When Miss Pearl called her name, she stood right up, holding her book firmly before her chest and not waggling it around the way the boys had. She read distinctly—and so well that even the older students in the rows further back stopped working and raised their heads to listen to her...until a glance from Miss Pearl sent them ducking back to work.

When Mary finished, she sat down promptly and did not look at Miss Pearl; she knew she had done well, and she did not need to look at the teacher for approval. She just hoped she had done well enough to wipe out her initial bad impression because of being late to class.

"That was very well done, Mary Walker," Miss Pearl said. "I assume your father has been teaching you?"

Mary looked at her, feeling pride for her papa welling up inside. "Yes, Ma'am," she said.

Miss Pearl smiled slightly. "He should've been a teacher...or a preacher," she said in what Mary thought was a cryptic tone. She started to ask a question, but Miss Pearl called on the next student, who happened to be Opal Sparks. Opal looked dismally at Mary before beginning to read. As Opal stumbled over even the simplest words, Mary realized with deepening chagrin that her own performance in effect had "set up" her best friend for failure and embarrassment. She wished she could shrink into her desk and vanish.

When the school day ended and Miss Pearl rang the wood-handled brass bell on her desk, the students put their books and materials away and walked from the schoolhouse...then exploded into yells, scuffles, catcalls from the boys to the girls, and races and chases. One of the Kauffman boys bumped Mary as he ran past, then turned and stuck out his tongue.

"Smarty-pants!" he sneered. "Just 'cause you're Flute Walker's—"

Before he could finish, and before Mary could attack him, his older brother cuffed him across the side of his head. Dan Kauffman followed the cuffing with a curt, "You watch your tongue, Brian, or Daddy'll whip you good!" He dragged Brian away by one arm.

Mary sighed angrily, unclenching her fists. She then became aware that Opal was standing near her. She glanced at her friend as they began to walk northward across the churchyard toward the crossroads. Maude and Hazel Lewis fell into step beside them as Veech raced past, chased by Alma, whose pigtails were flying.

Mary glanced again at Opal, who saw her look and smiled. Mary, reddening, said, "I'm sorry, Opal. I didn't mean to—"

"You can't help it if you're smart," Opal said easily, "or if your daddy is." She sighed, looking down at her high-topped, hook-laced shoes as she scuffed the yellowed dry grass of the churchyard. "I just wish my daddy could teach me half as good as yours does."

Mary looked at Maude and Hazel and saw by their soft, almost sorrowful expressions that they agreed with Opal. For an instant, Mary felt the beginning of a pridefulness that she knew her papa would whip out of her if he caught even a whiff of it, so she swallowed and drove down her pride. Quietly, awkwardly, she asked, "Can I help you with your lessons? Maybe Miss Pearl would let me take a book home. That way I could read to you as we walk to and from school."

"Would you do that?" Opal asked with a hopeful tone.

"Surely," Mary said, knowing in her heart that she could do the same thing Miss Pearl had been doing with the classes. "I'll teach you the words and how to say them right."

Opal glanced at Maude, grinning, and Maude said, "You sure could save us a heap of trouble...and a blistering. Daddy said if either of us failed a grade, he'd tan our hides."

The following day during recess, Miss Pearl stood listening to Mary's suggestion while the other students played "shinny" with sticks and a tin can, "blind man's bluff," and the scary "crack-the-whip" in the schoolyard. Then she sat behind her desk, set her elbows on the desk top, and placed her hands together so that her fingertips were under her chin. "I'll tell you what, Mary: Not only may you take a book or two home to help your friends, but you may help me with the rest of the first-graders. I don't get to spend as much time with the older children as I need to, even though Velma Cox has been tutoring some of the eighth-graders and Rodney Smalley works with the seventh-graders. However," she added with a warning rise in her tone, "as Velma and Rodney will tell you, you will take a certain amount of teasing for being 'teacher's pet' and 'too smart for your own good.' As I feel your father could tell you, intelligence often is a liability—something that gets you into more trouble than it may seem worth around here." She studied the expression of her young pupil, and slowly she smiled. Mary relaxed when she saw Miss Pearl smile, and she relaxed further when she said, "You remind me of myself when I was your age."

The next day, after Mary's first attempts to be patient and to tutor well, she came up the trail from the road to her house and was greeted by Millie tottering toward her with open arms. Mary picked up and kissed her sister, but then she saw her father coming out of the house. His fists were on his waist, and the look in his eyes told Mary that she was "gonna get it." Half-ducking her head behind Millie's, she went toward the back porch, hoping somehow to escape the wrath she felt sure was coming.

"Millie, you go on inside," Papa said. He waited until Mary had set the child down and she had gone unsteadily up the steps and into the house before he said anything to Mary.

"Your first day at school seems to have been less than a good start."

"Yes, Papa, but...."

"In fact, it seems you were more than an hour-and-a-half late."

"But Papa...."

"You were dawdling, weren't you?"

She hung her head, hating her cousins Veech and Alma for telling her aunt on her; she was sure Aunt Ella had called her brother as soon as she heard from her children about Mary's embarrassing entrance, and Mary could almost hear Aunt Ella's whining telling of the tale.

Victor lifted his daughter's chin with one fingertip.

Mary took heart from his silence. "But Papa, Miss Pearl is letting me tutor Opal, Maude, Hazel, and some of the other first-graders in their reading and numbers, and...."

His look again became stern, silencing her and wilting her hopes

of making him "proud as peaches" of her. He spoke solemnly.
"Being smart is fine; being educated is even better. But *showing*
how smart and educated you are will only cause jealousy and
resentment among the people near whom you must live."

"But Papa...!"

"Don't you 'But Papa' me anymore!" he snapped. "You tell Miss
Pearl that your father appreciates her confidence in his eldest
daughter, but that he wishes her to be nothing more or less than
the other students. You will tutor no one. I will not have Luther
Lewis or Otto Sparks spreading talk about my 'uppity' daughter.
Do you understand me?"

Dutifully Mary nodded, her hopes trodden into the dust of
ordinariness.

She knew how inflexible he could be, and she dutifully told Miss
Pearl of his wishes...then burst into tears. The other students were
outside for recess, and Miss Pearl came around her desk to steady
Mary with one hand on her shoulder. But she did not hug her.
Instead, she waited until Mary stopped crying somewhat and
glanced at her. "Miss Mary, you will listen to me now." Mary
nodded, wiping her cheeks with the backs of her hands. "You
must always obey whatever your father says, for he is a good
man." She waited until that soaked in, then said, "But you must
not stop learning or thinking. You are *not* to become resentful,
either. Dear, please learn to love learning for the sake of
learning—never to show off or to please someone else. If you learn
to learn just because it's fun to learn, and if you learn well and
wisely, someday...*someday* it will be put to good use. The Lord
God lets nothing precious go to waste."

Mary looked intently at her, heard well, and believed.

The days began passing in a steady routine that Mary grew to
love. She did begin learning for the sake of learning—not to please
Miss Pearl or her father and certainly not to show off before the
other students, whom she had great difficulty not being contemp-
tuous of for their dullwittedness and frequently apathetic attitudes.
Before school had gone on two weeks, Mary was placed in the
second grade—a fact which made her school life even more satis-
fying, for there the challenges were more at the level of her ability, and she surged ahead in devouring the lessons that Miss Pearl
observantly gave her when she was ready.

Meanwhile, at home, Mary became aware of increasing tension;
her mother's baby was long overdue, and Dr. Powell had come
to the house twice to examine her mother. Each time he left shak-

ing his head. As if in explanation, Mrs. Walker assured her husband in an exasperated tone, "I *know* how to count, Fluty. This one just wants to stay warm longer."

But Papa didn't laugh. Mary saw that he was worried, and she did everything she could to help her mother and to keep Millie out of her father's way at night while he sat at the bookcase-desk reading. She frequently went into her parents' bedroom to ask her mother if she needed anything, but all her mama would do was smile tiredly and say, "Just keep up your studies, Mary, and see that Mildred doesn't fall into the ash bucket or something."

Grandma Smith was called, and she came bustling in, portly now and often out of breath from her flurries of activity. She barely had time to set the house in order and take the edge off Victor's impatience when Lucy cried out to her.

The baby was born two days before Mary's birthday, and Mary jumped straight off her chair when Papa came pounding out of the bedroom yelling, "It's a *boy*...thank God, it's a *boy!*" Frantically he began cranking the telephone handle and paced back and forth in a small oval until Grandpa Smith answered. "Hey, Grandpa, you've got a grandson!...Yes...yes! He'll be James Walter. Yes, Sir...thank *you!*" When he hung up, he couldn't resist calling several of his close friends to tell them the good news...as Mary took Mildred by one pudgy hand and led the bewildered little girl into the bedroom. Mary felt bumped even further aside, but this time she did not resent it, seeing how overjoyed her father was. And what made him happy made her happy. So she put Mildred up onto her parents' bed and watched lovingly as her mama gently laid the large baby boy on Mildred's lap. Millie began to cry, holding up her fists and waving them.

Mrs. Walker laughed and took the baby from her, then held him out to Mary. As her eldest daughter took the boy and carefully pulled back the flannel blanket to count fingers and toes the way she had seen Grandma Smith do, Lucy Walker lay back against the pillows with a deep sigh. Looking at her mother and silently crying, Lucy mumured, "Victor's so happy now...so happy." Mrs. Smith nodded, tightening her lips and watching her daughter drift into sleep.

It occurred to Mary that babies were born in winter so their parents and grandparents could adore and play with them during the months when there was very little work to be done. She watched her grandparents and parents hover around the boy's crib, cooing at him and wiggling their fingers toward him, then

laughing delightedly if he happened to seize one of their prof-
fered fingers. "What a grip the lad has!" Granddaddy Walker
declared, looking proudly at Victor.

Mary also noticed a rather strange and unsettling development.
Her mama and papa clearly had loved her and had given her all
the attention and affection she had wanted while she was very
young; and they had done the same with Mildred, although after
Mildred was born, Papa seemed to lean more toward Mary while
Mama leaned more toward Mildred. But now, with the birth of
James Walter, there was something different in her parents' attitudes. She puzzled over it as she walked with her friends down
the rutted, snowy, and slushy roads to school, trying to remain
as motionless as possible inside her thick woolen coat, long scarf,
and knitted hat pulled down below her ears, trying to let no icy
cutting air inside to chill her more than necessary. Her feet, despite
galoshes, high-topped shoes, and wool socks were nearly numb;
her hands, despite her thick mittens (Oh! how she yearned for
real gloves, with fingers in them, instead of the childish mittens),
were numb. She walked without thinking of the cold any more
than she had to, unconsciously avoiding the ice-skimmed pud-
dles and the snow between the wandering ruts where freight
wagons had passed. And she thought...and thought. It seemed to
her that her parents had been waiting so long—and praying so
hard—for a boy that when he finally came, they more than fell
in love with him. It seemed to Mary—and this idea somehow
frightened her—that they worshiped the boy.

After the spring thaw and when warmer weather soaked into
the barely greening land, but before the steady labor of plowing
and planting began, school was interrupted by an event that Mary
had been to before but had never paid as much attention to as
she did to this year's event. It was a "protracted meeting," a
revival that lasted two full weeks at the Pleasant Ridge Church.

Reverend Oral Painter came in to lead the meeting, and Victor
Walker—more energetic and determined than ever—was his
"right-hand man," as Mr. Painter became fond of telling anyone
who would listen. Victor rode Belle's stallion son—named Flag
for the proud way he carried his tail high behind himself as he
trotted—far and wide to round up people and bring them to the
meeting.

School was let out for the meetings, which began after dinner
and lasted from an hour to an hour and a half. There were other
meetings in the mornings and evenings, but it was the afternoon

meetings—one in particular—that Mary remembered.

That particular meeting, in the second week of the revival, was the one in which, for the first time in his life, Victor Walker preached. Reverend Painter had talked himself hoarse, and at his urging—or command—Victor prepared a sermon. Unlike the other preachers Mary had heard, including Uncle Charley Hickman and Oral Painter, her father surprised her with his gentleness. Apparently he surprised a goodly number of other people, too, for the crowd that had jammed into the church was unusually attentive. Mary afterward recalled that her father preached on the fourteenth chapter of John, beginning and ending with the words of Jesus, "He that hath my commandments, and keepeth them, he it is that loveth me: and he that loveth me shall be loved of my Father, and I will love him, and will manifest myself to him." Her father explained that "manifest" meant to "make real or visible," then paused to look at his listeners one by one.

"Do you believe," he asked them—and Mary felt as if her were asking her personally—"that the Lord Jesus is *real,* that He is here among us and within *you,* able to change your very heart and soul and mind into the shining light of goodness that He Himself is?"

A number of people apparently believed that Jesus was, or could be, real in their lives, and they seemingly accepted Victor Walker's challenge to do what they said they believed, for 11 of them came forward to accept salvation that afternoon...and Mary Susan Walker was one of them. She had not thought beforehand that she might go forward, as several of the other students from the school already had done; she had formed the habit of thinking for herself, so their professions of faith had not swayed her; one thing and one thing only had moved her: She felt as if the Spirit of Christ Himself had taken her by the hand. But when the deacons went to those who had come forward and knelt with them to listen to their confessions and to their professions of faith, they avoided her, glancing at Victor. He himself came down from the platform and went down on one knee before his daughter.

"Are you sure?" he whispered.

She nodded, pressing her clasped hands against her chest to try to stop herself from crying.

"And you want to be baptized?"

"Yes, Papa."

"You're not doing this just to please me?"

She gave him a hurt look that made him flinch. "Papa, I love the Lord Jesus...and I always have," she managed to murmur. "I want to *belong* to Him...like you said."

He cleared his throat and began to say what she saw he did not really want to say: "Mary, we've never believed that anyone under the age of accountability should be baptized; other religions have infant and child baptism, but...." He stopped, embraced her awkwardly, aware of the congregation watching him, and stood; he stroked her hair before he went to talk with others who had come forward.

Mary was crushed by his refusal to allow her to complete what she knew Jesus Himself had begun, so at the first opportunity she worked her way, head down, to the back of the church. She was standing there, under the coatrack, vaguely aware that singing had begun, when she felt a soft hand on her head. She looked up at once, ashamed, and saw Anna Gentry standing beside her, looking down with tears in her eyes and a radiant smile on her full, rounded, lovely face. Impulsively Mary buried her face against Mrs. Gentry's bosom and relaxed as the woman held her. "Darling child, will you follow me outside?" Mrs. Gentry asked.

Mary nodded; wiping her cheeks, she followed the woman out of the church. They walked slowly toward a tall, conical-shaped cedar tree, and Mrs. Gentry began talking to her.

"Mary, I believe you need to know something. At this very special moment, you need to *know* that what you experienced as you listened to your father preach, and what you experienced as you walked that aisle, and what you likely have experienced before this day, is called the *joy* of the Lord." She fell silent as Mary stared up at her, realizing why Grace Ash had wanted her to speak with the woman. "Some folks never know the *joy* of the Lord; other folks have it for a time, then do their best to forget it, as if they were ashamed. But you know that joy now, and I was told to let you know not to forget it." Smiling still, she looked firmly down at Mary.

"You were...told?" Mary stammered.

"Yes, darling. By the Spirit of the Lord Jesus, by his Holy Spirit."

Mary had not heard that word—Spirit—used in connection with Jesus before; she had heard "Holy Ghost" but not "Spirit," and never in immediate conjunction with Jesus. She was confused and showed it.

"Dear child, listen and believe me if you can. My home is eight miles from here. My husband doesn't go to church, and he won't even hitch up the horse so I can go. But this morning, I woke up *knowing* I had to come here today, no matter what. So I did. You're the reason I was brought here, and I saw it when you were left standing at the altar. But you weren't alone. You *aren't* alone. And," she added, raising one forefinger to forestall Mary's budding questions, "even if you aren't baptized—which I don't expect you will be until your folks are sure you're accountable, as they say—you *must* know that you are *saved*. You forevermore *belong* to Jesus Christ. You are hid in Him, and you cannot be taken away from Him! Do you understand?"

"Yes, Ma'am...but...."

"I know," Mrs. Gentry said mildly, nodding with her eyes shut, "I know that understanding is not believing and that believing isn't faith and faith isn't assurance. But, darling child of Jesus, give glory to God all the days of your life—sing to Him and for Him, clap your hands and dance as David did if you feel led to, and play piano or teach or paint or whatever you've been given to do for Him—and your faith will grow and grow endlessly and can never be taken from you. Then, someday, you will have assurance." She nodded with such calm, radiant certainty that Mary did believe her. Mrs. Gentry again raised her forefinger. "Remember, glorify God—not yourself—in *all* that you do so that faith and joy will be your rewards long before eternal life in God is accorded you." She bent down, kissed Mary on one cheek, and turned to go to her buggy and climb in. Mary watched her drive away without looking back.

Mary did not go with the others over to the pool in Grant Creek beneath the giant elm tree for the baptizing. Instead, she went a roundabout way home, crossing the creek near Daddy Walker's house and slipping into her own home and upstairs. There she took her Bible from under a stack of books and began to read. For the remainder of her life, she did not miss one single day of reading it.

Neither James Walker nor Lucy had gone to the meeting that day for fear that their presence would embarrass or restrain Victor's first endeavor as a minister of God's word. So, at the supper table that night, he told the family what had happened and how many people had been saved. He seemed both awed and humbled by the response to the message he had been given. But he made no mention of Mary's decision or of her disappearance from the meeting, though several times he looked almost regretfully at her. Refusing to be hurt, she stared at her plate, remembering Mrs. Gentry's words and going over and over them instead of recalling her father's refusal to have her baptized. She flinched when her father spoke her name, evidently for the second time.

"I said, someone told me you'd been talking with Mrs. Gentry," he said, watching her eyes closely.

"Yessir," she admitted, wondering what was wrong with that.

"Well," he said carefully, "Mrs. Gentry is an...emotional woman. Very fine and upstanding in her own way, but...emotional. I'd not pay too much attention to whatever she may have told you, if I were you."

She managed to look him straight in the eyes and say, "No, Sir." But as soon as she could, she lowered her gaze and asked God to forgive her lie; she felt an immediate assurance that she was forgiven.

The weather turned rainy, then sweltering, then rainy again...and again. The men were kept from the fields, and Papa and Daddy Walker spent long hours sitting gloomily in the living room, staring out the front windows and grumbling about the time they were losing.

"It'll be a bad year," Daddy Walker said to his son one afternoon as Mary lay on the living room rug and worked on her homework. "Started with that comet last year and's gone from bad to worse—'cept for James Walter's comin'."

Mrs. Walker came into the house with some onions from the garden, brought baby James into the living room, and deposited him on his father's lap. "Here's a load for you to take your mind off the soggy ground," she said, going directly back into the kitchen with the onions. She trimmed the tops and roots from them and put them into the ashes of the kitchen stove fire. When they had cooked, she began mashing them with croton oil, holding her face away from the pungent fumes.

James, who was almost eight months old, stood strongly with one foot on each of his father's thighs and pumped up and down as Victor held up his hands. As Mary watched the way both men were smiling fondly at the boy, baby James bent over and coughed. All puckered up, he sat down with a plop and coughed again. Mrs. Walker stuck her head into the living room and quietly said, "Listen to his chest, will you?"

Victor put one ear to the boy's chest and listened, his frown deepening. "When did he get that cough?" he called to his wife.

"Two...three days ago," Mrs. Walker answered. Mary detected the restrained concern in her voice, and she looked up as her mother came into the room with a reeking poultice and a length of flannel. "Here, hold up his shirt while I tie this onto his chest. Maybe it'll open up his nose and chest."

"Mustard poultice'd be better," Daddy Walker grumped.

Mrs. Walker straightened and stared at him. Patiently she said, "If this doesn't work, we'll try a mustard poultice."

The cough did not loosen, much less go away. In fact, as his father continually held him—giving up all thought of going to work—his cough became deep and hacking. Mrs. Walker was close to tears, and she sat wringing her hands after putting a mustard poultice, then later a skunk oil poultice, around the boy's chest. Victor had called Dr. Powell, but he was away over east in the county, so Victor called Dr. Law.

The short, pudgy, and balding doctor arrived hours later in a Buick dragged through the muddy ruts by Ed Kauffman's best team of workhorses. Ed and the doctor took off their mud-coated galoshes on the front porch and hurried into the house. Dr. Law pulled his stethoscope from his black bag, put the earpieces into his ears, and warmed the round end of it before placing it against baby James's chest. He listened to only two places before straightening and giving Victor and Lucy a grim look and a single shake of the head.

"What is it?" Victor asked. "Whooping cough?"

"If it was, the poultices I smell might've done some good. It's pneumonia."

"Oh, Lord," Mrs. Walker groaned, sinking into a chair as she unfolded her arms and let her hands lie helplessly in her lap.

"What can we do?" Victor asked, his face distorting as he spread his hands toward the doctor. "Isn't there some medicine...maybe in Princeton? Could we take him to Dr. Powell's hospital?" He stared toward the baby lying along Daddy Walker's thighs. The older man was looking down at the baby, and Mary saw in his expression a full return of all the sadness and depression he had had when he first came to live with his son.

Dr. Law sorrowfully shook his shiny head and put his stethoscope back into his bag.

"But surely there's *something* we can do!" Victor stormed angrily.

Dr. Law looked utterly helpless, and Mary watched her mother raise her apron and cover her face, then begin to tremble as she silently cried. Mary choked back tears and hurried to put her arms around her mother, desperately fighting her own fear; Mildred followed Mary, crying.

Her mother looked almost wildly at the girls, then at the doctor and her husband. "I've tried everything I know...done everything I could! Surely to goodness there's something more, something I don't know...or did I do something wrong? Did *I* cause...."

"No, Mrs. Walker," Dr. Law assured her, going to grip her by one shoulder. "I've seen too many cases like this one." He held his breath for a moment, then slowly sighed, shaking his head. He turned to leave. "I'll send Dr. Powell out as soon as he gets back from the Mercer farm," he said glumly. In silence he went with Ed Kauffman onto the front porch, sat on the steps, and stared out over the muddy fields before working on his galoshes.

As the night wore on, baby James's coughing grew tighter and deeper. Frantic by then, Mrs. Walker even tried sucking the phlegm from his nose and lungs. She worked on him until she fainted from the effort. Victor laid her on the bed by baby James and knelt on the floor near them. He cried out, "Lord God, *please* put his sickness into *my* body; let me die, but save my son!" The house was utterly silent after his words ended, and Mildred stared at her big sister as tears ran down her rounded cheeks.

Within an hour, little James Walter Walker choked, turned blue, and became rigid as he strained to breathe. He died in his father's arms.

Dr. Powell came about midnight—with Reverend Oral Painter, whom the aging doctor had sensed would be needed. Dr. Powell forcefully shook Victor by the shoulders, then took the baby's body from his arms, saying, "No!" when Victor tried to take him back. The doctor examined the stiff little form as Lucy mechanically got from the bed and went into the kitchen.

She soon returned with a pan of soapy water and a cloth. She took her baby from Dr. Powell, laid him on her bed, and began to wash his arms, legs and body. When she was done, she got a long, lacy dress from a chiffonier drawer and put it on the baby. When she was done, she moved him to the center of the bed and stood back. "Victor," she said quietly, "you and Daddy Walker go build the coffin. Baby James is ready."

Dr. Powell watched the men leave the room, then he went to Mrs. Walker and placed one hand on her back. "Lucy...Lucy...."

Mary, watching from the doorway with Millie, saw that her mother did not move at all.

"Lucy, you did everything you could. You're a *good* mother. Everyone knows that. You did the best you could!"

Mrs. Walker turned with an expression as hard as stone. "My

best wasn't good enough, was it?" she said, empty-eyed and deathly gray. She let her gaze drift to her daughters, one behind the other, watching her, and she went to them. She led them to the big rocker by the stove and gathered them into her lap. Squeezing their heads against her face so hard that Millie winced in pain, Lucy began rocking, murmuring, "My babies...my babies...."

James Walter Walker was buried in the Pleasant Ridge cemetery among the graves of his grandmother, his uncle, his great-grandparents, two other children from earlier generations who had died in infancy, and a great-aunt. Of the many people who stood in drizzling rain for the service, only a few wondered at the angry expression fixed on Victor Walker's face. It was a look that Mary could not disconnect from her father's outraged demand of Reverend Painter late the night before: "Why? In God's name, *why?*"

Ella went to her brother as they all were leaving the cemetery; she stopped him as the family gathered around and softly, meekly said, "Fluty, if you went to a garden to pick a rose, wouldn't you pick the prettiest one there?" She smiled through her tears...but Victor merely glared at her and went on, ignoring her crushed expression. Mary walked away with her Aunt Ella, watching her father with a sense of dread.

The Dark Before the Dawn

A fter that May in 1912, winter seemed to come within the Walker household. Daddy Walker worked silently with his son, then silently returned to his old house as Victor went home, bathed, ate, and went to bed without reading his Bible or any of the other books, as had been his habit. Mrs. Walker seemed to have no time for anything except work. Mary, understanding the why of the change, said nothing, but in her spirit she grieved more for her parents than she did for the dead baby, who she felt assured was far happier where he was than any of them were where they were. But if the death split and separated the parents and children, it had one rather odd benefit: Mildred began to mature.

She did not go through a "Why!" stage because Sister, as Papa insisted on calling Mary, explained everything to her before she had a chance to do much more than hint at a question. That explaining on Sister's part helped produce the fact that Mildred grew up quickly and securely, seldom pausing in her play to wonder "Why?" because she felt sure that if something needed explaining, Sister would do it when the time came. Another reason she grew up securely was because Papa was not standing over her, glaring at her every thought and gesture. She was free to putter around where she chose—often, when she was in the yard, followed by assorted cats and a goose or two.

During that summer of silence, the girls found things to amuse themselves that required no contact with the adults—contacts that were unproductive at best and painful at worst. So, here and there on the farm while the incessant work went on unnoticed by them, they played house with the broken pieces of china that Mary had collected; they played with the dolls and dollhouse that Grandpa Smith had made and with the doll clothes they themselves had sewed from scraps in imitation of the better doll clothes that Grandma Smith and Mama had made. They "baked" mud pies and "iced" them with brick dust. They made parachutes from squares of cloth with strings tied to each corner and a rock hung from the ends of the strings. High, high into the white-blue summer sky they threw the parachutes and watched them drift slaunchwise on the hot wind.

In July, their contacts with Papa began to improve. Periodically he would come to them after work or on Sunday afternoons and seem to shake off the gloom that encased him the remainder of the time. During those contacts, Mary and Mildred watched him carefully, expecting an explosion at any moment. As if to reassure them, he would make them whistles out of long hickory sticks, whistles on which they actually could play simple tunes by fingering holes cut through the bark into a groove in the loosened core. He made loops of string and put one over his thumbs, then taught them to finger-weave "crow's-feet," "Jacob's ladder," and the terribly intricate "cat's-cradle" that took *forever*—it seemed to Mildred—for them to learn. Mildred was never as good as Mary at making the string figures because her fingers were too pudgy and her patience quickly ran out. But she loved Papa's magic tricks—like driving a straight pin through the palm of his hand and even through the top of the dining table. And she was delighted with the merry-go-round he made for them by placing a wheel hub and axle securely on a stump and bolting seats to each end of the axle. If Mary would push the axle as fast as she could, then hop onto her seat, they had whirling, windblown rides...as their father walked away smiling.

That summer, since her talk with Mrs. Gentry and since baby James's death, Mary felt the development of two strong urges: One was to feel the rush of the wind through her hair and against her face; the second urge emerged as a desire to be *alone*. The first urge was a yearning for flight—like the pigeons that wheeled above the barn into the sky in complete freedom. They and the other birds soared and flashed, rose and dove through the clear element with an ease and speed that thrilled her. She envied the birds. She began to love them and to watch them, learning their habits.

Her desire for wind on her face and through her hair was intensified when Daddy Walker took her and Millie to the county fair. Mary later remembered only one event: They went for an automobile ride around the dirt track at the fairgrounds arena. For the huge sum of a dime each, a man in a white cloth cap, long cloth coat, goggles, and gloves lifted the girls into the front seat of the car while Daddy Walker—rather disgruntled-looking— climbed into the back seat. The car sputtered off...and began to speed up. Mildred shrieked in fear and clambered into the backseat by her grandfather, but Mary leaned toward the windscreen as the dirt track became slightly blurred from the speed. She glimpsed faces of people watching them from behind the fence, and she loved flashing past them. It was over all too soon.

Her urge for wind and speed found a way of matching her other urge—to be alone. She liked to play with Mildred, and they played together for hours and hours on end. But, after all, Millie was *little* and she was *slow.* She had almost no patience for the complicated things that Mary really enjoyed. Plus, Mary still felt bubblings of her old jealousy—such as when Papa brought home some bananas.

The yellow fruit was a special treat, and late that summer Mr. Gregory got some in at his grocery store. Victor happened to be there when the small supply of bananas went on sale, and he bought a bunch before they were quickly snatched up. He brought them home and gave two to his father, two to his wife, and two to each of his daughters. Mary did not remember until later that he kept none for himself. She watched Mildred immediately peel and devour her bananas, then turn a long, greedy look upon her sister's. Mary held hers against her chest and turned away, then ran. Later, when she heard her mother take Mildred outside, she sneaked into her parents' bedroom and hid her bananas under their chiffonier against the wall. Satisfied, she went out to help her mother. Unfortunately, she spent so long gloating over her hidden hoard that when she returned two days later to enjoy her bananas, she found that they had turned brown, soft, and smelly. Choking back tears, she took the bananas outside and flung them toward the fields, hating Millie.

The banana incident made her more than ever want to be alone. She had to *think,* and she resented *always* having to watch and take care of Mildred. Fortunately, the conjunction of her two main desires happened. It was her job to go to the mailbox each afternoon. From the very first time—when her mother had taken her by one hand east along the road to the corner, then north up the road to the next corner by the Lewises' dairy to the mailbox—the trip had been an adventure. She could take her time, and she could be *alone,* since Millie did not like to walk that far...especially after Mary had described in great detail the snakes and other awful creatures that she would meet along the way. Mary could meander off the road and over the hills if she chose. Doing so, she once had discovered a rabbit's nest hidden in the grass. She had pulled aside the tall grass stems and peered into the down-lined hole. There were three motionless, soft-brown babies hiding there. She had run home and forced her mother to come see...but when her mother and she had looked into the rabbit nest again, her mother sprang backward and screamed: A blue racer snake was coiled in the hole, very full.

Though she had hated the snake for eating some or all of the baby rabbits, she felt none of her mother's terror for the creature. After all, it was one of God's creatures. And it too had become part of the adventure of going to the mailbox.

She finally worked up the courage to ask Papa if she could ride one of the horses to fetch the mail. She had reasoned that if she could ride one of the horses, she could feel that delicious rush of the wind through her hair and against her face that had been whetted by the automobile ride at the fair. Her father ignored her first few requests, giving her a look that told her he thought she was being silly. But she persisted...and her mother began complaining about how long she was taking to go for the mail. So one day he saddled and bridled old Belle, placed Mary on the saddle, and handed her the reins. He slapped the horse's rump to head her in the right direction. Proudly Mary kept her feet in the stirrups and kicked her heels against the mare's sides; she wasn't *very* old, Mary knew, and surely she could run.

Run she did—almost to the end of the drive. For a brief while Mary felt the thrill of speed and freedom. But when Belle realized that her little rider could not dominate her, she stopped, turned, and began walking back to the barn, determined despite all the girl's kicking and pleading and crying. Papa was waiting for her, chuckling. Mary was chagrined, and she despised Belle from then on, glaring at the mare as the beast walked with dignity into her stall and began tearing hay from the rack.

Mary persisted. Her father finally saddled Mack, with whom Mary had grown up. The horse was not a runner, so Mary was not as happy as she had been with the idea of riding Belle. But a horse was a horse, and horses meant speed and going anywhere you wanted to and going faster than you could walk. So she let her father set her upon Mack, her legs sticking almost straight out from his broadly rounded sides. "Hup!" she commanded him, kicking her heels into his sides. He did not move.

"Git-up!" Papa shouted, whacking the horse on the rump. Slowly Mack moved off...until he was out of sight of Mr. Walker. Then he too turned and went back to the barn despite all Mary's desperate efforts to yaw his head around by pulling mightily on the reins. He turned his head in the direction she was pulling, but he kept walking back to the barn. What an insult, what an indignity to Mary's pride! *She* was supposed to be the master of those dumb brutes, yet *two* of them had mastered her! It was so humiliating that never again did she ask her father to let her ride.

Soon after Flag, the Arabian stallion, was first used as a stud, he began refusing to be put into a stall and began giving Victor fits on every trip...and, wonder upon wonders from Mary's point of view, her father purchased a bicycle. It was a heavy-framed, thick-tired man's bicycle, and on it he rode to Goshen Baptist Church to preach one Sunday and to various other places. But he fussed and fumed about having flats, and Mary frequently squatted to one side of him while he upturned the bicycle, pried off a tire, dug out the tube and patched it, then reassembled the wheel and pumped up the tire with a hand pump. Evidently the frequency of flats discouraged him from putting Flag out to pasture in favor of the machine, so it began to sit idly in one corner of the barn.

Mary rescued it. She wheeled it out into the backyard one afternoon during harvest when everyone was away except Mama and Millie, who were in the house. Mary hiked up her dress, leaned the bicycle to her, and struggled onto the hard seat. With her right toes she pushed herself upright and began pedaling—wobbling and weaving and finally toppling over. But she stopped herself before she fell completely, caught her breath, and with dogged determination she tried again...and again...and again until she got the heavy bicycle going fairly fast down the drive toward the road.

The drive crested a rise, then sloped downward toward the deep ruts of the road that ran at right angles to the drive. The wind began going faster and faster past her as she pedaled harder and harder. Oh, it felt sooo good! Her hair was flying behind her, her dress was fluttering, and the wind was caressing her face. She looked up in time to see the oncoming road and remember that she did not know how to stop the thing.

The bicycle hit the ruts, bounced, bounded, and flew sideways through the air to land with a clatter on the hard clay ruts. Mary flew the other way, landed hard, rolled sideways, and came to a stop in one of the ruts. She lay still for a while, trying to figure out what had happened. Then she began to hurt. She picked herself up, sniffling, and looked at her cut and scraped elbows, hands, and knees. Fortunately she had kept her face up when she landed, so it was not harmed...but her dress! Oh, she knew her mother would have Papa whip her for ruining a practically new dress. She plucked at the torn places, crying. Disconsolately she went to pick up the bicycle...and discovered that both its tires were flat. Wheeling the heavy machine a quarter-mile up the dirt lane with two wobbling, flat tires, and herself with bleeding cuts and scrapes, plus wounded pride and growing fear, made her entirely forget the thrill of the wind in her face and hair...for a time.

But she was patched up, not whipped, and she herself patched the tubes, reassembled the wheels, and pumped them full. Within a week she was on the bicycle again, this time knowing how to backpedal for braking.

Her papa and mama watched her ride off toward the mailbox. Papa shook his head, smiling proudly as he watched his oldest daughter determinedly wobble down the drive. "I'll say this for her: She's got gumption!"

Lucy gave him a hurt look, which he did not see because he was gazing proudly toward Mary. Lucy turned and walked dejectedly toward the house, murmuring, "I'm glad at least one of your girls has."

Victor glanced at her, then resumed watching his daughter, hoping she did not fall again. She did not. She had gumption.

A third main urge began to grow stronger in Mary's life soon after school started that year and the snows began to come. She always had loved music. In fact, she loved it in direct proportion to the degree she hated the almost perpetual silence of her home. And the closing in of winter, which kept her in the house, made that silence nearly unbearable.

Jane George continued to be the organist at Pleasant Ridge Church, and she continued to allow Mary to turn pages for her during the services and to sit on the bench and play after the services while the others ate dinner around the church's stove. Mary quickly learned to play as well as Mrs. George, which the older woman laughingly said "Isn't much!" Mrs. George, in her kind and gentle way, spoke with Mr. Walker about the advisability of letting Mary take music lessons.

"She's got a gift, Mr. Walker," Mrs. George sincerely told him one Sunday afternoon. "You have the gift for expressing yourself and speaking to people." She paused, puzzled when he clenched his lips and looked away; cautiously she added, "And your daughter has the gift of music. I don't have to tell her things; she just does what I do and plays. I'd like to let *her* play next Sunday. She knows six hymns."

"We'll see," Victor said gloomily, walking away and leaving Mrs. George to wonder prayerfully when, if ever, he was going to stop grieving.

The next Saturday, despite what Victor Walker was going through within himself, he told Mary's mother to get her dressed up; he was taking her to town. Delighted to go anywhere with him, Mary raced upstairs, stuck out her tongue at Millie, and declared, "Papa's going to take *me* to town, and *you're* staying here!"

Millie began to wail, and she followed Papa and Mary all around until they drove off in the buggy. Papa glanced back at Mildred, who was sitting on the porch with her head thrown back as she wailed. "Sometimes I don't know what ails that girl," Papa muttered. Mary said nothing as she stared straight ahead, her hands clasped in her lap, her coat and hat and birthday-present gloves as prim and tidy as her mother and she could make them.

They went to the home of Mrs. Hazel Armsby Lindsey, the wife of the owner of the Princeton music store and a piano and organ teacher like her husband. Mr. Walker paid her what seemed to Mary an incredible sum—50 cents—and went off to town shopping, saying he would be back to collect her in two hours or so. Those two hours were pure heaven to Mary.

Mrs. Armsby Lindsey was tall and matronly in her lace-fronted, bustle-backed long dress, and she played with a precision and style that left Mary stunned with the realization of what she herself did not know...and of what there was ahead for her to learn. She set her mouth tight and began.

By the time her father returned, her fingers were cramped and her back ached from sitting as upright on the stool as Mrs. Armsby Lindsey demanded, but she was quietly proud. She had learned much, and she took with her sheets of music to study and a small book about how to read music. It never had occurred to her that you *read* music, since Mrs. George just played what she had learned by ear. A whole new world had opened up to Mary.

As Papa and she were leaving, Mrs. Armsby Lindsey stood in the open doorway and said to him, "She's got talent, Mr. Walker. She's got talent and persistence and she *listens*. She'll do." Victor was standing with his left arm across his abdomen, his hand pressing his side, and Mary, looking at him, could not tell if he was pleased or not. He smiled and thanked the music teacher and promised to bring Mary back whenever the weather allowed.

Mary's head was swarming with new possibilities: She could

play and her father could preach. They could be a protracted meeting team! He would be oh so proud of her because she would play oh so well! Bubbling with excitement during the long drive home, she tugged on the sleeve of his thick, almost-shapeless woolen overcoat. "Papa," she began timidly, "could we get a piano or an organ for the house?"

"We'll see," he muttered without looking at her. She saw that he was slumped forward, one boot up on the dashboard, staring over the horses' backs at the wintry countryside with what seemed to be his usual glum, solemn expression. Mary sighed, clasped her hands in her lap, and shivered.

Back home, Papa climbed down from the buggy and held up his arms to catch Mary as she jumped to him to be set down. As he caught her, she heard him moan sharply as he twisted to the right and hurriedly set her down. She caught her breath, watching him clutch his right side before straighteneing and walking to the rear of the buggy. He made an effort to smile at her as he said, "Got something for you and Mildred to play with this winter." He pulled out a huge square book and presented it to her. "Mr. Casteel gave it to me. Said it was out of date and would make the perfect thing for little girls to...." He winced, holding his right side near his waist, then stiffened and began unloading the other parcels from the back of the buggy.

She stared at the book, trying not to think that something might be wrong with Papa. Not Papa! But she could not shut out the piercing thought, *"What if he.... Like baby James? Oh, what if...?"* Tears swam in her eyes as she turned back the book's heavy cover...and saw that it was a sample book of wallpaper. She flipped through the book and saw a multitude of colorful, fascinating samples—some with pictures, some with designs, some with fuzzy raised patterns. She hugged the book against her chest and looked at her father. "Papa, thank you...thank you for thinking of me...and Mildred."

He nodded and went toward the house with his arms full of parcels. She trailed behind him, noticing that he was making an effort to walk normally and not lean to the right.

She and Mildred played with the wallpaper sample book all afternoon, cutting out pictures and pasting them on the backs of other pages with flour paste. She played silently, wondering if she should tell her mother that something was wrong with Papa. But no, she decided; surely, he would tell her...except that they hardly seemed to talk anymore. By rolling back the rug at night and pressing her ear to the floorboards, she used to listen to their voices as they lay in bed. But that was before baby James. *"Oh, what'll we do if Papa...dies?"* she fretted. *"We might have to wander the roads...or...or go to the poorhouse!"*

"Look," Millie said, interrupting Mary's thoughts. Millie was pointing at a picture of a big, black-hulled ship. Rows of the ships were arranged in diagonal lines across the page. Mary read the ship's name.

"Titanic," she said gloomily. "remember last April? The *Titanic* was *supposed* to be unsinkable—the biggest, bestest ship ever built. But on its first trip, it hit an iceberg in the North Atlantic and *sank*. More'n fif-teen hun-dred people *died,"* Mary said solemnly to properly impress her little sister with the magnitude of the disaster. They were seated cross-legged on the rug in their bedroom; the sample book, scissors, and paste pan were between them. Millie was staring openmouthed at Mary, her knowledge that Mary would explain having been confirmed again. Mary held up her head and rather dreamily said, "The ship's band was playing 'Nearer My God to Thee' while the *Titanic* sank." She squinched her lips and began cutting out one of the pictures of the ship. "When I heard Papa and Granddaddy talking about it, I ran and asked Mama, 'But Mama, if you were in a lifeboat, you couldn't sink, could you?' "

"They *all* died?" Millie asked, greatly awed.

"No. Some were saved. Other ships came and pulled them out of the *icy* water." Mary continued cutting out the picture, making sure she cut exactly along the outline. She worked slowly and patiently, while in her head flitted her collection of thoughts and memories concerning death: the hundreds drowning, her mother's stories of how Uncle Alex and Aunt Chloe and her baby had died, baby James turning blue and stiff, what Daddy Walker muttered about his Suzie, and, worst of all, the suddenly real possibility that her own papa could die. Why, if *he*—with all his strength and goodness—could die, then...then *she* could, too. *"Will the Lord Jesus come and take Papa away? Will He come for me, too?"* she wondered, then wondered what heaven was like. She heard voices below and quickly turned back the rug and pressed her ear to the floorboard.

Faintly she heard Papa's angry voice. "I will *not* call the doctor. What can he...." His voice faded as apparently Mama shushed him. But soon it rose again: "Yes, I know my side's feverish and hard. Where's that bottle of Adlorika we...."

Footsteps went toward the bathroom, and Mary heard the cabinet door jerked open. Then she heard a thud, her mother's sharp outcry, and running footsteps. Panic-stricken, Mary scrambled up and ran pell-mell down the stairs. When she burst into her parents' bedroom, she found her mother trying to help her father to the bed. He was clutching his right side in agony. Lucy grunted and lifted his arm higher across her shoulders and dragged him toward the bed. Mary ran to her father's other side and started to help, but her mother snapped at her, "Go telephone Dr. Powell!" As Mary ran and cranked the telephone, she heard her mother muttering, "Hardheaded man! Wouldn't say anything if it killed you!"

Breathlessly, her heart pounding, Mary waited for the switchboard operator to ring the hospital, then she waited for a nurse to go and bring the doctor. By the time he finally answered, Mary had gotten control of herself and was able to slowly and specifically tell Dr. Powell the symptoms of her father's illness.

"Appendicitis," Dr. Powell concluded. "We'll be right out."

Mary hung up and went back into the bedroom to see her mother and Mildred standing at the foot of the bed, staring at Papa. Mama noticed Mary and said, "Take a pan outside and fill it with snow. Mildred, you run down to Granddaddy's house and fetch him."

The girls raced off. When Mary returned carrying a pan mounded with pure white snow, her mother pulled up the nightshirt she had managed to get onto her husband, took a handful of the snow, and held it against the red, distended area low on his right side. Mary watched silently, trying to think what else she could do. But her thoughts collapsed in a whirl, and she began to cry. Mrs. Walker noticed that the pan was shaking, and she looked at her daughter.

Mary whispered, "Mama, he's not...he's not gonna die, is he?"

Mrs. Walker looked tired and grim. "We must pray he won't."

"B-but we haven't p-prayed in a long time...n-not as a family," Mary said, jerking as sobs racked her slender body; but she continued holding the pan by its handle straight out before her.

Her mother took the pan from her, set it on the floor, and held her close, patting her back. "We must try...and not give up. We *can't* let him die, can we?"

"N-no!" Mary said, tightening her lips and setting her lower jaw; she looked around her mother's face at her papa. His face was distorted by pain, and he seemed asleep. Mary looked at her mama. "Now? Can we start now?"

They knelt on the floor by the bed, gripping each other's hands.

When Daddy Walker came in, he placed one broad, gnarled hand on his son's side, stood back for a time lost in thought, then went into the living room and sank into the rocking chair by the stove. "I'll keep the fire going," he said to no one. "Least I can do."

After dark they heard the putt-putt-puttering of the doctor's car coming up the drive; they ran onto the front porch. Flickering lights stopped near the house; the lights faded slowly as the Model-T engine coughed and backfired a number of times before it died. Two men in black suits strode to the house, each carrying a black leather bag. Dr. Powell, in the lead, stepped onto the porch with a long stride and went past Mrs. Walker into the house. "Where is he?" he asked as he went.

"In the bedroom," she answered, waiting for Dr. Stacy to go in. Dr. Stacy was Dr. Powell's anesthetist, shorter and plumper than his colleague. Mrs. Walker, Mary, and Mildred went after them. Before the girls and Mrs. Walker got to the bedroom, they were met by the two doctors carrying Victor between them.

Dr. Powell commanded, "Quick, go clean off the kitchen table!"

Mrs. Walker ran, dragged the long worktable into the middle of the kitchen, and cleared it of the dinner caster and pickle caster. She raced back into the bedroom and returned with a sheet; the doctors lifted Victor so she could slide the sheet under him.

"You, big girl," Dr. Powell snapped, jerking off his coat and undoing the cuffs of his shirt so he could roll them above his elbows, "bring a full lamp and hold it *steady* where I tell you to." He went to the sink, pumped hard on the handle, and began washing his hands with lye soap. Over one shoulder he said, "Mrs. Walker, bring me a pan and get another lamp. Little girl, you go in with your grandpa."

While Dr. Powell prepared the site of the operation, Dr. Stacy held a cloth over Victor's nose and mouth and dripped ether onto the cloth. Mary forever after remembered the vulnerable whiteness of her papa's abdomen exposed to the scalpel, and she forever after dreaded the smell of ether. She kept her eyes riveted on Dr. Powell's sweating, age-worn face as he cut and worked. She was aware of the small amount of blood and of the sight of what lay inside, but she watched Dr. Powell's face as she held both hands tightly around the lamp base, making sure the flame did not waver. Once Dr. Powell gave her a quick grin. "You're pretty tough, aren't you? Most girls would've fainted long before now."

Holding her head stiffly, her mouth set, she nodded slightly.

Dr. Powell soon slumped to one side and looked at Mrs. Walker. "It burst. I almost had it, but it burst on me. Ripe as a...." He shook his head and began to clean Victor out inside with disinfectant. Mary felt nausea sweep through her as she saw him take intestines out and cleanse them carefully; the smell and sight made her almost pass out on her feet. But the lamp flame barely quavered.

Dr. Powell sewed Victor up and left a tube sticking out of the incision. As he worked he told Mrs. Walker, "You'll have to keep the tube clear and draining. Otherwise the poisons'll build up and...." He glanced at her. "Call me each day and tell me if he has fever; he likely will have for a long time." He pushed his glasses higher on the bridge of his nose and stared at her. "He may not make it."

"Can I do anything?" Mrs. Walker asked weakly, gripping the table edge near her husband's head and leaning forward.

Dr. Powell shook his head. "I've done all that can be done. You just make sure that tube doesn't clog up. The rest is up to Him." He jerked his head toward the ceiling as he finished the final stitch. He cut the black threads, tied a neat knot, and looked at his work. Then slowly he began packing up.

When Victor had been settled into bed, the doctors stayed until the ether wore off and their patient roused slightly, moaning. Opening his watery eyes, Victor tried to focus on the people around him. He struggled to rise, but Dr. Powell forced him down with one hand on his chest.

"You're mighty sick, Fluty, and you won't be going anywhere for a long time." He gave Victor an assessing look. "You haven't forgotten how to pray, have you?"

"Yes," the feverish man replied, turning his head slightly from side to side and squinting in pain.

"Well, you'd best remember," Dr. Powell said, nodding to Mrs. Walker as he started to leave the room. He stopped in front of Mary, looked down at her for an instant, then went on, followed by Dr. Stacy.

The hours, the days, passed more slowly than the ticking of the new Waterbury eight-day clock atop Victor's bookcase-desk. Mrs. Walker silently went through her rounds of duties—cooking, washing, tending to her husband. Daddy Walker, true to his word, kept the stoves going, and he tended to the animals and did the other outside work. Neither he nor Mrs. Walker spoke for hours and hours on end, and the girls gave up on the possibility of hearing a happy sound in their home ever again.

Most of the time they remained upstairs, cutting and pasting pictures from the wallpaper sample book. Mary frequently stared at the book, remembering that her father had thought of her in getting it; she realized how deeply he loved her, despite his sternness and his grief over his son's death. And crying in the night with the thought that he might die, Mary had Millie come closer to her in the bed so they could hold each other. It was then that Mary taught her sister how to pray.

Victor drifted feverishly through a realm that was neither entirely in contact with his surroundings nor entirely in "that other place"—wherever it was. That other place consisted of flowing rivers of dark memories, of vague voices calling or talking to him, of fleeting faces that hovered near him for a while but sped away when he reached for them. Repeatedly he saw images of his son— laughing and playing—and his mother as he remembered her from his childhood. And, after three weeks of delirium and fighting against the damp covers and his wife's restraining hands and soothing words and cool cloths, Victor encountered his brother, Alex. He seemed to see Alex above him in the darkness; he rose to that level and found a calmness there. There was nothing around them, but Victor seemed to sense a great dome of light somewhere far above him; however, he could not look upward to see that dome or vault of light, and when he looked at Alex, he saw that his brother was smiling at his efforts to look upward.

"It'll be all right," Alex said quietly.

"What?" Victor demanded.

"I said, it'll be all right."

"What will?"

"Everything. Everything will be all right."

That was all. Alex's face faded into the dark, flowing, and confusing the rivers of images that surrounded Victor. He felt deeply annoyed and disappointed; he thought that if he must have a vision of the dead, Alex might at least have brought him an answer to the question that had been burning through and through him for months: "Why? In God's name, *why?*" Didn't God *care* about him? Didn't God care that he was lost in confusion and doubt? Surely...*surely* if God were *real,* He would provide some explanation other than simply, "It'll be all right."

The days and nights passed on, mingled in an incomprehensible tangle. Victor struggled to move his body, but each effort was met by a gentle resistance which occasionally he could identify

as either his wife's hands or Mary's. Once or twice he managed
to focus on their faces, and within their expressions he read the
seriousness of his condition before he drifted back into delirium.

Then Alex came to him again, and again came the gentle, patient words, "Fluty, it'll be all right."

"What will be all right?" Victor stubbornly demanded.

"Everything. Everything will be all right."

"But how do I *know* that?"

The inexplicable rivers of images were silent. After a long while,
as waves of bitterness lapped at his soul, he began to hear his own
voice—talking to his own father long ago in the Spickard grocery
store-apartment. He seemed to be saying something about walking away step by step...step by step until darkness intervened.

It was then that he realized that he was indeed lost...and the
thought occurred to him that he never had been saved, that what
he had thought was a salvation experience was nothing more than
a sham, an illusion like all the other illusions drifting with him
in nothingness. He began to cry, to sob, and from the depths of
his being came fears and doubts, anxieties and feelings he long
had absorbed and contained with all his quiet stubbornness,
obligation to self-sufficiency, and high expectations. In the dark
night of his soul—his true and full realization of lostness—all that
mass of inner infection flowed upward, and he cast his tears of
remorse into the dark rivers of images that surrounded him. Into
them he poured resentments against his father and mother and
brothers, jealousies such as those that had so triggered his anger
against Mary, bitterness against the plaguing he had taken from
various people, and self-hatred and disgust for having failed to
live up to his own standards. On and on came the upswelling of
memory-feelings.

As he became emptied, he felt the emptiness inside as a clean-
ness. He seemed to recall a hand in his side, and that hand was
rummaging around, muttering something like, "What else...what
else?" He felt lighter and lighter and seemed to be rising into a
realm that was more gray than dark, less filled with disturbing
images and confusing voices and faces. He then began to recall
moments of his life that had been "almost" this or that. He almost
had gone back to see old Mrs. Scholwalter, and he grieved as he
envisioned her alone in her back room. He almost had gone to
Tom Fairly after Alex's death to assure the young man that no
hard feelings existed, to offer forgiveness. He almost had told his
mother how deeply he loved her before she had died; but in his

father's silence, he had remained silent. He almost, any number of times, had taken his father in his arms and hugged him. He almost had agreed with Anna Gentry, against commonly held beliefs, that the "joy in the Lord" was an important Biblical principle and that she was right in claiming that "the Spirit brought her that joy to share." He almost had had Mary baptized...almost had....It went on and on for what seemed an eternity, and he sobbed and ached inside at all the opportunities that had slipped ...no, that he had *let* slip...through the woven pattern of his life.

He became aware that the gray void around him was becoming paler and paler, lighter and lighter. He tried to look upward, but something prevented him. He struggled against the restraint...and realized that it was keeping his spirit from looking higher. He fought with that restraint and seized it. Twisting in the void, he turned...and came face to face with a being at whom he blinked and stared. It was himself, but it was himself in a way he never had seen before, in a way that disgusted him. He saw a set jaw, staring blue eyes, ears that protruded almost sideways, an arrogant head of auburn-red hair...and pride. There was so much stubborn, ingrained pride in that other face at which he stared that he wanted to turn away, to stop facing it and allow it to return to wherever it had been. But with a cry of hatred he wrenched it from himself and flung it downward. Immediately his spirit soared.

He became aware of tiny particles of light, like snowflakes. He could not tell if he were rising through the light flakes or if they were falling past him, but he was fascinated nevertheless. He looked toward their source, and gazed up and upward. The entire sky seemed to be sending down the particles of light, and when he followed their progress downward, he saw that the particles were slowly falling in among the flowing images and faces of the dark rivers below himself. He looked upward again as he came into the source of the particles, and he became aware of a vast sky of light. The light was diffused, horizonless, and at first pleasant. But as he rose into it, it became more and more painful to his sight. He wanted to turn away, to look downward again, but he found that he was held in an inexorable current lifting him. He had thought that he was rising of his own volition, but he discovered that his will had absolutely nothing to do with it. Nor could he will himself to look away from the light source toward which he was going. It became as dazzling as a field of unblemished snow in bright sunlight...then became the sunlight itself before becoming brighter than the sunlight, more total and surrounding, warming and comforting and yet somehow painful. His sight ached, and he wanted to turn away, for he could not stand the light in such intensity. As it burned into him and throughout his spirit, though, he found that it itself was not painful; rather, it was his own reaction to that light that was painful; the hurt was caused by his lingering desire to flee back into the drifting nothingness.

As the light filled him to the point that he lost all awareness of himself as a separate entity, he felt his lingering desire to return to the realm below leave him...and he lost all memory of himself as a separate entity. He was unborn. Joy pure and unalloyed filled him. At the height of that vibrant joy, he again heard his brother's voice—only now it was something more than Alex's voice: "Victor, it will be all right. Everything...*everything* will be all right."

When he did not resist, when his complete submission was proven, certainty entered him. He opened his eyes and looked toward the western windows. He saw—with a keen sense of disappointment because the overwhelming joy was being withdrawn to a distance from him—that snow was falling gently. Snowflakes drifted past the windows, stirred by a breeze. He slowly regained his hearing and turned his head toward a sound. It was the sound of his wife crying. She was saying, "But Dr. Powell, the tube *came out*. How will I get it...." She paused, then seemed to repeat the doctor's words: "Sharpen the end and put it back."

In a while she came into the bedroom. Victor took one long look at his wife and saw the terrible struggle that she too had been undergoing. His restraint dissolved into love for her; he adored her more freely than ever before, no longer holding back his love for fear that she, like his mother and Alex, would die. She bent over him, unaware that he had regained consciousness. He watched her as she stared at the wound, her lips trembling as tears fell from her eyes. Then, with an effort that showed throughout her body, she set her lips, straightened, and worked the tube back into the hole in the incision. "There!" she said to herself, standing back and folding her arms.

Victor had felt no pain; he marveled at that fact as he also marveled at the change he saw in his wife. She had grown up. Despite the years of work, of marriage, of tragedies and triumphs, she had retained the childlike quality he had been so fascinated with when he had courted her. But now it was gone. He felt a sharp sense of regret...until he realized that his regret was because he now no longer could feel superior to her because of her childlikeness; now he would have to accept her as truly equal. She was woman. She felt his gaze upon her and started as her eyes met his.

"You're awake," she murmured as if returning from her own thoughts. She went to him and placed one cool hand on his forehead. "Still have fever, though." She looked at his moisture-filmed eyes. "Can you eat?"

He nodded, unable to speak for fear he would choke and cry.

She hurried away...and soon returned with chicken broth in a cup. She fed him spoonful after spoonful, then went away again. In a few minutes Mary and Mildred ran into the room, slowed as they approached the bed, and began to grin. Mary whispered, "Oh, Papa! You're all better, and we've been praying so hard...so hard that you would be!"

He smiled and reached toward her, seeing in her the joy of the Lord. She clasped his hand as she and Mildred cautiously climbed onto the bed.

In the days that followed, Victor's sleep was peaceful. He returned to a warm whiteness not unlike the snow outside, where the white winter sky lowered and seemed to touch the land. He awoke once to watch Dr. Powell remove the tube from his side and stitch the hole. The doctor smiled encouragingly at him and left. The next time he came, he pronounced Victor well enough to eat more solid food, get out of bed for a few minutes at a time, and begin to regain his strength. "After all," Dr. Powell said, "plowing time's almost here, and if I know you, you'll be out there behind a team of horses with the rest of them."

Victor pushed himself upright and scooted against the pillows and headboard. "How long have I been sick?" he wondered aloud, amazed to think that it had been longer that a few weeks.

"Fluty, you've been sick for five months," Dr. Powell said, turning to look admiringly at Lucy. "And Lucy has managed as well as any woman I've ever seen." He removed his glasses and assiduously cleaned them with his handkerchief.

Victor frowned, "It didn't seem...."

"When the gangrene set in...."

"Gangrene!" Victor exclaimed, horrified.

Dr. Powell nodded, resettling his glasses on his nose. "When it set in, I told Mrs. Walker that there was just no hope, that only a miracle...." He nodded sharply and began to smile. "I love it when the Lord proves me a fool."

Victor blinked and closed his eyes as a deep, awed gratitude swept through him. "Lucy," he murmured, opening his eyes as he held out his arms to her. "Oh, Lucy, I love you so much!" he whispered as she came against him. He stroked her hair, smelling her sachet scent and savoring the soft touch of her cheek against his face. "Please forgive me." She stiffened and would have drawn back had he not held her against him.

"Fluty, I forgive you," she whispered, hearing the doctor leave the room and close the door behind him. "And my love...my husband...I'm so glad you were sent back to us." She held her head back, her eyes brimming with tears as her gaze roved his face. "We...*I* need you...*so* much."

"I know," he whispered, holding her tightly. "Believe me, I know...and I need you the same." He laughed and kissed her strongly on her lips.

Called

S ure enough, Victor plowed that spring. Stumbling over curled chunks of the rich-brown, rich-smelling furrows behind Mack and General, he plowed in his fields while Daddy Walker follwed with the disc harrow pulled by the second team they had bought the year before. The men then went to work on the new land where James had felled part of the forest and where he had dragged the trees to one side to be sawn as wood was needed. The stumps resisted the efforts of all four horses straining at their utmost, but eventually the stumps yielded and were dragged off to be burned. Victor and his father dug rocks from the earth, carried them to a wagon, drove it to a ridge where a windbreak was needed, and stacked the rocks to make a wall. They then plowed and planted the soft earth of the forest floor. And the work made Victor stronger and stronger.

It was after the crops were all planted and the work slacked off slightly that they came: Ed Kauffman and his son Bill with Otto Sparks, Ed Ash, and Dad Bohring, as well as ten or so other men from the Pleasant Ridge Church. The men began to assemble in the front yard of the Walker place as Victor, Lucy, and their girls came outside, followed by Daddy Walker, wondering what on earth was going on. When all the men had gotten out of their buggies or off their horses, and when a few had come from shiny black Model-T Fords, Ed Kauffman cleared his throat and stepped forward.

"Fluty...ah, Mr. Walker, we've formed a committee from the church. Like you know, Uncle Charley Hickman has decided to do only protracted meetin's. That leaves us without a reg'lar minister." He looked at his neighbors—their faces sun-browned, their blue or white shirts wrinkled but fresh—who patiently were waiting for him to say his piece; their thumbs were hooked behind the straps of their overalls, and some of them slowly were chewing tobacco. One spat a stream of brown juice to the side, and another scuffed a heavy boot in the grass.

Ed—tall and slab-muscled and red-faced—cleared his throat again and said, "We all know you for a godly man; we've known

189

your family back to your great-great-granddaddy; and we know you're a learned man. We've heard you preach, an' we've been prayin'—us and our missuses. We're all of a mind. We believe it's God's will that you be called to the ministry. If you do half as well preachin' as you've done as Sunday school super'tendent...." He broke off and coughed once. With a more concerned expression, he added, " 'Course we can't pay you much. Reckon you'd have to keep farmin; and prob'ly go elsewheres a Sunday or two a month to make ends meet. But...we're of a mind it's His will." He nodded emphatically, his lips clenched, his piece ended.

Victor shook hands with each of them and invited them inside. But each politely refused, saying they'd taken time enough out from work. Victor and his family watched them leave.

Mary was delighted. After hearing him preach that one time, it seemed obvious to her that her papa was meant to be a preacher. She hurried to the house and held the screen door open for her parents and grandfather...and noticed that her mother appeared far from happy.

Daddy Walker stopped his son in the kitchen and took him by the arms. Mary came into the kitchen and noticed the way her grandfather's eyes were shining with tears as he said, "Son...I'm *so* proud of you." They embraced awkwardly, slapping each other on the back. Daddy Walker murmured, "Thank you, son...for the future," then released Victor and walked quickly to the back porch and out the door.

Victor watched him go, sighed, shook his head, and sat at the kitchen table. Lucy set a cup of coffee in front of him. She sat near him, motioning slightly for the girls to join them.

"All right, Mama," he said, grinning from ear to ear, "what is it?"

She gently flapped the end of her apron, looking at it until she had the right words to say. "Victor, I agree with the men that it's the Lord's will that you become a minister. I've known it since I was 15." She gazed toward Mary and Mildred and smiled. "That seems *so* long ago." Looking back at Victor, she said, "But it'll mean that the girls and I will be here alone a lot of the time."

"You don't see me much now," he said regretfully, "what with me hiring out as well as doing our own work."

"Yes, but I know how preachers are. The few good ones travel all over. And if I know you, you'll set into this like you do everything else and won't be content just to preach at Pleasant Ridge and Goshen.''

He leaned toward her and took her hands; rubbing the backs of her hands with his thumbs, he looked into her eyes and said, ''Lucy, it'll be all right.'' He smiled. ''Believe me, it'll *all* be all right.''

She returned his gaze for a long while...and slowly nodded, smiling as she sighed.

''You've been called, too, you know.''

She nodded again as he drew back and sipped his coffee. She clasped her hands in her lap and looked at them, at the redness and swollen knuckles; softly she said, ''That doesn't make it any easier to be without you. But,'' she added, smiling at him, ''it's like you said: I did finally grow up. It's time I started *being* Mrs. Walker.''

He leaned forward and hugged her...grinning at the girls when they giggled.

The ordination service was as impressive as the congregation of Pleasant Ridge Church could make it. Mary, dressed in white linen and thin white gloves, sat on the front bench beside Mildred and her mother. Daddy Walker in a new suit sat next to her. Matt and his wife and Nanny and Tom McClary sat at the end of the bench. Across the aisle were Aunt Minerva, Uncle Matt, and Walter Smith and his family. Behind them, filling the church, were many of the farming families of Lower and Upper Tennessee, as well as some families from Moriah and West Pine—including, of course, a number of Georges and Kauffmans. A few families from the English had come, and State Representative Arnold Jewell gave the main address. After it, the deacons assembled in front of the platform, and Victor knelt facing the altar for the laying on of hands. Victor himself then preached—on assurance in the faith— and closed the service with a prayer that made Mary feel certain that Jesus' spirit was with her father, speaking through him. She wiped her eyes as the prayer ended, and she adoringly watched her father as men went forward to clasp hands with him as an expression of fellowship.

The Lord had His man; he was 37 years old, not very tall or impressive-looking, with a rather wide mouth and rather long nose, with auburn-red hair combed to the right side, and with ears that stuck out. His eyes were twinkling blue, and in them shone a light that drew people to him and made them feel comfortable and reassured in his presence. He never preached in a large church, though later he did become pastor of the First Baptist Church of Princeton; it was there that he preached old Mrs. Scholwalter's funeral. He never preached before huge crowds, but he did lead hundreds to accept Jesus Christ—including Half-Millie from over near Goshen. He was never well paid, and often he was paid no money at all for serving the Lord, but he served his scattered flock so well—particularly in times of bereavement— that more than 3000 people came to his funeral. He never lived in a house that had more than six rooms, but he did bring a used organ the next spring, and music from then on banished the silence of the house. He never owned more than one suit at a time, but for his family small luxuries appeared regularly, and they never suffered any lack of the necessities. Most of all, he loved as his Master bade him...and was loved in return, deeply...gratefully.

By his side year after year in partnership and communion was his wife. She bore other children as well as other griefs and sorrows. She reared orphans, took care of aging relatives and others, and worked incessantly until she no longer could care for herself, much less for others. She outlived her husband by 14 years, and she outlived three of her children...yet her faith did not waver. She stood strong in the Lord.

●   ●   ●

"Those were my parents—your grandparents—ordinary, but very special...sharing love's majesty."

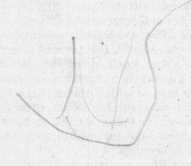